CELLAR

OTHER BOOKS BY

KAREN E. TAYLOR

THE VAMPIRE LEGACY SERIES:

Blood Red Dawn

Thirst

Crave

Hunger

COLLECTION:

Fangs and Angel Wings

CELLAR

Karen E. Taylor

CELLAR

ISBN-10: 0-9860868-1-9

ISBN-13: 978-0-9860868-1-6

Author's Note:

CELLAR is a re-issue of my previous published book (Twelve Steps from Darkness, Copyright © 2007 Karen E. Taylor.) The story, while essentially the same, has been edited and expanded upon in certain areas, resulting in several new scenes and an epilogue.

Published by:

Karen E. Taylor

Alexandria, VA

http://www.karenetaylor.com

DEDICATION:

CELLAR is dedicated to all of my loved ones, family and friends, who have passed on.

CHAPTER ONE

"Refill?"

Laura looked up from her study of the melting ice cubes in her glass to the grizzled face of the Sea Shell Cafe's bartender and gave him a half-smile. "Better not, Ted. I really should be getting back to work."

He stared over his shoulder at the clock behind the bar. "Why bother now?"

She followed his glance. "Damn." Once again she had allowed the dark comfort of the bar to steal hours of her life; time that could have been better spent. Too much of her life was like that now, wasted hours that stretched into days, weeks, even months.

I should have stopped at one, she told herself, beginning the silent lecture she'd delivered too many times before. *I should have gone back to the real estate office and spent the day on the phone, making contacts and trying to set up new appointments. Instead, I wasted the whole damn day.* She lifted her glass and drained the last of her drink, mostly water but with enough of a lingering vodka tang to kick in the craving for another. Laura sighed, wrapping her hands around the empty glass, and looked at her reflection in the mirror behind the bar. She was pale, her complexion looked pasty and dry, seeming even fairer in contrast with her chin length black hair. Her features were blurred, a combination of the smoke-tinged mirror and the many martinis she'd had. As always, she saw three people in her reflection: a dim suggestion of her mother in the droop of her mouth; herself, that shady sadness looking back at her from alcohol-reddened eyes; and Lizzy.

With the thoughts of her youngest daughter, Laura smiled and a spark of life seemed to jump into her face. She would call tonight and talk to both Lizzy and Mandy, her eldest. The happiness of the thought was only slightly overshadowed by the worry that Tony might answer the phone. And if he did, she knew she'd better be sober.

"Actually, I'd like a cup of coffee, please, Ted."

"Coffee?" Ted raised an eyebrow, his thin lips twisted into the closest he ever got to a smile.

"Yeah, coffee." Laura's voice grew stronger in her resolve. "I'm going to talk to my girls tonight."

"Funny," Ted said, pouring a mug full of dark strong coffee and setting it in front of Laura, removing her empty glass and making a cursory sweep at the bar surface with his rag. "You been coming here for close to a year now, I'll bet, and I never knew you had kids. Never even knew you were married."

"Not married now," she took a cautious sip from the steaming cup, "but yeah, I have two little girls, although they're not that little anymore. They live with their father. I guess I never talked about it."

Ted snorted. "People don't come here to talk much."

"No, I suppose not."

"You got pictures?"

Laura glanced at him briefly. He seemed genuinely interested so she leaned unsteadily from the barstool and grasped the straps of her purse. She set it on the bar and rummaged through the contents, coming upon a small frayed fabric-covered album. Flipping quickly to the last few pages, she pulled out the most recent school pictures that Tony had sent. "This one's Amanda, she's twelve."

"Pretty."

"Yeah," Laura gave a small smile and took another sip of her coffee. "She takes after her father's side of the family. And this one is Lizzy. She'll be eight in a few weeks."

Ted picked up the picture and looked from it to Laura's face. "She looks just like you."

"Yeah, everyone says that." Her stomach twisted as she took the photo from Ted's fingers and stared at it herself; the resemblance *was* striking, but Lizzy's face held promise and youth. Laura knew that most of her youth had been leeched away by too many hours spent in places like this. She gathered up the photos, hurriedly crammed them back into her purse, and pulled out her wallet. "So what's the damage?"

He went to the cash register and printed out her tab for the afternoon. She grimaced at the total, pulled two twenties and a ten from her billfold and placed them on the bar. Crawling from the barstool shakily, Laura blinked, swaying on her feet, and drained her coffee. "Keep the change, Ted."

"Yeah, thanks. You okay? Want me to call you a cab?"

"No, I don't live that far away, I'll be fine."

Outside the bar, Laura cursed the bright June sunlight and fumbled in her bag for her sunglasses. Ignoring the disdain in the glances of passersby, she shook her head and mumbled to herself until finally, beneath wads of tissues and crumpled receipts, she located the glasses. She put them on with unsteady hands and fished once more for her keys before looking around to get her bearings.

Locating her car, she got in and started it, adjusting the rear view mirror. She put it into reverse, it sputtered and stalled. Frustrated, she jammed the gearshift into park, restarted the engine anc the motor. She could still feel the alcohol surging through her sy and wondered briefly if she should go back inside and have Ted c her a cab. Or at least have another cup of coffee. Except she fearea reentering the bar, knowing that the extra coffee might turn into another vodka martini or two and for once the longing to talk to her daughters was stronger than the urge to drink. “I can have coffee at home,” she told herself firmly, and shifted over in the seat to look into the mirror again, this time to check her appearance. Laura combed her bangs back with her fingers and removed her sunglasses. One glimpse was all she needed; she put the glasses back on to avoid looking at her eyes and the puffy bags underneath that had formed over the past few years.

“Great,” she said, “just goddamned great,” and shifted her car into reverse. Her foot slipped off the brake and hit the gas pedal at full force. This time the car did not stall, but surged backward, directly into a car just pulling into the parking lot. When she recognized the red and blue lights and the uniformed man emerging, she said nothing. She didn’t even swear. Instead, she went back into her purse, rolled down her window and extended her wallet to the policeman. He took one look at her and she gave him a rueful smile. After the questioning and the breath test he returned to his car to make the necessary arrangements. Laura folded her arms over the steering wheel, rested her head on them and slowly, desperately, began to cry.

Three months went by in a blur of appointments, appearances, signing papers and waivers, seemingly countless interviews by clerks and mental health counselors. Eventually, it had been decided she would qualify for the ARD program — Accelerated Rehabilitative

Disposition. Her final courtroom appearance was just a state-mandated necessity.

Accelerated Rehabilitative Disposition. She rolled the social services jargon over in her mind with a cynical laugh. *Fancy words for getting my ass in gear,* she thought, *words to justify locking me away for four weeks, taking away any defense I have against the world.*

She panicked slightly at her thoughts, and then tried to calm herself down. Even as a passenger, the cab ride from the courthouse had almost completely unnerved her; one of the reasons she worked and lived in the suburbs was to avoid the downtown traffic. As inconvenient as not being able to drive had been the last three months, she hadn't missed bumper-to-bumper traffic. Her father had promised to take her to and from the courthouse. That he supported her and offered to drive was not a surprise, but then neither was the fact he'd had an "emergency" at the last minute and canceled. Their telephone conversation that morning was typical of their relationship: brief, but vaguely loving.

"Take a cab, honey. I'll pay."

"Thanks, Dad," Laura said.

"And remember, don't let the bastards get you down. I'm with you on this, honey. Take care, I've got to run."

Laura hung up the phone and indulged in a bitter chuckle. Of course he was with her; he'd faced the same situation so many times himself. He'd gone the rehab route without much effect over the years. She couldn't remember one special occasion in her life when her father wasn't drunk: birthdays, anniversaries, funerals. Laura, herself, had discovered the dubious comfort of alcohol at the age of seventeen. It filled the empty spot her mother's death had left, an emptiness that Tony and the girls had, for a time, alleviated.

"Life's a bitch, and then you die." With a brief smile, Laura read the words from a parked car's bumper sticker, and directed the driver the last few blocks home. The area was residential, very suburban and very quiet. Not quite the typical neighborhood for a divorcee, but the housing values were depressed due to some unsolved kidnappings in the neighborhood years ago. *And,* Laura thought sadly, *I've no children to worry about.* The cost of the new house had been hard to turn down, especially since Laura was able to finance the whole thing herself with the divorce settlement.

They pulled into the driveway and she paid the driver. He waited a few moments for a school bus to pass, backed out when it went by. Laura stood at her door, house keys in hand, and watched the bus stop a few doors down.

When Mandy and Lizzy were younger and they were still a family, she had looked forward to the arrival of the bus. They would burst through the door, flushed and grinning, hungry for the afternoon cartoons. That was all in the past; with the death of her son, Matthew, before he'd even reached two months old, Laura turned once again to alcohol. And although Tony had begged and pleaded with her to stop, she didn't. She couldn't. Each new day, each movement reminded her of the life that she'd carried so close to her, now lost forever.

Tony had left her, finally, taking the girls with him. That had all happened in a different neighborhood, a different house. Here she was making a fresh start.

Laura frowned at that thought as she opened her front door. She'd honestly tried to stop, had tried to discipline her drinking; but eventually it came down to the fact that she had no reason to do so. Tony had seen to that; in one blow he removed her reasons for trying, her reasons for living.

"Shit, Laura, don't get morbid on me," she admonished herself, her voice echoing through the house. Then she smiled when she heard a soft padding up the cellar stairs. A scrawny black head appeared through the cat door, followed by a stringy body. "Hi, cat," she greeted the animal, reaching down to scratch his head. "Did you miss me?"

The cat gave a pitiful, quiet meow and ran to the kitchen. Laura laughed softly, went to the refrigerator and spooned some food into his dish. Leaning against the counter, she watched him eat with a maternal satisfaction. He'd finally begun to fill out since she'd found him outside her new home, no more than three weeks ago, drenched and terrified. It had taken a lot of coaxing and even more patience, not to mention cat food, to convince him to move in with her. But now he belonged here and to her, and Laura felt comforted not to be entirely alone.

He finished his meal and jumped up to the counter, rubbing up against her sleeve. "Hey, baby." She put her face down to his and let him lick her cheek. Then he jumped up to her shoulder and wrapped himself around her neck, his throaty purr tickling her ear. She walked back to the bathroom of the small ranch home. *I'll have to make arrangements to have him fed while I'm in rehab,* she thought with a grimace.

"Rehab," she said aloud, wincing as the cat dug his claws into her shoulder before jumping down. "Beats jail, I guess, but not by much." She started running water into the tub, added bath oil, lit three votive candles, stripped off her clothes — the low heeled pumps, navy suit and white blouse worn to impress the judge with her professional status — and kicked them across the room. She turned out the light and tested the water. Satisfied with the temperature, she walked away and went to the medicine cabinet. She opened a bottle and swallowed two Valium, with no water. "A second chance, they called it," Laura said to herself in the mirror as she ran her fingers through her hair. Her eyes looked better, less red, although the dark circles underneath had not gone away. In the candlelight she looked younger, prettier. Laura smiled at her reflection, stepped away from the mirror, and lowered herself into the tub with a grateful sigh. "I guess we'll see about that."

The hot water relaxed her thoroughly and she leaned back and closed her eyes. She shifted her position slightly so that the water covered her ears. The soft drumming in her head was rhythmic, soothing, almost hypnotic. Laura lazily soaped herself, observed by the watchful eye of the cat, sitting in the hallway, grooming himself after his meal. Suddenly he stiffened and arched his back. With a low throaty growl, he took off and ran to the bedroom at the end of the hallway.

Laura sat up and smiled. "Dumb cat," she said settling back into her previous position. He was so spooked, she thought, but not without cause. The last time she bathed, the phone rang and as she hurriedly tried to answer it, she'd lost her balance and fallen, accidentally dousing him and the entire bathroom with half a tub of water. *I guess cats think they're better off dead than wet,* she thought, succumbing to a pervading drowsiness.

The phrase filtered into her consciousness: *better off dead, better off dead, better off dead,* blending into the pounding of her ears and the beating of her heart.

Laura lay immersed in the water, her body inert and limp, her mind drifting slowly. She was aware of the feel of the water, the scent of the candles and bath oil, but made no connection between these senses and reality. She knew that the words spinning in her head were the only reality.

Better off dead, better off dead, the words lost their meaning in the repetition, like a child's sing-song chant.

Child, children...the words kicked off warning signals, but her mind, aided by Valium and an unnatural languor, floated past them and replayed the events of the day, then the events of the past few years. Dismally she viewed her life, solitary now and doomed to be forever. She saw all her mistakes magnified; she saw all of the chances she'd lost, the opportunities she'd never pursued. *Will it ever get better,* she wondered, *will it ever stop?*

Easy enough to stop, her mind advised.

And the chant continued — *better off dead, better off dead.* The walls pulsed with the words in her head.

Detached and disinterested, she watched her arm reach out of the water and find the razor she used for her legs. Her father's old safety razor, its stainless steel sparkled in the candlelight, glinted coldly on the water's surface. Laura turned it over and over in her hand. This too had no reality.

A new refrain was added, silently, internally, but somehow it echoed through the empty house.

Do it, Laura, do it.

Her fingers moved of their own volition, removing the double-edged blade from its holder. Vaguely she could remember replacing it recently. When had it been? Was it only yesterday? No matter, she knew it would be sharp, not dulled by hair or skin.

Do it, Laura.

There would be no pain, it would not be real.

Do it, Laura, nothing is real.

Yes, her mind answered and the voices that were no part of her agreed.

No pain, no problems. It will be over soon, all be over soon. Do it, Laura, it will be easy, easy enough to stop.

"Yes," she whispered over the cooling water.

"Yes," she whispered and watched, uncaring, unfeeling, as her fingers deftly slit her wrists open to the bone.

Yes, the voices sighed.

The water darkened, the room darkened. Before blackness descended she saw the blade drift, gently and silently, to rest on the bottom of the tub.

CHAPTER TWO

Officer Mike Gallagher drove slowly through the residential streets, surprised how normal the neighborhood seemed. Children were everywhere. One group of young girls stopped jumping rope to smile and wave as he drove by. He smiled back, turned the sirens on for one second and laughed as they scattered, giggling. Five years ago you would not have seen one child unattended; if the adults were not outside supervising the play, you would see them looking out windows and doors, observant and alert. Still, despite the vigilance, the final count had been six — six children gone, with no clues and no trace. Four boys and two girls, they might have been the brothers or sisters of some of these who played.

There were more houses now and fewer trees; the name "Woodland Heights" no longer quite as appropriate as it had been. Most of the houses had been built since the disappearances.

The Woodland Heights cases had been his first assignment after transferring to the suburban department from Detroit where he'd started his career. It remained their only unsolved case. Of course, most of the occurrences in this township were domestic problems, traffic violations and drunk driving — a complicated kidnapping case was somewhat out of their scope — but to this day he would see pictures of those children on milk cartons and remember his failure.

His supervisor thought he took the whole situation much too personally. "Jesus H. Christ, Mike," he finally blew up one day, "this isn't your fault. You didn't even work here when those kids disappeared. If this thing stumped even the Feds, you know we don't have a chance in hell of solving it."

Mike had said nothing, and thereafter had kept his investigations of the matter to himself.

He slowed and made a right hand turn. *It's odd,* he thought and not for the first time, *that Laura Wagner should live here, on the very street where the children had last been seen.* Even knowing it was only a coincidence, he had still been shocked when he saw the address on her license. His first thought had not been the DUI arrest he was making, or the procedures involved. Mike only knew that here was someone who might know something they had missed. In the car on the way to the station, he had found she'd been in the neighborhood for only a short time; she had lived out of state at the time and never even heard about the kidnappings.

Still he saw her as a link, and tried to cultivate her as such. He acted gentler and more considerate to her than was normal given the circumstances. She seemed to warm to him because of this and when he had offered her a ride home the next morning, she accepted graciously. Mike discovered that her eyes, when they were not reddened with the booze, were a soft shade of green and her hair curled onto her cheeks like black wings. Even a night spent in a jail cell seemed to have no effect on her looks. *She's so fragile,* he thought, and remembered watching her profile as they drove. She was pale and ethereal, as if she were a statue of an elven queen cast in porcelain. Her soft, petite face had intrigued him and Mike wondered if he would ever discover how she had fallen into her present state. He'd wanted to contact her during the time between her arrest and her trial, but knew that would be crossing the line. So he'd waited until today, the day of her trial, to see her again.

His fascination with her hadn't faded, he discovered. Even though Laura hadn't met his eyes in court, Mike sensed a connection between them still. After the trial ended with her sentence being suspended in lieu of rehabilitation, he walked up to her and shook her hand. "Good luck, Ms. Wagner," he said. The touch of her hand felt electric. *There's something there,* he thought. *Something I should pursue.*

Mike knew firsthand what Laura was going through, knew she'd be feeling lost and confused and completely unable to cope with it all. He smiled to himself and pulled into her driveway. Here he was, Officer Gallagher to the rescue, to provide a shoulder for her to cry on, to give her the benefit of his experience. With an expectant grin on his face, he rang the doorbell on Laura Wagner's house.

Laura's next awareness was of a sharp stabbing pain in her cheek. She opened her eyes to a blur of black as a small body sped back through the bathroom door. She sat up in the water and put a hand to her face. From far away she could hear a faint ringing, and she tried to pull herself out of the stupor into which she had fallen. Confused and disoriented, she glanced around her, trying to remember what had happened. It was something important, something monumental, but her mind felt hazy and drugged.

The doorbell rang again; this time Laura recognized the sound. She stepped out of the tub and grabbed an oversized pink terry robe from the hook on the door. As she put it on, the fabric brushed against her wrists and she flinched. A panic-filled memory of the gaping wounds she had inflicted suddenly surfaced.

Don't look at them, she advised herself, *just get to the door.* Desperately clutching the robe around her, Laura slowly worked her way down the hall. The doorbell rang again. "I'm coming," she called and was surprised to hear her voice sounded clear and loud.

Just get to the door, Laura, she told herself again, *it's not too far now. Whoever it is, they can help.* The thought sustained her as her vision darkened and she frantically groped at the walls in an attempt to stay upright.

Though seemingly endless, the hallway dwindled at last and Laura reached the living room. *Just a few more feet now,* she urged herself to keep moving forward. *It's not that big of a house, just keep moving.* She winced at the vision of the bloody streaks she was leaving on the carpet and walls, knowing that answering the door was the only thing of importance now.

Finally she arrived with a sigh of relief. Ignoring the cold stab of pain in her arm, she reached down with difficulty and turned the knob. Only when the door opened did she succumb to the pain and the weariness. The last thing she saw was the smile on the policeman's face fade away.

Mike reached out and caught her before she hit the floor. He lifted her in his arms and carried her to a couch. She seemed to weigh no more than a child, but as he laid her down, her robe fell open exposing her breasts. He tried not to react; instead he averted his eyes and tucked the robe back around her body. When she was completely covered he regained his professional demeanor. Now she seemed nothing more than a person in trouble. *When I hoped to comfort her in her hour of need,* he thought, *I had no idea she would really need it.*

Mike checked her pulse; it was racing. Her face was ashen, her skin cold and damp. She had been in a state of shock when she answered the door, he knew; her pupils had been dilated and her expression, one of severe panic. But there were no marks on her, seemed to be no reason for her response. He checked her breath and found no trace of alcohol.

Drugs, maybe an overdose? He picked up her cordless phone on the way to the bathroom. Dialing for an ambulance, he turned on the bathroom light and began to check her medicine cabinet. The paramedics would want to know what she took. All he found was a bottle of Valium, properly prescribed for Laura Wagner. It was completely full and he could see no evidence of any other drugs.

He tested the temperature of the bath water as he completed his call and realized the cold water might account for the clamminess of her skin. Mike returned to the living room and found Laura as he had left her, but with some color returning to her face. Her pulse slowed and was now steady and strong. He knelt down next to her and called her name.

Laura fought her way back into the light. The voices had softened, relinquishing their hold on her when the doorbell rang. She felt them still, their anger and disappointment — she should have been dead by now. As she struggled to open her eyes, she thought she heard a soft wailing and a promise of later.

"Later," she whispered even as her eyes focused on the concerned face hovering by her.

"Laura?" The strong, deep voice seemed to pull her up to the surface of reality. "What happened? Are you okay?"

She recognized the face, searched her mind for the name. *Flannagan? No, Gallagher. Mike Gallagher.* She managed a confused smile. "Hi," she said, "what are you doing here? What's happening?"

"You don't know?" he questioned. "You opened the door and then fainted."

"Fainted?" She realized she sounded stupid, but couldn't help herself. "The last thing I remember was taking a bath. And then I wake up here and find you. What's going on?" She knew she should be upset over the black out and embarrassed by her half-dressed state, but for some reason her only feeling was one of relief. He had saved her. *But from what,* she wondered, shook her head and sat up.

"I called an ambulance," he snapped, "they should be here soon. Maybe you should tell me what you've been taking."

She cocked her head at him, wondering why he sounded angry. *Did he think she didn't want to answer?* "Nothing out of the ordinary," she replied, "I took two Valiums, got into the tub and fell asleep. I think I—" She rubbed at one of her wrists in confusion. *What had happened?* "—I think I had a bad dream."

"Bad dream, huh? I guess so." He smiled at her briefly, then scowled, intently watching the compulsive movements of her hands. "Why are you doing that?"

"Doing what?"

"Give me your hands."

She placed her hands in his. He gently turned them over and looked at her wrists. They were slender and delicate, marked only by blue veins. She watched his face, knowing there was something there other than question and concern, some unremembered pain and despair. Pulling her hands from his, she clasped her robe closed, rose from the couch and slowly walked back to the bathroom.

It didn't feel the same as before. She went to the tub and looked at the water. She picked up the razor, the blade was still inside, clean and unused. Suddenly the dream — surely it was a dream, her fevered mind supplied — came back to her. With a gasp she dropped the razor into the tub and turned to run from the room.

Mike blocked her way and she tried to push him aside. He stood in the doorway, unmoved.

“Let me out,” she pleaded. “I’ve got to get out.”

“Why, Laura?” His voice was soft and compassionate now, “What’s wrong, what happened here?”

“I don’t know,” she whispered, not fighting her tears any longer. She felt a sadness flow from her in a great, dark stream, like the blood in her dream.

“Oh, God,” she said softly as his arms came up to enfold her, “let it only be a dream.”

CHAPTER THREE

Laura watched as Mike walked back from the men's room. He stopped before he reached their table and, leaning on the service counter, exchanged greetings with one of the waitresses. She watched him, realizing she'd had never had a chance to look him over. The first time she met him, she'd been drunk. The second time, when he drove her home from her night in jail, she was so embarrassed she could barely meet his eyes. After the trial, she'd felt the same way. And this afternoon, well, everything had been so disjointed, so confused that she'd really paid little attention to him. Even when the ambulance left and he remained, he still seemed only a vague, protective presence. She was surprised at his invitation to go out for something to eat, but accepted. Only after she got into his car and they began driving, did Laura become aware of him as a person, a man.

She smiled as he continued his banter with the waitress; Laura liked what she saw. Mike was tall, well over six feet, she guessed. His light brown hair was cut short and speckled throughout with grey, but his body looked strong and youthful. She remembered the feel of his muscular arms around her and she felt her stomach tighten in nervous excitement.

Sometime during that afternoon, he had asked her permission and changed from his uniform to the street clothes he said he always carried in his car. He was now dressed in a faded work shirt and jeans that were well worn, but, she thought with an appraising glance, tight in all the right places. She supposed him to be in his early forties, but he had kept himself in shape — great shape, she amended, taking another long look.

As if on cue, Mike turned around and gave Laura a wide smile and a nod. He collected the two mugs of coffee from the waitress and walked to their table. With his smile, her stomach twisted again; she dropped her eyes and felt a blush creep up her neck.

"You're starting to look better," he settled himself into the booth across from her, brushing her knees with his. "How are you feeling?"

"Okay, now, I guess," she said, taking a sip of the hot coffee. "Mostly I just feel stupid."

"Why should you feel stupid? After all, I was the one who called an ambulance for nothing more than a bad dream." He looked at her intently, his brown eyes narrowing. "But when you opened the door, you were in shock. I've seen enough people in that state to know. And, although I know better now, I could have sworn you were injured somehow."

Laura shivered and rubbed her wrists together, wincing.

"And why the hell do you keep doing that?"

She looked at him, startled at his sudden anger and tears began to brim in her eyes. "I really wish I knew."

"Look, Laura, don't cry. I didn't mean to be so harsh. I just want to know what happened. None of this makes any sense. You hadn't been drinking, you couldn't have accidentally taken too many Valium since the bottle was full. Nothing that I could see could have happened to cause such a reaction." He reached over and grasped her hand. "Why can't you tell me?"

Laura pulled away from him, reaching in her purse for a tissue. She wiped her eyes, discreetly blew her nose and managed a weak smile. "I'd tell you what I remember, but I'm afraid..."

"Afraid of what?"

"Afraid you'll have me committed. I mean you've already arrested me and thrown me in jail. My guess is the funny farm is your next step." She gave a small, strangled laugh, to help disguise the truth in her words. *Maybe,* she thought, *I really am crazy. That would explain it all.*

"You're not insane, I'd put money on it." Mike's voice was calm and steady and his statement reassuring. "Just tell me what happened."

The words began to fill his mind as she related the dream. Every detail became vivid as she spoke: the reaction of the cat, the soothing heat of the water, the hypnotic nature of the voices that somehow did not come from inside. As Mike watched, the color she had regained in her cheeks drained away. Laura's voice became emotionless and empty, a soft drone that, nevertheless, drowned out the noise of the diner. As she talked, he realized with a sharp sense of panic that he felt he had entered into the dream himself. He winced as she described the razor and the sharpness of the blade. He felt the insistence, the urgings, the irrevocable wisdom of the voices that Laura had heard.

And then it was over. The restaurant noises intruded once again and Mike shook his head and shoulders, as if to repel an invisible presence. "Jesus," he said softly, rubbing his hand over his eyes. "That's one hell of a dream."

"If it is a dream."

Mike glanced at Laura sharply. She seemed composed and sure of herself, the telling had strengthened her somehow. "What do you mean, if it *is* a dream?" Her statement angered him; he wasn't sure why. Because it was like the stories he once exchanged with adolescent friends, stories that would pull them all in and frighten both the listeners and the teller? Because she spoke of it in the present tense, as if it were still happening? He had felt its immediacy, the fear and the gut-wrenching pain, and when he looked at her earnest face, she gave no indication her story had been a deliberate attempt to scare him. She didn't deserve his anger, he finally realized, she had been through too much.

Laura shook her head slightly. “I don't know, Mike. It seemed more than a dream — even now it seems as real to me as sitting here with you.” Looking across the table, she met his eyes. “I have a strange feeling about it, that's all. It's as if by ringing the doorbell you saved me.”

“Yeah, I woke you up.” Mike drained his cup and signaled the waitress for more.

Laura reached over and gently touched his hand. “It's more than that,” she said, her voice trembling. “This is going to sound crazier than everything else, but I truly believe that if you hadn't shown up when you did, I'd be dead.”

Mike didn't comment on Laura's statement and as the evening wore on, he felt reluctant to pursue the subject further. Their talk drifted to other matters while they ate and as her initial shyness abated, she began to open up to him. He realized as she laughed at one of his more inane jokes, that he was genuinely attracted to her. He knew the reason he had given himself for driving to her house that afternoon was just an excuse. She obviously wasn't connected to the Woodland Heights kidnappings. That she lived in the area was only one of life's strange twists. Mike went to her house merely to see her again. And looking across the table at her, her elfin face animated and happy, he was glad he had. They were good for each other.“So,” he said, pushing his empty plate to one side of the table, “when do you go into rehab?”

Laura's smile twisted into a grimace of distaste. "Monday, and thanks a lot for reminding me." Then her green eyes lit mischievously, "But that gives me three more days to go on one hell of a binge. Care to join me?"

"I can't, sorry."

"You're not still on duty, are you?"

"Of course not," Mike smiled at her. "I went off duty before I stopped at your house. I'm on early this week."

"Well, then why not?"

"I don't drink, Laura."

"Great, then you can drive. After this afternoon, I really could use a drink."

Mike studied her. "You don't need to drink, Laura. And you certainly don't need one last binge. You're better off without it."

"And just who the hell are you to tell me what I need?" Laura's eyes flashed angrily and her lower lip shook. "My life is shit. I lost my job because I've lost my license. I won't have any money soon, because I won't have a job. I used up most of my savings, for Christ's sake, just to pay for rehab. I lay in the bathtub this afternoon and felt my life drain from me, and I was relieved. I was *relieved,"* she repeated, her voice rising, her face flushed. "Not scared, not terrified. Just goddamned relieved it was all over."

"Laura, look, I know you're going through a bad time, but let's talk about this somewhere else, somewhere more private."

She glanced around her, intercepting the stares of the other diners before they glanced away in embarrassment. "I'm sorry, Mike," she said in a soft voice, blinking back tears again. "I didn't mean to blow up at you — it's just that this whole thing sucks."

"I know, Laura. And I really do understand. Are you ready to go?"

At her nod Mike stood up, threw some money on the table and escorted her out of the diner.

Laura did not talk on the drive home. Mike made an attempt at conversation, but when her only responses were yes and no, he gave up and they finished their ride in silence. When they pulled up into her driveway, Laura rummaged in her purse and swallowed two more Valium. Mike gave her a sidelong glance but said nothing as he turned off the car.

In the darkness and relative seclusion of the car, Laura began to feel more at ease. "Mike," she began tentatively, "I'm really sorry for making such a scene. You've been wonderful today. Hell, you were even wonderful when you arrested me and hauled me off to jail." She glanced over at him and saw his broad grin.

"I like that, Laura. I never had anyone I arrested tell me how wonderful I am. I must associate with the wrong kind of criminals." She winced at the word and he paused, softening his voice. "I'm sorry, Laura, I don't think of you as a criminal. You made an error in judgment. And now you have a chance to correct that error. Oh, it won't be easy, nothing like this ever is, but I promise you if you stick it out things will get better. You can trust me on that."

"Okay," Laura agreed meekly, "I'll trust you. Would you," she hesitated for a moment, picking an imaginary piece of lint from the car seat, "would you like to come in for a while?" She tried to make the question casual, teasing, but she held her breath waiting for his answer. *I don't want to go inside alone, she thought, it's so dark and empty. But I've made myself enough of a fool in front of him, I can't ask anything else of him. If he wants to go, I'll let him go.*

He heard the urgency in her voice, felt the tension build up in her small body. I shouldn't get involved, he thought, it can only mean trouble later on. Now that my life is straightened out, I can't let myself get drawn into someone else's problems, especially hers. But he remembered her ashen face this afternoon, the way her body had fit against his, the glint in her eyes at the diner. *What the hell?* he thought. "I'd love to."

"Put something nice on the stereo," Laura instructed as she went to the kitchen to make a pot of coffee. After checking the cabinet for a minute she called back out to him, "All I have is caffeinated, is that okay?"

"Fine," he answered, taking his attention from her CD collection for only a second. "You've got some real interesting stuff here, but nothing new."

"New stuff is awful," Laura said. "Give me the 70's and 80's any day."

"Okay, then, what do you want to hear?"

"Anything — you choose." She measured the coffee, poured the water and set out mugs and spoons. She took the milk out of the refrigerator, and after smelling it, promptly poured it down the drain. "I don't remember, do you drink it black?"

"Yes," he answered.

"Good."

Mike walked into the kitchen, a CD case in his hand. She glanced at it and saw he'd picked one of her favorites. "This okay?" he asked and she nodded with a smile.

"Perfect," she said, "Costello fits my mood exactly."

Mike went back to the living room and turned on the player.

"Coffee'll be ready in a minute," she called, "and turn it up a bit, please." Laura glanced over her shoulder and saw that Mike was still studying her odd assortment of CDs, removing some from the stacks and setting them aside. *If we listen to all of those,* she thought to herself with a smile, *he'll be here all night.* The idea was comforting, but she needed something more, so she opened the cabinet under the sink and brought out a small bottle of brandy. *Just a touch,* she promised herself as she poured some into her coffee cup. She looked around guiltily, but he hadn't noticed, he was too busy adjusting the controls on the equalizer. She filled both cups with coffee and carried them to the living room.

"That sounds fine," she said, handing him a cup. "Quit fooling with it. I'll just have to change it all again when you leave."

He sniffed at his cup appreciatively and an odd look crossed his face. Laura thought he seemed angry, but at the same time saw a sad longing fill his eyes. Suddenly she realized she had given him the wrong cup.

"This is yours," he said tightly, "I like mine plain."

"Oh, shit...I mean sorry, I must have gotten them mixed up."

They switched cups and Laura blushed.

"Look, I'm sorry," she began, "but I've had one hell of a day and..."

"Laura, I'm the one who should be sorry. I told you I understand and I do really. When I said what I did at the diner, I was out of line." He moved across the room and sat down on the couch. "I'm not your keeper. I don't have any right to tell you what to do. You're in your own home and I guess if you want to drink yourself blind, you can. Just go easy, okay?"

"Okay," she agreed, "I'll only have one."

"If you can do that, then you don't have the problem I think you do. But we'll drop it for now."

"Thanks," she said, feeling more than a little bit stupid, but when she took a sip of her coffee she relished the soothing warmth of the brandy. “I wonder,” she said wistfully, as she curled up in an armchair, her hands cradling the cup, “if you ever lose the craving.”

“No,” Mike admitted, “you never lose it. But as time goes on it does get easier.”

“You sound so sure, I wish I could believe you.”

“Believe me, please. I know what I’m talking about. And it’s not just textbook knowledge. I learned it the hard way. Five years ago, I left rehab, and I’ve not had a drink since.”

Laura stared at him in shock for a minute. “You?” she stammered, “but you’re not a drunk, you’re not the type.”

“There is no type, Laura. You should know that right off. You don’t have to be stupid or disturbed or unbalanced. Some people just can’t drink; their minds and bodies can’t handle it without overdoing. I’m like that, and I think you are too. After you realize that, you can get on with your life.”

Laura took another sip of her coffee.

“But I said I’d drop it so I’ll quit lecturing right now. Let’s talk about something else.”

“Like what?” Laura asked with a smile.

“Well,” he began, “we could start with your music collection...” Before he could continue an angry screeching echoed from the cellar.

Laura jumped up from her chair and spilled her coffee. “What the hell?” she said, moving towards the hallway, but stopped when the wiry black body erupted through the cat door. “You bonehead,” she scolded, “look at the mess you’ve made. I ought to throw you outside for that.”

The cat gave her an aloof glance and began to groom himself, smoothing the raised hair on his tail and back.

“What’s eating him?” Mike asked, going into the kitchen for a towel.

"He's a little strange." Laura took the towel from him and began to mop up the spill. "He doesn't take to people much, do you, boy? And he's very easily spooked. He probably saw another cat outside the sliding doors."

"That's a lot of noise from such a small cat." Mike reached down to him tentatively and Laura was surprised to see the cat respond. "Have you had him long? He seems awful scrawny to me."

"You should have seen him when I found him. He looked one step away from starvation. Since then he's done nothing but eat and make trouble." Laura's voice sounded stern, but she couldn't help smiling. "Most of the time he's good company."

The cat allowed Mike to pick him up and Laura laughed, "He likes you, you should feel honored. And he's usually so choosy."

Mike ignored the good-natured insult, "I like him, too. What's his name?"

"Mostly I call him Bonehead, and he'll answer to almost anything if he feels so inclined. Or nothing. But his formal name is Anubis."

"Why Anubis?"

"Why not? It seemed appropriate when I found him. He was soaked to the skin, and so skinny that his most noticeable features were his pointy nose and his ears. He really has incredibly large ears for a cat. Somehow, he looked like those jackal-headed creatures you see in Egyptian pictures. So Anubis it was."

Mike sat on the couch, petting the cat and listening to her explanation. He looked up at her suddenly, "You know, he's been hurt."

"Hurt? Where?"

"Here." Mike carefully pointed out a nasty looking scratch on his left rear leg.

"Now, where could he have gotten that?" Laura bit her lip as she examined the wound.

"Does he go outside?"

"Not unless I let him out. He hasn't been out for days, he really seems to prefer the indoors."

"Well, this is fresh." Mike showed her his fingers, dappled with blood. "What's in the cellar?"

"Junk, mostly — boxes I haven't unpacked yet, a washer and dryer, you know, standard cellar material.

"Anything he could scrape himself on?"

"I think there's some old boards stacked in one of the corners. To tell you the truth, I don't go down there too often." She grew aware that her tone of voice changed and she wondered if he could hear the underlying fear. He looked at her questioningly. "I just don't like basements," she admitted, "they're damp and dark and the ceilings are always too low. So I go down to do laundry and change the cat box. Otherwise, I stay away. I guess in addition to everything else, I'm slightly claustrophobic."

"Do you mind if I check it out?"

"I'm not hiding anything illegal down there," Laura smiled, "so be my guest." She watched him open the door and go down the stairs, then walked to the kitchen and poured herself another cup of coffee. Anubis came in and rubbed himself against her legs, purring.

"Let's see what we can do for your leg first, baby, and then I'll give you some food." She picked him up and carried him to the bathroom. He tensed in her arms as they entered, but relaxed as she whispered to him. Laura managed to daub a small amount of antibiotic ointment on his scratch, before he expressed his displeasure with a quick swat of his paw. "Okay, food now," she agreed and let him down. He stopped for a minute at the top of the cellar stairs, gave a small hiss, and ran into the kitchen.

Laura was putting away the cat food, when Mike came back upstairs. "Find anything?" she asked casually as she closed the refrigerator.

"Not really, he could have done it on any number of things. You might want to check with the vet and see if he needs shots or anything."

Laura walked to the cellar door, locked the knob and put the bolt into place. "Thank you," she said, "do you want some more coffee?"

"Just a little bit more. I'll have to go soon." Mike smiled, glancing back at the door. "Do you have another animal in the house? A tiger, maybe?"

"What?"

Mike laughed. "That's the biggest cat door I've ever seen in my life. And did you know you have more locks on your cellar door than most people in this neighborhood have on their front door?"

The locks were already here when I moved in," Laura said. "I guess I never really noticed how many there were." She turned away from her lie and went into the kitchen.

"And the cat door?"

Laura shrugged, and mumbled an answer, holding out the coffee pot to pour him another cup.

Laura walked him to the front door, wishing he wouldn't leave. She understood he had to go to work tomorrow; he'd already explained he worked the early shift. Her mind shouted for him to stay, *Please don't leave me alone*, but outwardly she tried to stay calm and reasonable, saying all the standard phrases for an awkward first date. *Yes, I had a nice time, and yes, I'd like to go out again, thank you very much.*

He hesitated before going outside. "You're really short, you know that?" He ruffled the hair on her head in an affectionate gesture, moving his hands down to her shoulders. "I know I was pretty rough on you tonight, Laura, with all my lecturing and advice. I don't want to be pushy, but could you answer just one more question?"

She looked up at him, and saw the intensity of his eyes. "I'll try."

"Tonight, in the diner, when you were talking about your dream, you said you felt relieved that it was all over. Is that the way you really feel? Are you seriously considering suicide?"

If I said yes, she thought, *he would stay with me. But sooner or later he'd leave; I can't keep him here forever. Sooner or later, I have to face myself.* "No," she said, her voice steadier than she expected, "I'm not considering it now. I've never been of that frame of mind before."

"Good." Mike said, grasping her shoulders and pulling her closer to him. "I'd hate to lose you," he whispered quietly into her hair.

Laura didn't acknowledge the words, but she caught his meaning. She reached up and pulled his face down to hers. His hands fell to her waist and he lifted her for one long, searching kiss. Mike held her against him, then gently set her down and kissed the end of her nose. "See you later," he said as he opened the door.

"You bet." She watched as he got into his car and waved as he drove away. After shutting the front door and turning off the porch light, she walked into the kitchen to get her drink.

Once the small bottle of brandy was gone, Laura got ready for bed. She brushed her hair and teeth, humming to herself one of the songs Mike had played earlier in the evening, something about angels and red shoes. Laura sang it softly as she turned out the lights and crawled under the covers.

She stretched, rubbed one finger over her lips and smiled. "He's nice," she whispered to the dark room, "I really like him." The cat door clicked open, not once but several times, accompanied by a light thumping on the cellar stairs and a faint scratching noise. "Dumb cat," she murmured, rolling over into a fetal position. Only in the second before sleep claimed her did Laura's drunken mind register the fact that Anubis was with her, awake and watching at the foot of the bed.

CHAPTER FOUR

"No, Mommy. Mommy, Mommy, no..."

Tony Wagner had been awake from the first moment of his daughter's restlessness. He lay in bed and listened to her thrashing and hoped, as he always did, she would just fall back to sleep. But when her terrified screams began, he was at her side.

Night terrors, the doctor called them. Something that some children suffered from; most children, Dr. Wilkins had tried to reassure them, didn't even recall the incidents the next morning. Not a sign of psychological problems, it was only a phase, like baby colic, that would be eventually outgrown.

Tony refused that textbook comfort as he held his youngest daughter's trembling body. Although it had been four years since she last suffered this torment, he remembered the symptoms vividly. He knew she was still asleep, despite the fact her eyes were wide open. And he knew that tomorrow her fear would be forgotten. But tonight, like every other night, it seemed all too real.

She struggled against his embrace for a moment, then relaxed as he crooned her name over and over, smoothing her damp hair. He thought he recognized the signs of the dream's abatement, when suddenly her body tensed again. She turned in his arms and looked into his eyes. He repressed a shudder at her lifeless stare, knowing it was normal in her state. Always in the past, if she talked at this stage, the words were nonsense, without any connection to reality. But now she spoke to him, really spoke to him as if she knew the meaning in her words.

"Mommy's hurt bad, Daddy. They say she has to die. They say she's going to die. Why does Mommy have to die, Daddy?"

"Jesus," Tony swore under his breath.

"I saw her, in the bathtub. And the water turned all red. It hurt bad, Daddy."

"Oh, Lizzy," he hugged her small body to him. "It's okay, honey. It's only a dream. It's only a dream."

Lizzy murmured something he couldn't hear. He continued his crooning, rocking her gently back and forth. Eventually her body stopped shaking and relaxed completely. He shifted her in his arms and looked at her face. Lizzy's eyes were closed now and her breathing calmed and slowed. The terrors were over.

For tonight anyway, he thought as he lay her back in bed and tucked the sheet around her chin. So small and delicate, she had inherited Laura's build. Her looks, too, Tony thought as he pulled a tress of dark hair away from her face.

As he walked out of her room, he felt the familiar pangs of guilt about separating the children from their mother. Laura, when not drinking, had been a good mother. There was no doubt that she had loved her children, almost desperately. She had never been brutal or abusive; and the drinking hadn't started until after Matthew died. Maybe he hadn't been sensitive enough to her grief, to her suffering, but he'd been grieving too. And when Laura had turned to alcohol for comfort instead of him, he'd become cold and distant, so much so that he always felt that Laura's problem had been partly his fault.

Tony opened the door of Amanda's room; she still slept peacefully. It always amazed him how she never woke during one of Lizzy's spells. Mandy must be, he thought, the most self-sufficient, stoic twelve-year old ever. And although she would admit now and then that she missed her mother, she had taken the separation well.

Gently easing the door shut, he went to the bathroom, and got a drink of water. Then he returned to his bedroom, reassured by the soft breathing from Lizzy's room.

"Poor kid," he muttered as he climbed back into bed. She was the one most affected by the divorce. There was a bond between her and Laura, closer than he ever thought possible. There were times when she looked and acted so like her mother, that he found it difficult to believe they were two different people. Even now — and they had been apart for over a year — Lizzy would sit at the breakfast table, using mannerisms and expressions that were pure Laura. And Tony, although he knew the marriage was over for good, would feel a strange longing for the old days.

"I guess I miss her, too." The confession surprised him a little.

As he tried to sleep again, he hoped Lizzy's dream would not reoccur. Every time he closed his eyes her tortured words rang in his ears.

"They say she has to die."

Tony sat at the kitchen table over his third cup of coffee. Getting up from the table, he checked his watch and went to the bottom of the stairs. "School bus comes in about fifteen minutes, girls."

"Okay, Dad, we're ready now." Amanda was the first down the stairs.

"Good morning, pumpkin." He kissed her cheek and marveled at how grown up she was becoming.

"Aw, Dad," she protested the use of the childish nickname. These days she even balked at Mandy, preferring that people use her full name.

He checked out her outfit as she walked past him to get to a tray of muffins. "Where's your uniform?"

"It's a free day today, we don't have to wear them."

"Then why don't you tell me again," he shook his head, smiling, "how much I paid for jeans that look like they've been worn for twenty years?"

"You don't want to know," she mumbled, her mouth full.

"You're right, as usual, Amanda. Is Lizzy ready?"

"Getting there." She crammed the rest of the muffin into her mouth and brushed the crumbs from the table. Then she raised her eyes to him, serious and thoughtful. "Bad night, huh?"

"How did you know? You slept straight through."

Amanda began to pack books into her bag. "You look like you haven't slept at all and she has that look again."

"What look?"

"You know, that little waif look, like she just lost her best friend." Amanda pulled a compact out of her purse and set it up on the table. She rearranged her hair, and although Tony couldn't tell the difference, she smiled her satisfaction and put the mirror away. "What was it about, do you know?"

"Your mother."

Amanda raised an eyebrow and seemed about to make a comment when Lizzy burst into the kitchen.

"Mandy, have you seen my shoes?"

"By the door where you left them, dummy."

Lizzy ran to retrieve them and sat down in a chair to put them on. Amanda took one look at her and rummaging once more in her purse, produced a brush and began to style Lizzy's hair, who sat patiently for her sister's ministrations, not complaining even when Mandy hit a particularly nasty snarl.

Tony smiled, watching the two of them together. They had both inherited Laura's coloring: the dark hair, pale skin and green eyes. But where Lizzy was small for her age, Mandy had grown tall and promised to be long-legged and willowy. Model material, Laura had always said.

"Daddy?" Lizzy looked over at him, a hesitant expression on her face.

"Yeah, Pixie, what is it?"

"After school, can I call Mommy? I want to talk to her."

Tony studied her face, hoping that she had no memory of her ghastly dream last night. "Of course you can. But Susan is coming this afternoon to take you girls shopping."

"Can I call before we go? It's important."

Tony nodded. "I'll tell Susan it's okay. He smiled reassuringly. "You know, honey, last time I heard from your mother, she was fine."

"I know, but I want to hear her say it, too."

The sound of the school bus rumbling down the hill toward their house interrupted the conversation.

"They're early again," Amanda complained as she grabbed her jacket and handed Lizzy hers. "Come on, Liz, we'll miss the bus."

With a flurry of good-byes, kisses and a slam of the door they were gone. Tony sighed and poured the rest of his cold coffee down the drain. He checked his watch again and realized he had almost an hour before he had to leave for the university. His first class didn't start until ten. He cleaned off the table and put the butter into the refrigerator. When he closed the door, he saw the note in Lizzy's cramped, childish handwriting...*Mommy's new number...*

He started another small pot of coffee, lit a cigarette and went to the phone.

The telephone rang five times before Laura was sufficiently awake to reach for it. She dropped the receiver on the floor next to the bed, then picked it up. "Hello?" Her voice sounded fuzzy, so she cleared her throat and tried again. "Hello."

There was a small silence then a tentative question. "Laura? Did I wake you?"

"Hmm, yeah, sort of..."

Tony gave a small grunt of impatience. "Sorry," he said gruffly, "I thought you'd be up and ready for work. Or aren't you going to work today?"

Laura heard his voice sharpen with a sudden rush of anger, and knew that he was thinking of the days she did just that, allowing the children to fend for themselves while she slept off the previous night's binge. She tried to ignore his sarcasm. "Good morning to you, too, Tony. How nice of you to call."

"Sorry, Laura." The anger dropped out of his voice, replaced by what sounded like pity. "How've you been?"

"Pretty good," Laura, finally awake, crawled out of bed. "Listen, can you hold on a minute while I get the portable phone."

"Sure."

While he waited, Tony smiled to himself. He could almost see her. She would be naked, she never wore anything to bed. Chances are, he thought, she wouldn't even put a robe on, but would sit talking to him, at the dining room table, totally nude. The situation seemed obscene to him somehow, and totally incongruous, but his body responded, and he shifted uncomfortably in his chair. *I guess old habits die hard*, he thought with a wry smile, when she picked up the other phone.

"Tony? You still there?" Her voice was indistinct and distant.

"Hang up the other phone, Laura."

"Oh, okay."

There was a slight pause and then a click. "Is that better?"

"Much, thank you." Now that he had her attention, he couldn't think of what to say. He knew what he wanted to say — the kids miss you, I miss you, even though I'll be getting married again in ten weeks — but somehow that seemed a bad way to start the conversation.

Fortunately, Laura took the initiative. "I'm glad you called, Tony. I have some news for you."

"Good news, I hope."

"Well, bad and good, both. But I think in the long run it will be good. I got picked up for drunk driving."

Tony ran his fingers through his curly hair. "Oh, Laura. You really should be more careful. Next time, take a cab."

"There won't be a next time. Monday I go into rehabilitation. They tell me there's a good chance I can stay sober after that. I thought you'd be happy to hear that."

"I am happy, Laura. That's great news." He tried to sound enthusiastic, but could only remember the other times she had quit. Each time it had been for good and each time it had failed, leaving her more and more depressed with every attempt.

"So," she hesitated a bit, "if I do quit, can I have the girls for a while?" She rushed her words together, and he recognized the tactic, knowing that she thought if she just spoke fast enough he might give in. The girls did the same thing to him and he held back a chuckle. "Not too long, maybe two or three weeks. I miss them so much; and I think it would be a good idea for me to see them. A sort of reinforcement for good behavior, don't you think?"

"We'll see, Laura. We can talk about that later. Will you be home this afternoon? Lizzy wants to talk to you."

"Great, I'll be home all afternoon. I look forward to it."

Tony could hear the happiness in her voice. "I have some news for you, too."

"Okay, hit me with it."

"I sort of wish you didn't use that expression. You see, Susan and I are getting married."

Tony wondered if he imagined that slight pause on Laura's part, and her sharp intake of breath, because when she did speak, her voice seemed bright and sincere. "Tony, that's wonderful. I'm very happy for you, she'll make a good professor's wife and she'll be great with the kids. Tell her I said hi and congratulations."

"I would have told you sooner, Laura, but I didn't know how to tell you." He was relieved that she took it so well; he had always tried to be completely honest with her, and holding back on this news had bothered him. "I wasn't quite sure how you would take it; I mean we've not been divorced that long, and you and Susan were best friends at one time..."

"Tony, I understand, I really do. It will take some getting used to, I suppose, but it seems like a good match to me. You two always got along."

"Laura, we never, you know, when you and I were..."

"I never thought it for a moment." He knew she was lying. "And even if you had," Laura continued, "who could blame you? Let's face it, I wasn't much good at the wife and mother thing, was I?"

There was a short silence on Tony's end.

"Hey, Tony, don't jump too quickly to my defense. Anyway, how are the girls?"

"God, they're growing so fast. But they're adjusting well to the new school; Mandy is trying out for the cheerleading squad and Lizzy's on the chess team."

"Tell them I miss them, okay?" Tony could hear the tears in her voice.

"Sure. And when Lizzy calls this afternoon, please let her know you're doing well. She had a nightmare last night and is still pretty shook up about it this morning."

"A nightmare?" Her voice acquired an edge. "What was it about?"

"Well," he hesitated. It was a difficult thing to tell Laura that Lizzy had dreamed her dead. "Actually, she wasn't very coherent, but it had something to do with you. I got the feeling she thought that you were in some sort of danger."

Tony knew he didn't imagine Laura's pause this time.

"Oh, no, I'm okay. Where would be the danger here? Just tell her I'm fine, and that I'm looking forward to our talk this afternoon. Oh, and Tony?"

"Yeah?"

"Don't worry about you and Susan. I really do think it's great. I had a date last night, myself."

"That's nice. Anyone I know?"

"No, I doubt it. Actually, we met because he's the one who arrested me."

"Oh," Tony remarked flatly. He didn't know how to deal with that information, so he left it alone. "I've got to run, Laura. It's been good talking to you."

"Same here, Tony. Take care."

Tony hung up the phone with a small shake of his head. Same old Laura, no matter what sort of trouble she got herself into, she always came out ahead. And now she's dating the policeman who picked her up. *Maybe*, he thought, *he'll be a steadying influence on her. It might be the best thing for her.*

Later, between his morning classes, he phoned Susan to discuss the phone call. He didn't mention Lizzy's dream had prompted the call or that he'd told Laura about it. But he did tell her about the rehabilitation and that she was now dating the policeman who'd arrested her.

"So, I was thinking, honey," Tony was trying to convince himself as well as her, "that if she really does stop and if this policeman thing continues, we might want to let her have the girls while we're on our honeymoon."

Susan considered the matter. "I don't quite see that it could hurt, Tony. She is their mother and she does love them." She paused for a minute and thought how pleased Laura would be to have them back, if only for two weeks. "Yes," she said determinedly, "I think it's a good idea. Provided that Laura's not drinking, of course. I mean, what harm could it possibly do?"

CHAPTER FIVE

Nursing her cooling coffee, Laura remained at the dining room table long after she hung up the phone. She worried over the dream Lizzy had, Tony's upcoming marriage and the next four weeks of rehab. She studied her reflection in the remaining coffee, then swirled the cup to watch it dissolve and took the last swallow.

She had read all the AA literature she had been given. Propaganda, her father had said, yet their philosophy made sense to her — live one day at a time and don't worry about the things you can't change. "Let's start today, Laura," she told herself. The resolution was easy because her head still ached from the brandy she had drunk last night. She stood up and swayed a bit; the alcohol hadn't yet worked its way out of her system and she felt slightly woozy. Laura put her cup into the sink and began to walk down the hall.

Anubis burst through the cat door and Laura swerved to avoid him. As she stepped back she stumbled over the shoes she had left there last night, and in trying to check her backward motion, she overcompensated and ended up face down in the hallway. Laura lay there for a moment, stunned until she realized she wasn't really hurt. A small gust of air blew on her naked back from under the cellar door and she felt the hair on her arms raise. The cat nestled against her and began to lick her face and neck. She pushed him away and sat up, grimacing. "God, Anubis," she scratched his ears, then eased herself up from the floor, "your breath is foul. You need kitty mints or something." Without warning, the combination of the fall, last night's brandy and this morning's coffee overcame her and Laura fell to her knees and began to vomit.

When it was over, she sat back on her heels and looked at the mess. Fortunately, there had not been much in her stomach. *Thank God I didn't have breakfast,* she thought as she stood up unsteadily. Pulling a towel from the linen closet, she saw Anubis sitting in the doorway to her bedroom. If she hadn't felt so weakened she might have laughed at the expression on his face. Reproachful and indignant, he looked at her as if he wondered whether she would get her nose rubbed in it.

"Don't be so superior, Bonehead. Yeah, I did it, but I'm also the one who has to clean it up." He turned his back on her and walked into the bedroom.

"Thanks a lot," she called after him, "I always clean up your mess."

She scrubbed at the carpet. It seemed to be only coffee, she decided, and probably wouldn't stain. As she finished, the ridiculousness of the situation struck her — here she was, a grown woman, stark naked and hung-over, throwing up no more than four feet away from the bathroom. And no more than four minutes after she had decided to take control of her life. Laura began to laugh, tentatively at first and then boisterously, hysterically, until tears streamed down her face.

"Shit," she exclaimed, still laughing as she stepped into the shower, "what a way to start the day."

After the shower, Laura felt refreshed and revitalized, and threw on a pair of cut-off shorts and a T-shirt. Pouring herself a glass of diet soda, she sat at the dining room table with her laptop, and listed the items to be done before she went to rehab. There really wasn't much to do, she realized, most things could be taken care of by a phone call or two. But at the top of the list was cleaning the house, something no phone call would accomplish.

She turned her stereo on full blast and after three hours she had finished. The sheets were changed, the floors scrubbed, the tables dusted. On her bed sat stacks of clothes, carefully folded for packing.

"Now," she addressed Anubis solemnly as he watched from the foot of her bed, "all I need is a suitcase." She walked out of the bedroom and down the hall to the cellar door. Throwing back the upper bolt, Laura hesitated, listening. Over the blare of the stereo she could hear the faint ring of the phone. "Damn," she said and locked the door again, turned down the stereo and went into the kitchen. Her hand shook as she reached for the receiver. "Too much booze," she told herself and answered the phone.

"Hello?"

"Laura, I'm glad you're there."

"Susan? Hey, it's just like old home week, huh? First Tony and then you. How have you been?"

"Are you okay? You sound funny."

Laura ran her fingers through her hair. "I'm fine. I was just surprised to hear your voice, that's all. And it's been sort of a strange week."

"So I gathered." Susan's voice sounded odd; it could have been the phone line, or maybe, Laura thought with a smile, a guilty conscience. "Listen, Laura, about Tony and me, I wanted to tell you a while ago, but I just couldn't." The sadness and regret in her voice were apparent.

"Yeah, Tony said practically the same thing this morning. Susan, we've all been friends since college. Don't tear yourself up over this. I always expected that Tony would get married again, not this soon maybe," *and not to you*, she mentally supplied, "but it's not exactly going to ruin my life at this point. Now that I've had a chance to think about it, it seems an ideal solution for everyone."

"Everyone but you." Susan's voice was now soft, apologetic.

"Hey, no one can take responsibility for how screwed up I am but me. But things will change." The determination in her voice surprised Laura, but she felt good about the statement, so good she said it again. "Things will change."

"Tony told me you're going into rehab."

"First thing Monday morning. I was just getting ready when you called."

"But you've got two more days. What will you do over the weekend?" Laura thought she detected a note of disapproval and bristled.

"Drink myself blind, probably, what's it to you?" In the shocked silence that followed, Laura regretted her words. "Look, I'm sorry, I didn't really mean that. I don't really know what I'll do — maybe Mike will call or something."

"Mike — your policeman friend? What's he like? Tony wouldn't tell me anything." They were on more familiar ground with this conversation; the subject, something they had discussed many times at school together, made Laura feel years younger. Suddenly, the intervening events of their lives did not exist and if she closed her eyes, she could clearly visualize the dorm room they had shared.

"Oh, Susan, he's gorgeous," Laura confessed, her voice slightly breathless, "tall, muscular, strong. I could really fall for this one, you know? And he seems to like me, although I'm not quite sure why. I mean, I've been such a mess every time I met him, but he understands me, knows what I'm going through.

"And he saved my life," she said quietly, and shivered, "or at least it seems like he did."

"What?"

"Oh, nothing. He's really a great guy and I hope to see a lot more of him."

"Wow," Susan said, "he sounds wonderful. I can't wait to meet him."

Laura laughed, "No way, toots, this one is off limits."

Susan returned the laugh. "Okay, but maybe I can meet him some day anyway. I've got to go now; I'm picking the girls up from school — we're going shopping."

"Is Mandy still so picky about her clothes?"

"Worse."

Laura groaned in appreciation. "Well, then you'll all have a lot of fun. Sorry I'm missing it. Take care and tell them I said hello."

"Sure thing. We'll be back around five or so. Lizzy wants to talk to you, will you be there?"

"I'll be here. Thanks for calling, Susan."

"No problem. And Laura?"

"Yeah?"

"Good luck in rehab. You can do it, you know. It'll be wonderful when you do."

"Thanks."

Laura hung up the phone. "Now, where was I?" She looked around for a bit and remembered. "Suitcase," she said and opened the cellar door.

She flicked on the light switch and was rewarded with one bright flash, then shadowy darkness. "Shit," she turned off the switch, walked to the hall closet and found a light bulb. "Damn things are always burning out when you need them." Carefully gripping the rail in one hand and the bulb in the other, she slowly went down the stairs. Laura grimaced as she stretched to reach the light from the second stair and squinted her eyes in concentration. The fixture was lightly covered in cobwebs; she sucked in a quick breath as she reached through them, but eventually got the bulb replaced.

She relaxed slightly when the cellar was lit again and picked up her largest suitcase. When she felt its weight, she remembered that she had filled it with books on her arrival. It was too heavy to carry up the stairs, so she sat down on the rippled cement floor and began to unpack it. By the time the books were neatly stacked, Laura felt chilled, and her bare legs, one mass of gooseflesh. She zipped the suitcase and stood up slowly, straightening her stiff back with a small sigh. "I'm getting old," she said wearily and the empty room with concrete block walls made her words sound distorted and strange. She put her hand down to the handle of the suitcase and grasped it, only to drop it with a thump a second later.

"Shoo. Scat. Go away," she said to the spider perched on top of the case. It wasn't that large, but it was also not so small that she wanted to brush it away with her bare hand. She kicked the suitcase over and the insect scuttled away to hide in one of the shadowy corners.

"If I had my shoes on, you wouldn't get away alive, buddy." Somehow the words sounded angrier than Laura intended and the walls in the near-empty cellar seemed to magnify that rage and bounce it back toward her. Laura held her breath for a second, expecting some sort of retaliation. *Retaliation?* she thought. *From whom? The spider? What the hell is going on?* She shook off the thoughts, but they left her feeling dizzy and weakened; her legs trembled and she felt as if she'd been stuck to the floor. With great effort, she moved, picking up the overturned suitcase and walking toward the stairs. At the bottom of the steps, she noticed with shock that the door was beginning to swing shut. *I can't be left down here alone. I'll never get away.* The sheer fright of that thought gave her a rush and she moved faster, running now, the case banging loudly against the wall and her legs. When she reached the top, she pushed against the almost closed door and practically fell into the hallway. She threw the luggage into the living room and slammed the door shut, resting there a moment, eyes closed, waiting for the sudden panic to subside.

When her heart rate slowed and the awful chill subsided she opened her eyes to see Anubis at the end of the hall. He meowed at her and she smiled, feeling silly. "Just a spider," she said to him, locking and moving quickly away from the door, "a draft, and an overripe imagination."

CHAPTER SIX

Watching Susan and the girls get out of her yellow SUV in the driveway, Tony knew instantly that it had been a difficult trip. Amanda's mouth was set in a rigid frown, Susan scowled, struggling with the bags, and Lizzy's eyes were red and puffy. She trailed behind the two others, dragging her feet as if dreading each step to come, looking for all the world as if she'd lost her best friend.

He opened the door and they all filed in, silently. *Definitely not a good sign,* Tony thought, but smiled anyway in an effort to diffuse the situation. "How'd my ladies do?"

Susan rolled her eyes. "Great, just great." She dropped the shopping bags in the foyer corner. "Rooms, girls."

Lizzy was still crying as she walked by Tony, he gave her a pat on the shoulder. Amanda stalked up the stairs and once there, slammed her bedroom door only to open it a second later and yell down the stairs. "You're not our mother! So you should just quit trying to be!"

Tony had draped an arm around Susan's neck and they both flinched when Amanda slammed her door again. "Want to talk about it?" Tony led them both to the kitchen and they sat down at the table.

Susan shook her head. "Things were going just fine, until Lizzy started crying. Did you tell her she could call Laura right after school?"

Tony sighed. "Yeah, I probably did."

"Anyway, that's what started it all off. Lizzy kept insisting she had to call Laura. Laura was in danger and she had to warn her. Where on earth did that come from?"

"She had a nightmare last night, I thought I told you about that."

"Maybe you did. It's kind of hard to keep track of it all when I don't live here. When she started making a fuss, I gave her my cell phone to use and the battery had run too low to get a signal, so we plugged it into the car lighter and went into the mall. She seemed better at first, but after a while she ended up dragging behind us, crying. Quietly, you know? Just sniffling a bit with tears streaming down her face. I tried to jolly her along a bit, but nothing helped. Eventually I lost my temper, told her that she should quit being such a baby and that both you and I had talked to Laura in the morning and she was just fine. And *that* set Amanda off." Susan rubbed her hand across her eyes. "You know how they start playing off each other."

Tony nodded. "Years of practice."

"There we are, standing in the middle of the mall, one girl is crying and the other is ranting about how I get to do anything I want but they're practically prisoners and I don't care about them and I ruined their mother's life and theirs as well. And I'm feeling like a wicked stepmother." Susan gave a dry chuckle. "You get the picture. I got them out of there as quickly as I could."

Tony reached over and held her hand. "I'm sorry, sweetheart. It's been a bad day for everyone."

"Yeah. I love you, Tony. But sometimes I don't know if us getting married so soon is a good idea..."

"It's just one day, Susan. Most of the time we get along just fine, the four of us. Now, why don't you order us pizza? And I'll go upstairs and talk to the girls."

Tony knocked softly on Lizzy's door first and when she didn't answer, cracked open the door. Lizzy lay sprawled out on top of the bed, fully dressed and sound asleep. He whispered her name, but didn't push her any further. *Poor little thing has been through enough,* he thought, regardless of how irrational her fear of a nightmare was.

He stopped next at Amanda's door, across the hallway. He knocked softly there too, at first, then turned the knob to find the door locked. "Amanda," he called and knocked again several times; each successive knock becoming louder. Eventually she opened the door wearing her iPod earphones around her neck.

"Yeah?"

Tony hated the tone of voice and the defiant set of her mouth. "I want you to apologize to Susan. And quit playing that damn music so loud! The whole house could fall down around you and you'd never know a thing! And don't get me started on hearing damage."

Amanda gave an exaggerated sigh. "Okay."

"We're having pizza for dinner. Come down in about ten minutes and set the table. Lizzy's asleep; try to wake her if you can."

"She'll probably sleep through the night now. She was really worked up. And you know how she is."

Laura sat at her dining room table and stared over at the kitchen clock in disbelief. After she'd finished her packing, the day had just dragged on. Ordinarily, she never noticed the passage of time; in fact she rarely had enough moments in the day, work and drinking stole away her time. But now she had no job and was determined to stay away from the bottle, at least until she talked to Lizzy.

Even so, Laura thought, *just one won't hurt; and while I drink that, I can toss the rest of it.* She got up from the table and opened up the kitchen cabinet below the sink. She kept most of her liquor here, although there were bottles stashed in various places around the house: vodka chilling in the freezer with wine and beer in the refrigerator, a flask of scotch nestled in bottom of her purse, and yet another flask, the one with whiskey, tucked away in her bedside table drawer. "Fully stocked," Laura whispered with a small smile. Fully stocked was good — it meant she could handle any situation that came her way. Being fully stocked made her feel secure, comforted. But now... *now those bastards want to take it all away from me. This is all I have left. Otherwise, there's nothing. No comfort. No love. Oh, no, not for me. Bastards.*

As had happened earlier in the cellar, the vehemence of her thoughts surprised her. Anger was far from her mind. She'd been intending to have one drink only. And then meant to pour all of it down the drain, throw it all away, in preparation for her new life of sobriety. "Shit." She began to pull the bottles out from under the sink, one by one, and lined them up on the counter. The late afternoon sun through the window shone on and through the row of bottles, bathing the counter top and kitchen tile in a wavering colored reflection. Glancing again at the clock, Laura cracked the seal on a bottle of port she'd been saving for a special occasion. Pouring a generous amount into a juice glass, she held it up and admired its rich color. "Cheers," she said, "Now's about as special as it's ever going to get."

The first swallow tasted harsh, but the liquid flowed easily down her throat and into her stomach, spreading an innocuous warmth. She gave a sad, small smile and took another drink.

The next two glasses went down slowly; Laura savored each and every drop, oblivious to everything else around her — lost in her lover's embrace. But when she finished the third glass, she came to with a jolt and looked around. While she'd sat drinking and daydreaming, it had grown dark outside and the normal noises of a suburban neighborhood — laughter, lawn mowers, the spin of bicycle tires, the clatter of skateboards — had all ceased. The quiet fell so deep, Laura felt like she could hear the air moving in and out of her lungs, the blood rushing in her veins. The darkness of the house engulfed her. Only the pulsing green power light of her laptop, on the table in the dining room, was visible. She timed her breathing to its rhythm, inhaling and exhaling, until that seemed to be all that existed. As her breathing grew louder, she felt a brief moment of panic, thinking that if the light went out completely she wouldn't be able to draw her next breath.

Would that be so bad?

"Yeah."

How could it be bad? You have nothing on earth to live for, nothing but all those bottles. And they're taking that away.

"I have my girls if nothing else."

You think they care? Did you notice the phone ringing tonight? You're out of their life and they're well rid of you.

The cat door clicked; Anubis came over and butted his head against Laura's leg. She reached down and scratched his head. "But I have you, Bonehead, don't I?"

The moment of despair forgotten, Laura scooped up the cat in her arms and cuddled him, carrying him out to the kitchen. She flipped on the kitchen light and opened the refrigerator. "You want some food, baby?"

Watching the cat eat voraciously as usual, Laura had a sudden thought and gasped. "Shit," she said, shaking her head, "I forgot to find someone to take care of you while I'm gone. Damn."

See, you can't even take care of one little cat. What good are you?

“Shut up.” Laura poured herself another glass of port. “I’ll go out tomorrow and talk to the neighbors. Maybe get one of the kids to check in every so often.”

That dilemma solved, Laura checked the clock again, then picked up the phone. Tony answered on the third ring, just as she was about to hang up.

“Hi, Tony. What’s happening?”

“We’re just watching a little television before bed.”

“And are the girls around?”

“Sleeping, Laura.” She could hear his disapproval through the phone. “It’s pretty late for them. Don’t you know what time it is?”

“Yeah, but it’s Friday and not a school night. Isn’t this a bit early?”

He paused. “Yeah, I suppose so. But they had a rough day. Lizzy’s been sleeping since they came home from shopping. Apparently they had a small altercation at the mall.”

“What happened?”

“She was upset because Susan didn’t let her call right after school.”

“Ah. Well, that was the plan, wasn’t it? I’ve been waiting by the phone. It’s not as if I don’t have other things I could be doing.” Laura winced at the sound of the whine creeping into her voice.

“Cutting into your drinking time, are we?”

The sheer unfairness of that question surprised and angered Laura. For one brief second she pictured Tony and Susan, snuggled together on the couch in her old living room. They could each have a drink of wine or a nightcap — that wasn’t a problem for them. But God forbid Laura, with no responsibilities, no one to answer to, should do the same. “Fuck you.”

“Excuse me?”

She remembered how that particular profanity bothered Tony and smiled. Not a pleasant smile at all, the sheer nastiness of it sent a shiver down her back. Still, she didn't take it back. "You heard me."

"You've had quite a bit to drink, haven't you?"

"And if I have, so what? It's none of your business, after all."

"Laura, you are still my business. We all care about you, about what happens to you."

Yeah, right, as long as what happens to me is what you want to happen. "Do me a favor, Tony. Quit patronizing me. I hated it when we were married and I hate it a hundred times more now. Just go back to whatever you were doing and have Lizzy call me tomorrow."

"Can't. Not tomorrow. We're heading up to my Susan's parents' house early in the morning."

Laura sighed. "Sunday then. Please. I go away starting Monday and there'll be no phone calls for a while. I'm only allowed to make calls one day a week and only emergency calls can come in."

"Really? That seems a bit extreme."

"Yeah, it's not exactly a resort." Laura gave a snort of amusement. "More like boot camp, I suspect. No phones, no laptops, no iPods. Visitors only once a week, on Wednesdays. I think prisoners have a better deal. Rehab is all group hugs and therapy, healthy food and clean living. Sounds like fun, doesn't it?"

"But maybe it works, Laura."

"Maybe. I'll give it a shot. Not that I have a choice in the matter. But maybe it'll work." She sighed. The anger she'd felt earlier flowed out of her and she felt completely drained. She sipped on her drink and refilled her glass, not caring if Tony's ears could hear the sound of liquid being poured. "But I really would like to explain this all to the girls myself. They need to know why their mother is being locked away for a while."

"There's probably no need. I've explained it to them."

"Fine. But *I* want to, as well." *Who knows what kind of stupid guilt trip Tony brought into the discussion.* "I am still their mother, Tony. And I have a right to talk with them."

"No one is disputing that, Laura."

"I don't know. It seems like between you and Susan, there's a plot to keep them from me."

"You really have been drinking too much tonight. You're paranoid."

"Whatever. I'm too tired to argue, Tony. And it never does me any good anyway. And just to make sure I get to talk to them, I'll call on Sunday. Good night."

Laura hung up the phone, and walked over to the dining room window, staring out into the night and feeling rather satisfied with the way the conversation went. For once, she hadn't let Tony walk all over her feelings; for once she actually said what she wanted. *Blame some of it on the alcohol,* she thought, *and the rest on the angry mood I've been in all day.* Oddly enough, she was normally a quiet drunk, but tonight she'd been raring for a fight.

"Nice of Tony to oblige," she said. "But still, I didn't get to talk to the girls." She made a face at herself in the window, then turned around, looked at the bottles on the counter and walked back into the kitchen. Anubis had curled up next to them and regarded her with sleepy eyes. "What do you think? Pour it all away tonight or save some fun for tomorrow?"

He put his ears back and she nodded, scratching the top of his head. "Yeah, tomorrow." She picked up the bottle of port and walked back to the dining room table. Sitting down, she poured another glass and bolted it down, then held the bottle up to the light. "This one's practically a dead soldier anyway," she laughed softly and poured the rest of it into her juice glass. “So that’s one less bottle to dispose of. We’re making progress at least.”

Her laughter turned into tears, though, at the sheer loneliness of her life. The only voice she heard most days was hers. The only thoughts were the tortuous doubts and self-loathing of her own making. “Shit.” Laura put her head down on the table and allowed herself to cry.

Weary from the emotional day, she felt herself dropping off to sleep as she cried. *I should get back to bed,* she thought, *but the bedroom is just so far away.*

“It’s okay.” She heard a voice, not hers. Soft, childish, with a bit of a lisp, it sounded so much like Lizzy and Laura gave a little smile as she felt the tiny hand on hers.

“It’s okay,” the voice repeated, “I know a place where you can be safe. Where you won’t be sad anymore.”

“That would be nice,” Laura told the girl in what must be a dream. “But I don’t think there is such a place, anywhere.”

“Oh, but there is.” The cold little hand tugged at hers. “And I know where it is. I can show you. Come with me.”

“Later. I just want to sleep.” Memories of being passed out on the couch on a particularly bad day washed over her. Her reply now, like then, sounded slow and slurred. “I just want to sleep now, Lizzy. I’ll look at your painting later.” Feeling guilty, she nevertheless put her arm up to cover her eyes and knocked her now empty glass on to the floor. She faintly heard the glass shatter.

“No. Please, Mommy, come now. Please? Pretty please?”

That last plea reached Laura and she finally submitted to the insistent pull of the hand. It led her across the room, heedless of the shards of broken glass on the carpet.

It led her past the kitchen, ignoring the bottles strewn around, ignoring the cries of the cat. They stopped in front of the door to the cellar.

"You need to undo the lock, Mommy. I can't reach it."

Laura's hand went to the brass slide. The coldness of the metal seemed to burn her hand and she pulled back.

"No," the voice whispered, "You can't stop. We're so close now."

CHAPTER SEVEN

Mike dialed Laura's number for the fourth time. The first two times he'd gotten a busy signal, but the third time, there'd been some sort of interference on the line. It sounded almost as if someone had picked it up before it could ring and then stood far away from the receiver and whispered. Mike hesitated calling again when he felt the hair on the back of his neck stand up, but he smoothed it down, feeling silly, and gave it one last shot.

This time the phone actually rang. And rang. And rang. Just as he was about to hang up, the ringing stopped.

"'lo?"

"Laura?"

"Yeah." She spoke slowly, as if she'd been sleeping.

"Did I wake you? I'm sorry..."

"No," Laura said, her voice still quiet and distant. "I wasn't sleeping. Or at least I don't think I was sleeping. It's weird — one second I'm sitting at the dining room table and the next I'm standing with my hand on the cellar door. I guess I planned on going down there. I've no idea why."

There was a long pause. "Hold on a second, okay?"

"Sure," Mike said and he heard the clatter of the receiver on the kitchen counter. He could tell she'd been drinking, but that didn't matter. He of all people knew about those last desperate days before rehab; he was sort of surprised, actually, to find her awake and functioning. No, the drinking didn't bother him, he realized, but her state of mind did. He remembered the dream she'd told him about yesterday when they'd had dinner; how could he have forgotten? And oddly enough, despite not having known Laura for long, the thought of her distress hit him right in the gut.

Mike strained to listen to see if he could figure out what was happening. He heard Laura say "Ow." And then, "Oh, shit."

"Laura," he said loudly into the phone, "are you okay?"

"Yeah," she picked up again. "Sorry. I cut my foot on some broken glass. Must've just happened, although I don't really remember. But it's fine now — I mean it's not real deep or anything. Nothing a bandage won't cure."

"Good."

Laura sighed. "Pretty much, it's the perfect end to a perfect day like today."

"Sorry to hear that. What's happening? And is there anything I can do?"

Again there was a long pause on Laura's end of the line. Mike could hear that faint whispering interference he'd gotten that one time he'd called. "Laura?"

"Huh? Sorry, I sort of faded off. It's been a really long day. I've been waiting all day for Lizzy to call. Finally, I called there only to get into a huge fight with Tony."

"Tony?"

"My ex. He was being controlling as always; I decided I'd had enough and called him on it. He's not fond of that."

Mike heard Laura give a soft chuckle. "No," she said, her voice growing a bit stronger now, "he really is not fond of someone calling his bluff. The whole time we were married, I barely put up a fight about anything. But, you know, I don't have to take it now, do I? And until Monday morning, I'm a free person — free to do what I want. Even if it means having a few more drinks over Tony's comfort level."

Mike detected a note of defiance in her voice as if she were expecting him to argue with her. Maybe he would, if they were married and had years of history. But now, their relationship, if that is indeed what this was, was fragile. Like Laura. And she would be tested soon enough. Besides, it seemed her ex-husband piled her with more guilt than anyone needed.

Mike jumped to her defense. "I already told you, Laura, I don't mind if you drink. After rehab, it'll be different, everything will be different, but you'll have had a month of practice and you'll learn different ways of coping with the cravings and the temptations. Alcoholism is a disease, regardless of what most people think, it's not a weakness. Expecting you to cure yourself without the proper treatment is ridiculous. So drink up. Just be careful, okay? I don't want you to fall down those cellar stairs and break your neck."

Laura laughed. "If so, you're the only one who doesn't."

"Laura."

"Okay, okay, I know, I'm fine. Much better now, actually. You seem to manage to always come to my rescue. Thanks for calling."

"Well," Mike said, "I wasn't just calling to wake you up out of another nightmare, I wanted to ask what you were doing tomorrow. I have the whole day off and I thought we might make a day of it."

"I have absolutely nothing planned for the rest of the weekend. Except to find someone to look after the cat while I'm gone."

"Tell you what," Mike said, "you give me your key and I'll do that for you. But for tomorrow, I thought you might have some errands to run and I'll provide the transport. Then I thought we'd just play it by ear. Maybe a picnic if the weather is nice. Plus, there's a Saturday night AA meeting I usually attend and I kind of figured you might want to see what goes on at these things. There's a woman there I'd like to introduce you to. If you hit it off she could be your sponsor."

"Whoa, cowboy, slow it down a little." Laura's voice grew light and teasing. "You're gonna sweep me right off my feet with all this fancy planning."

"So the answer is no." Mike failed to keep the disappointment from his voice.

"No, silly. The answer is yes. Of course I'd love to spend the day with you. It's very thoughtful of you."

Mike chuckled. "Thoughtful has nothing to do with it. I have ulterior motives, you know."

"Shhhh, don't spoil the surprise."

Mike could hear Laura stifle a yawn. "You should get to bed. I'll pick you up around nine o'clock tomorrow morning."

"Man," Laura said, "that really is early."

"Which is why you need to sleep now."

"Yeah, I guess so." A hesitant tone entered Laura's voice. "I'm not sure I can sleep, though." She paused again. "Mike?" Her voice wavered slightly. He wondered if she was crying.

"I'm here."

"Mike." She caught a breath. "I'm scared."

"Scared? Of what?"

"Oh, I don't know. Everything. Nothing. I've got this knot in the pit of my stomach that won't go away. And it's so dark here. And quiet. But not quiet. That sounds really stupid. Shit, I don't know."

"It's okay, Laura. I understand."

"Do you? Then maybe you can tell me what's wrong. Because I sure as hell don't. Nothing makes sense. So if you can explain it..."

"I can do better than that. I can help you sleep."

"How?"

"I'm going to wait on the line here. You do what you need to do to get ready for bed, put on whatever CD will relax you, crawl under the covers and I'll talk you to sleep."

"Really? You'd do that?"

The relief and gratitude in her voice made Mike happy he'd thought of it. "Of course I would."

"Okay, then, you hold on and I'll be right back." Laura set the phone down on the kitchen counter and smiled. He really was nice, even though she kept having hysterics when he was around. *Maybe tomorrow,* she thought, *I'll have a chance to show him my better side.*

She checked to make sure she'd locked the front door, then carefully walked into the dining room to pick up the broken glass so that the cat wouldn't get into it while she slept. "Although," she said, looking at Anubis curled up on one of the dining room chairs, "you usually have better sense than I do." Fortunately, the glass only broke into four large pieces, easily found and discarded. She lifted her foot and looked intently at the sole, but couldn't find anything wrong. "Weird," she said to the cat. "Let's get to bed."

She stopped in the bathroom on the way, washed her face, brushed her hair and teeth, took two of her Valium, stripped off her clothes and dropped them into the hamper. Then she padded out to the kitchen, picked the phone back up and deliberately left the light on. Back in her bedroom, she turned on her clock radio tuned to a mellow jazz station, and crawled under the covers, enjoying the feel of the clean sheets against her bare flesh.

"Hey." She giggled slightly into the phone. "I'm here. Are you?"

Mike's voice was like warm molasses, soothing and sweet. "You bet. Are you all settled in? Wearing your footed jammies?"

Laura laughed again. "I don't wear pajamas," she said, then blushed.

"Oh. That's good to know, I guess." Mike laughed a bit. "And here I'm all set to read to you from my favorite childhood book. Somehow knowing that you're naked doesn't really fit that image."

"So picture me in pink flannel jammies with a big bow in my hair if that makes you feel better. You're going to read to me? No one's done that since I was a small girl. What are you going to read?"

"See if you can guess. 'Chapter One: THE RIVER BANK. The Mole had been working very hard all the morning, spring cleaning his little home.'"

"Ooooh, this is one of my favorites too. How on earth did you know? I used to read this to Lizzy when she was real small."

"I just guessed. You seemed the type. I'm glad I'm right. Now be quiet and listen like a good little girl."

"Yes, Mike." Laura smiled, snuggled into her covers with the phone pressed to her ear, focusing on Mike's voice and allowing herself to relax and drift away to a simpler time. Anubis curled up next to her, purring loudly.

"Is that you?" Mike asked.

"It's the cat — he's enjoying this too. Please don't stop."

"I'll bet you say that to all the boys."

"Hey," she giggled again, "get your mind out of the gutter and just read. Please?"

And Mike did read. Laura remembered drifting off just as Rat was explaining to Mole about the Wild Wood.

When she woke up the next morning, she felt rested and refreshed. She must have said good night and hung up at some point, for while the phone still nestled next to her cheek, it was turned off. Laura smiled. What a wonderful thing that was, to be read to again until she fell asleep. "I'm sure those nasty old nightmares were greatly disappointed," she said to Anubis, who'd woken up and was stretching. "How about some breakfast for you?" She glanced at the clock, "And a quick shower for me. Mike'll be here in about forty-five minutes or so."

Mike had planned out a lovely day for the two of them: breakfast at a small Airstream trailer diner which had the best peppered bacon Laura had ever eaten; a picnic (with a basket Mike packed himself) at a local park for lunch; and dinner at a small Italian place, complete with red and white checkered table cloths and candles dripping down the necks of old twine-wrapped Chianti bottles.

In between the meals, they drove around, stopping at little shops in out of the way places. And they talked — about everything. Mike turned out to be very understanding and not at all judgmental. In fact, he seemed the total opposite of Tony, who always made her feel as if she lacked the elements needed to make her an entire person. As a result, the whole day proved something to Laura, something she desperately needed at this point in her life. She wasn't a bad person, not at all. Instead she felt worthy, of life and of love. Of Mike's love, although that would be something she wouldn't mention now. It was much too soon. And rehab still loomed over her, like a giant black cloud. *Let's get that out of the way,* she thought, *before I start building a life around this man.*

Even the AA meeting turned out to be an interesting experience. "It wasn't at all what I was expecting," Laura said, as they pulled into her driveway.

Mike chuckled a bit. "What did you expect?"

"I don't know. Something a bit more evangelical, maybe — with lots of Praise-the-Lord and arm waving. The literature is so God and

Jesus oriented. Not that there's anything wrong with that, but that approach doesn't do all that much for me..."

"I know exactly what you mean."

"It's not that I don't believe in God, I do, but, well, I'm not a religious person. I've not been to church since...well, not for a long time. I was too angry, I think. None of it seemed to make sense, worshiping a god who would allow a little baby to die, much less *my* little baby. It just didn't seem fair."

Mike nodded, reached over and touched Laura's hand lightly.

"I don't feel all that much like abandoning control to a higher power." She paused for a second, shaking her head. "I guess I'm still angry."

Mike held her hand now and squeezed it tightly. Laura ducked her head and smiled, in spite of the seriousness of their discussion.

"Although, maybe that higher power could do a better job — I've pretty much mucked everything up all on my own." She gave a sad laugh, then pulled away from his hand and picked up her purse from the car floor. "Want to come inside?"

"I was hoping you'd ask."

As she opened the front door, her good mood dissipated and all of the good feelings she'd been building seemed to disappear. The day had been very nice, but like everything in life, it was temporary. Deep down inside she knew she was worthless. Unlovable.

Laura sighed, walked into the kitchen and set her purse on the counter, checking the answering machine and finding no messages. As always. *Why would anyone call me?*

Mike came up behind her and laid a hand lightly on her waist, resting his head playfully on her shoulder. "So, you must've had quite a party last night."

"What?" Laura saw the rows of bottles lined up on the counter. "Ah, I see. I'd planned on pouring these all down the drain, but you called and took my mind off of it all."

"I'm proud of you, Laura. In the same situation, I'd probably have tried to drink half of them."

She smiled at him. "I did drink some of the port." She picked up the bottle and checked the level. "Correction — all of the port. But I need to get rid of the rest of this stuff, don't you think?"

"Yeah, but I have a better idea. I'll dump it all while you're in rehab, so that when you come home again, it'll be to a clean slate. I'm going to be here to feed the cat, anyway."

"That would be nice of you, Mike. I have to wonder, though, why you'd bother. What sort of ulterior motives do you have?" She gave him another smile to try to soften the sting of her words, hating herself for the sounds of the words, for the self-pity in her voice.

"Laura..." Mike gently twisted her shoulders, turning her around to face him. He reached over and smoothed the back of his hand gently down the side of her face and she leaned into his touch. "I know you're going through a bad time. I know that this thing between us has heated up much faster than either of us expected it to. But you have to know that I like you very much. You're a beautiful, intelligent and fascinating woman. My ulterior motives are only these: I wanted to give you a good day to remember while you were in rehab, one that you enjoyed without having to drink. And I wanted to make sure you'd remember me." He gave a soft chuckle and kissed the tip of her nose. "A month is a long time."

Laura wanted to believe him, but doubted in the back of her mind. *He's lying, he has to be. Who'd want a drunk like me?* "That's really sweet, Mike. I guess if I had to be arrested for DUI, I'm glad it was you. We might never have met otherwise." Her mind raced; now that the day was over, he'd be leaving soon. And she'd be alone again. Alone with all the bottles and the temptation to drink and the sick feeling in the pit of her stomach whenever she tried to envision a future without all the things that made her current life worthwhile. She pulled away from his embrace. "Want some coffee?"

"Love some, thanks."

"Go have a seat in the living room and I'll join you in a minute."

"Actually, I think I'll use the bathroom first, if that's okay."

"Make yourself at home."

Once she heard the bathroom door shut, Laura poured herself a shot of whiskey from one of the bottles sitting on the counter and bolted it down. She followed it quickly with a second then started the coffee maker. As she watched the coffee drip down from the basket, her mind started to wander, moving from thoughts of how pleasant the day had been into darker territory. *You know, of course, that he's only interested in one thing. And that one thing isn't you. Why would anyone want to spend time with you? You're a loser, you're worthless, you'd be better off dead.*

"Stop it," she whispered to herself. "He says he likes me and I like him. I won't let this be ruined with self-defeating thoughts."

The flow of the coffee into the pot seemed to slow down until it fell, a drop at a time. But the noise it made overwhelmed her, like a rushing in her ears. Mesmerized by the liquid, Laura stared at the pot — it sounded like rain drops trickling over dead, moldering leaves. Like an annoying leaky faucet. Like...like — the image flashed into her mind as clear as reality — like congealing blood dripping slowly from open wounds. The open wounds on her wrists after she'd slashed them — slashed them quickly, quietly, using one of her sharpest paring knives while Mike was in the bathroom.

The voices were right. She *would* be better off dead.

CHAPTER EIGHT

Mike flushed the toilet, lowered the seat and turned to the sink to wash his hands. When he reached for a towel, the light bulb blew out, filling the air with the odd smell of ozone and burning. With the main light in the room out, the nightlight clicked on, giving him enough light to finish. Mike smoothed his hair back a bit and bared his teeth a bit, turning his head side to side, checking his appearance in the mirror.

He noticed then that the bathtub faucet had a leak, a steady dripping that echoed in the small dark room. Everything else in the house seemed hushed, as if waiting breathlessly for the next drop. *Funny,* he thought, peering into the darkened corner where the tub sat, *it sounds like the tub is full of water.* He touched a hand to the shower curtain, hesitating for a second, remembering the dream Laura had the night of her trial. She'd been so upset by it. And so had he. His hand trembled. *This is stupid,* he told himself, *Laura is out in the kitchen making coffee.* Mike took a deep breath and pulled back the curtain. The tub was empty and the faucet was dry. He shook his head, then turned away to open the door.

The knob wouldn't turn. "This is just crazy," he said. He turned the knob again, this time with more pressure. It didn't budge an inch. Mike checked the lock, turning the center of the lock back and forth. "Crazy," he muttered and pushed his weight against the door. The door flew open. He turned back around and checked the knob one more time, shaking his head.

"You need to get the door to the bathroom fixed, Laura," he called, "I couldn't get it to open. Didn't you hear me rattling the knob?"

Mike walked into the kitchen to find Laura just standing there, with her back to the door. He could see her shoulders shaking and wondered if she were crying. He reached over and gently tapped her on the shoulder. "Laura?"

She took in a great gasp of air and dropped what she'd been holding. The knife fell, clattering on the tile floor and she turned around to face him.

"Mike?" Her eyes were unfocused, distant, her skin deathly pale, her lips practically blue. She shivered violently.

"Laura? What were you doing?" He pulled her close to him and held her until the shaking stopped and noticed that instead of feeling cold as he expected, she was incredibly hot to the touch. Mike put a hand to her forehead. "You're running a fever," he said. "Have you got a thermometer around here?"

She took another deep ragged breath, but said nothing.

"Let's get you into bed, okay?" Mike gently led her back to her bedroom, pulled the covers back and eased her down. Not quite the romantic ending to the day he'd been hoping for. He looked at her, pulled the covers up to her neck. She mumbled something he couldn't hear and her eyes fluttered closed.

He felt her forehead again. She definitely was running a fever, no doubt about it.

"Laura?" He said her name louder now. "I'm going to get you some aspirin, but I need you to wake up for a little bit so you can take them."

She mumbled again, then opened her eyes. "Mike?"

"I think you're sick, babe. I'm going to get you settled in, okay?"

She gave him a little sad smile. "I'm sorry I'm such a mess. You deserve better."

"Don't be silly. You can't help it if you're sick. I'll be back in a second with something for that fever. Don't go anywhere."

Mike found aspirin in the medicine cabinet and brought it to Laura along with a glass of water. He sat on the edge of the bed and propped Laura up so she could take the pills. Then he took the glass from her hand and set it on the nightstand, easing her back into bed. He felt her forehead one more time, and stroked her hair until she fell asleep, then settled into a chair in the corner of the room.

Laura awoke the next morning with no remembrance of the previous night. But she felt well rested and refreshed and slightly surprised to see Mike sleeping in a chair in the corner of the room, with Anubis curled up in his lap. She smiled, assuming the snoring was Mike's. It was a reassuring sound, somehow. Even more reassuring was to see him there.

He stayed, Laura thought to herself in wonder. They'd obviously not had sex, given the fact that she still wore her clothes from yesterday and that he slept in the chair. But still, he'd stayed. Which meant he must like her. *Right? So maybe I'm not as much of a mess as I think.*

Laura bent over him and dropped a light kiss on his head. Mike slept on.

Laura was sipping her second cup of coffee when Mike finally woke up. He came over to her and hugged her, then stepped back and felt her forehead. "Feeling better?" he asked.

"I feel great," she said, "why wouldn't I?"

"You were running a fever last night."

"Really?"

"Yeah, don't you remember?"

Laura searched her memory. "Vaguely, I suppose. I remember you putting me to bed. I must've been exhausted."

"Well, we did have a busy day yesterday."

Laura smiled. "A busy one, yeah, but also a very nice day, Mike. Thanks for making the effort."

Mike pulled her to him again. "It wasn't an effort, it was a pleasure."

She stood on her toes to kiss him, savoring the scent of him, enjoying the scratchy feel of his beard stubble against her skin.

The phone rang a second later and Laura jumped.

"Hello?"

"Mommy?"

"Hi, Lizzy. How are you, sweetie?"

Mike deposited a kiss on the nape of Laura's neck. "I'll freshen up a bit," he whispered, "then get out of your way. I'll need to get back to my place and change before my shift starts."

Laura nodded.

"I'm fine, Mommy. How are you?"

"Great." For once Laura didn't have to lie. She smiled. "I'm great," she said again, "but I miss you and your sister."

There was a pause on Lizzy's end. "I, um, had a nightmare about you the other night..." She seemed unwilling to continue.

"Yeah, your dad told me. But you know, Pixie, it was only a dream. Sometimes they can seem very real, but they can't hurt you. You know that, don't you?"

"Yeah, but..."

"I'm fine, sweetie. You shouldn't be worrying about me."

"Do you have to go away, Mommy? To that clinic place?"

"Yep. But this is a good thing. If I do better, your dad has promised you and Amanda can come and stay with me sometime. Would you like that?"

"I'd love that, Mommy." Lizzy paused again and Laura heard Tony's voice in the background. "Dad says I have to go now. We're going out for breakfast."

"Sounds like fun," Laura said, trying to keep her voice light and cheerful. "Is Amanda there?"

"She's already in the car," Lizzy said.

"Tell her I said 'hi,' okay? And that I love her. And you."

"I love you too, Mommy. Bye."

Mike came back into the kitchen. "She doing okay?"

Laura nodded. "She has nightmares. And night terrors. Kid's stuff." She suppressed a shiver, not wanting to even think about Lizzy's dream.

Mike put his arms around her and gave her one long, hard kiss. "I wish I didn't have to go," he said. "But I've no choice in the matter. Work's work."

"I know," Laura said, walking him to the door. "Thank you for everything."

"I'll be back tomorrow morning, bright and early, to take you out to the rehab center. Take it easy today, okay? And call if you need anything."

Laura sighed as she shut and locked the door behind him. It was going to be a long day. And a long night. She walked back to the bathroom and took two Valium, then went to the kitchen to open up a bottle of wine. She felt her tensions ease from the sound of the liquid pouring into the glass. She sighed and gave a half smile.

We don't really need him here. And we don't need anything from him, do we? Laura held up her glass and admired the deep red color of the wine. *As long as there's this, we're all just fine.*

The morning came too quickly to please Laura. She'd drunk the entire bottle of wine, fallen asleep too early, and woke up on time, but feeling fuzzy and confused. Where had all the time gone? She showered quickly, dressed, and checked her suitcase one last time. After being ousted from the piece of luggage several times, Anubis gave up and, perched high on the bed pillows, watched Laura intently. "I have no idea if I packed enough stuff or not," she said, "it feels kind of like summer camp." Eventually, she zipped the case shut and wheeled it to the living room by the front door. She sighed, wishing she could put everything back where it came from.

"I don't want to go," she said quietly. "It seems like I'm dying and going to hell."

Even Mike's arrival didn't dispel her dismal mood. She gave him directions for taking care of the cat and the house, but refused to laugh at his many attempts at humor. They didn't talk much on the drive to the facility and once there, Laura sat silently in the car. Mike got out, removed her suitcase from the trunk, and walked over to open her door. Laura still sat in the car, staring down at her lap.

"Laura, honey, I promise you you'll survive this. Just take a deep breath..."

"And dive right down," she answered, moving slowly out of her seat. "Into the murky depths of the underworld."

She gave Mike a brief kiss at the front desk before he left. Laura did not turn around to watch him go.

Rehab isn't quite hell, Laura thought at the end of her first week. *No, not quite.* She gave a wry smile, falling back on her lapsed Catholic upbringing. *More like limbo, actually.* She had a sense of a suspension of time, as if she were holding her breath, waiting. In fact, it was as if everyone here was waiting. Waiting for their sentence to be over, maybe, or just longing for the return to their normal lives, no matter how awful they may have been. And dreading the return as well, not knowing what would happen once they were free of this place.

This odd feeling had nothing to do with having too much spare time; instead, the administration seemed determined to fill most of their free time. They offered group and individual therapy, lectures and seminars, and films, both popular and informative. Then there were the nature walks, the fully equipped gym, an Olympic-sized swimming pool and the ever-ubiquitous arts and crafts. *God forbid,* Laura thought, *they should give you a moment by yourself to just think* — although she realized that was the point. She welcomed the presence of other people during the day and the many events that took her mind off the growing itch of her cravings. But once she went to her room, she felt lost. She hadn't yet been assigned a room mate, instead she spent her nights alone. Those nights dragged by slower than she'd ever have expected; she hadn't remembered it being so difficult to sleep before she became dependent on the assistance of alcohol or Valium or both. Maybe it hadn't been.

The loss of her Valium hit Laura hard. She hadn't been prepared to have them taken away — she had a prescription for them, after all — so when the pills were confiscated at check-in, Laura was surprised and indignant. Although embarrassed by her anger and the tears that ensued, she'd pleaded with the nurse, to no avail. Valium, like alcohol, was forbidden.

Wednesday was the day for visitors, but since Laura expected no one, she headed for the gym. After about a half hour on the bike, she heard her name paged. The tall African-American woman smiled when she walked into the lounge area; Laura thought she looked familiar, but couldn't quite place her.

The woman walked up to her and held out her hand. "Laura? I'm Renee Simpson, we met at the A.A. meeting."

Laura smiled. "Yes, of course we did. Nice to see you again. Do you want to sit down?" The two of them headed over to two of the empty chairs by a window.

"Good to see you, too," Renee said. "Mike thought I should come over and see you — he says you're in need of a sponsor. So I figured we could chat for a while and see if we get along. Although I have to tell you that if Mike likes you, you automatically move up on my list."

"Really? Why?"

"Honey, that man is a gem. And I was so thrilled to hear he met someone he liked. He's quite taken with you, you know?"

Laura blushed. "Is he? I find that hard to believe. I'm a bit of a mess."

Renee put her head back and laughed. "Well, mess or no, sweetie, you're the first woman he's ever brought to a meeting. In fact, you're the first woman I've heard him talk about in years."

"Have you known him long?"

"As long as he's been coming to meetings. Seven years, I think. It's hard to keep track of other people's sober time. Speaking of which, it's probably a good time for you to start running your own tally."

"Three days." Laura's voice wavered a bit.

Renee nodded her head. "Tied on a good one the night before, huh?" She gave a small laugh. "I remember that well. I don't think I was sober for weeks before my last go at rehab."

"Last go?"

"Took three times for me, Laura. Not everyone makes it the first time. Or the second. It's not an easy thing. So how are you doing?"

"I'm okay. Sleeping seems impossible. They took away my Valium."

Renee nodded again, sympathetically. "That's a hard one, isn't it?"

"I guess. To be honest, I was sort of surprised. I knew they were going to wean me off of the booze, but I didn't expect..." Her voice trailed off.

"Yeah." Renee reached over and patted Laura's hand briefly. "It does get better, I can promise you that. Not for a while, but it does. And when you get home, you can even have caffeine in your coffee. Trivial, I know, but that was one of the things that really bugged me."

Laura raised her eyebrows in surprise. "It's decaf? I must've missed that. It would explain the morning headaches."

Renee laughed again. "Ah, another coffee addict. At least it's still legal. I think we'll get along just fine."

Laura smiled. "Good. I'm kind of new to this part of town, and I don't know many people."

"Support is important." Renee looked at her watch and stood up, smoothing her skirt. "And speaking of support, I've got to get back to work." she grinned as Laura rolled her eyes at the pun. "I'll try to get back again before you leave." She reached into her suit coat pocket and handed Laura her card. "You can always reach me at this number. Anytime. Day or night. That's part of the deal."

"Thanks so much. I feel a little less lost right now." Laura reached out to shake her hand, but Renee gave her a smile and pulled her into a quick hug.

"Mike said to be sure to say that he sends his love." Renee moved away and winked at her. "Even if he didn't quite put it that way. He's a keeper, honey. If I weren't happily married, I'd fight you for him."

Laura blushed slightly. "Thanks," she said again.

"Think nothing of it." Renee turned and walked out the door.

Watching her leave, Laura suddenly felt close to tears. *I'm glad Renee came,* she thought, *but it's going to make the rest of the day seem very dreary.* She peered out the windows, noticing that it had begun to rain. "Great," she muttered under her breath and headed back to the gym to try to sweat it all away.

Mike struggled again with the key in Laura's front door. She never seemed to have this much trouble, but since he'd been coming in alone to feed the cat, he couldn't seem to get the lock to work. With each visit, it seemed to grow more difficult. To make matters worse, it was pitch black on her front step. He thought he'd left a light on, but apparently not. And the door still wouldn't open. "There must be a trick to it," he said through clenched teeth and jiggled the key in the other direction, while applying pressure on the door with his hip. Finally, it sprung open with such force he almost lost his balance. "Stupid son of a bitch," Mike said, unsure if he was swearing at the door or at himself. "What the hell is with the doors in this house?" *Maybe I should change the lock,* he thought as he flipped on the light. *At least Laura doesn't need to worry too much about people breaking in — you can't even get the door open with a key.*

He walked into the kitchen and called for the cat. Anubis sauntered out from Laura's bedroom, then stopped at the cellar door and hissed. "You know me," Mike said. "Come on if you want to eat."

The cat came over to him and twisted around his legs, purring. "So now I'm your new best friend? What was all that noise about earlier?

You don't fool me." He reached down and scratched Anubis around the ears, then opened the refrigerator and dished out the second half of the can he'd opened yesterday. "What are we going to do tonight? How about a nice cat box change? And I'll probably get around to finding the rest of Laura's stash and getting rid of it all. You'd like your mom to stay sober, wouldn't you?" Mike chuckled. "Although I doubt you care one way or another as long as the food hits the bowl at meal times."

Mike rinsed out the cat food can and tossed it in the recycle bin. "I'd like her to stay sober, at least." He felt sort of silly talking to the cat, but the sound of his own voice was comforting. Laura's house seemed so empty and dark and cold without her presence. And, although he hated to admit it, even to himself, the place creeped him out. Just a bit. The house was too silent and made him edgy and uncomfortable. Nothing had happened that he could put his finger on; he had no evidence to support the feeling. Mike relied on physical evidence in his life — it was something to hold onto, something he could trust. But regardless of the lack of anything concrete, the feeling persisted: a watchful, waiting atmosphere that had nothing to do with a hungry cat.

"But that's stupid," he spoke to the cat, wanting to hear the sound of his voice again. "It's just an empty house. I miss Laura — that's all it is."

His first day feeding the cat, Mike had noticed the bottles she'd lined up on the counters were gone. He knew she couldn't have drunk them all Sunday night. Since she lived alone, there'd be no reason to hide them, and yes, there they were, neatly stowed away in a kitchen cabinet. He'd left them there, until he had the time to deal with them. And now was the time. Mike removed all of them, rather impressed with the variety: vodka, red and white wine, whiskey, scotch. Tequila, and rum. He opened the bottle of scotch first and began to pour it down the drain. The smell of the alcohol wafted up to him. In one way, the scent repulsed him; in another, the fragrance called to him, beckoned him once more to fall into the bottle. The cravings the scent caused were as sharp as if he'd quit drinking only yesterday; along with them surfaced a small, frighteningly familiar, nagging voice in the back of his mind. *Go ahead, do it. Have a drink. Just one little drink. One won't hurt you.*

Jumping back from the sink, he lost his grip on the bottle and it crashed to the floor. "Dammit. I'm my own worst enemy."

He cleaned up the broken glass, dumping it all into the garbage can. His nostrils burned from the scent of the alcohol and he felt mildly nauseated and dizzy. Still, he glanced over at the cat as it finished off the rest of the food. "Yeah, I know. Cat box time."

Mike hesitated at the cellar door, slowly opening the locks, shuddering from the rush of frigid air that met him. He flicked on the light and went down the stairs. Recalling Laura's dislike of the place, he felt himself tense up. As if he were bracing himself for... *For what?* "What the hell are you expecting?" he said to himself, grimacing. "It's just a cellar: cold and damp and unpleasant. Like every other cellar in history." He breathed in a bit, "But at least it doesn't smell bad." In fact, he thought that the air smelled slightly sweet, a chocolate-type smell. "Or maybe hot cocoa." He smiled and inhaled deeper. "Mm mm. With just a touch of almonds."

Mike stood with his eyes closed for just a second and swayed, as if he were falling asleep on his feet. The cold flowed up his legs to his back and he jolted back to himself. "What was I doing?" He looked around, and then nodded. "Cat box," he said, "that's what we're here to do." He did the job quickly, opened the sliding glass doors, and put the bag of used litter in the garbage can outside on the small concrete patio. He stood there for a moment before going back into the cellar. "Funny. It feels warmer outside than it is inside."

When he made it back upstairs, the cat seemed to be pacing the hall, waiting for him. Although he'd planned to leave right away, Anubis wove around his feet with mournful cries. "Lonely, bud?" Mike picked the cat up and walked into the living room, sitting on the couch, petting him. Eventually, judging by the not too gentle swat Mike received on his hand, Anubis tired of the attention and wandered off.

Mike checked one last time to make sure the windows were locked and bolted the cellar door shut. Not trusting himself to crack open another of the bottles, he left them still sitting on the kitchen counter.

"I'll deal with them tomorrow." He emptied the cat's water bowl and filled it with fresh. "Maybe I'll invite my sponsor to come along — just in case." Although he felt rather odd about inviting someone else into Laura's house, maybe that wasn't a bad idea. With another human being around he probably wouldn't be so spooked.

With that thought, the silence of the house seemed to rise up and surround him. He shivered. A sharp crack behind Mike made him spin around and instinctively reach for his gun, realizing a split second later that he was out of uniform and had left his gun locked up in his apartment. Then he saw a black blur disappear down the stairs. The cat door swung back and forth, making that same clicking noise. Mike chuckled at his jumpiness. "Next time I come, I'll turn the television on for company."

Within seconds, though, he was out of the house and into his car. He noticed that he'd left a light on inside, but thinking that was a good idea, anyway, he turned the key. Before he backed out of the driveway he saw the outline of Anubis, sitting in the front window, his eyes eerily reflecting the headlights. *Damn cat must be a speed demon,*

Mike thought, shaking his head as he pulled onto the street. *I saw him go downstairs just a minute ago.*

CHAPTER NINE

Laura's roommate arrived on Friday. Cassandra Grabowski was a large blonde in her mid-twenties; her weight looked appropriate for her, giving an impression of comfort and rest. A Vicodin addict, Cassie had been arrested for forging prescriptions and, since it was her first offense, she'd been offered and accepted rehabilitation as a substitute for jail.

Laura liked her at first sight. Her warm smile and honest eyes made the cold institutional room seem warmer somehow. The shared problem of addiction created an instant bond between them, a fact that Laura embraced. When meeting new people for the first time, Laura had always tried to hide her habit, assuming that when they found out about her drinking, they'd dismiss her as weak and useless. That was how she thought about herself, after all. Why would others be any different? Here, though, the judgment or the fear of that judgment just didn't exist. Here everyone was an addict of some sort. That leveled the playing ground.

"So," Cassie said as she finished unpacking her suitcase, "what did they get you for?"

"DUI," Laura said. "I have the worst luck — I backed into a police car in a bar parking lot."

Cassie giggled. "That's pretty bad."

"Yeah." Laura paused for a second. "But there are compensations in everything I guess. I'm sort of dating the guy who arrested me."

Cassie gave a full laugh this time. "A man in uniform? Nothing better." She grew serious. "Are you sure that's not a conflict for him?"

"Not sure why it would be. We didn't actually start seeing each other until after my trial." Had that little amount of time gone by? Laura thought that it seemed much longer. In a good way, of course, and she ducked her head and smiled to herself.

"And what's the scoop on this place? Anything I should avoid?"

"Other than being here? Not really. I don't have anything to compare it to, this being my first stay, but it seems like an okay place. I've spent most of my extra time in the gym. The days are pretty full with events and sessions and such. The nights are dreadful, for me, at least. I get itchy, you know?"

Cassie nodded. "Yeah. I know the feeling well. At least we'll have each other for company." She walked over and looked out the window at the grounds. "The place seems to have decent vibes. I'm not looking forward to this, but..."

"It beats jail," Laura finished. "That's what everyone says. Me, I'm not so sure."

"Me either. How's the food?"

"It's not half bad. Healthy stuff and large portions. I've probably eaten more this week than I've ever had since I was a kid." Laura left out the part where she vomited for the first three days after arriving. She hoped that part was over, now, and there was no need to share the information with a stranger, roommate or not. "I'll probably gain some weight while I'm here."

Cassie gave her an appraising glance. "Not that a little extra weight would hurt you. And as for me," she gestured to her body, "What possible difference could it make?"

Laura started having the shakes Saturday night. *It is hell now,* she thought, when she had to stop writing a letter to Amanda and Lizzy because she couldn't read her own writing.

The nightmares began on Sunday.

"I understand you had a nightmare last night."

Laura rubbed her hand over her eyes and sighed. "Nothing escapes your notice, does it, John? Yeah, I suppose I did."

John Bryant seemed a decent enough sort. He didn't want to be called doctor and he didn't talk down to people. It was fairly obvious to Laura that he understood the problems of addiction from the inside out — his knowledge of the psychology seemed more than just textbook. "You suppose?"

He did, however, ask too many questions. She sighed again. There'd be no getting around it, she'd have to relate each and every detail. During their first session, he'd asked a question she didn't want to answer and they'd just sat in silence waiting for her response. "It seemed very real."

"Do you want to tell me about it?"

Laura gave him a sly smile. "Not really, but I don't have much of a choice, do I?"

He had the decency to look somewhat ashamed. She knew the gesture for a ruse, but appreciated his effort.

"I was sleeping, in my bed. Here. Which is what made it seem more real, I guess."

"Tell you what, Laura, why don't you try to keep your guesses and suppositions out of this conversation? Tell me the facts, tell me what happened, how it made you feel. Not what *you* think it's about. Okay?"

Laura nodded; took a sip of her coffee and set it back down on the table next to her chair. "I could hear Cassie snoring and the rain outside hitting the windows. I'd tossed and turned earlier, thinking I'd never get to sleep. But I must have at some point, since I woke up."

"In the dream you woke up?"

"Yeah. In the dream, I woke up. And Cassie was still snoring and the rain and wind were roaring outside the windows. I noticed then that the door had been opened a bit. The light from the hallway made a path across the floor and shone in my eyes. I blinked and when I opened them up again, I saw a person standing in the doorway. It seemed like a child, a little girl — I couldn't see her clearly, just her shadow outlined against the light. I sat up in bed then. 'Hello?' I whispered, wondering what sort of addiction this poor little girl might have to be staying here."

John nodded. "Just so you know, we have no children here. When there's a need for this sort of treatment for them, they go elsewhere."

"That's what I thought. But still, here was this little girl, standing in my doorway. I called out to her again. 'Hello? Can I help you? Are you lost?'

"'Mommy?'

"She looked a lot younger than Amanda. Or even Lizzy. So I knew this little girl wasn't either of mine. That wouldn't make sense, would it?"

John raised an eyebrow. "Do all your dreams make sense?"

"This one did, or seemed to. And at the time, I didn't realize it was a dream." Laura looked away. *I'm still not sure it was a dream,* she thought, but she wasn't about to open that particular subject right now. "Anyway, I called out to her again. 'Lizzy?' She shook her head and took a further step into the room. I heard a funny sound that wasn't snoring or rain. Her teeth were chattering. And I saw that her shadowy outline was shivering. 'I'm not your mommy, sweetheart, but why don't you come in and get warm?' I tossed my covers back and patted the side of the bed. The shadow girl nodded and I saw a flash of a smile. She walked quietly across the room to me and crawled into bed next to me. I tucked the covers up under her chin and I could feel the tenseness of her body relax. She still shivered though, so I wrapped my arms around her to warm her. She snuggled up against me, her arms wrapped tightly around my neck."

Laura took a deep breath, then put her hand up to her mouth and exhaled through her closed fingers. "You know how little kids grip too tightly? They hold on for dear life and you think they'll never let go? Well, it's okay for one's own kids. But for a child who is a stranger, it's weird. And kind of frightening. 'Not so tight, sweetie,' I said to her, 'it hurts.'

"'It hurts,' she whispered back to me. But she wouldn't let go, she just kept squeezing my neck, her poor little cold body shivering up against mine. I didn't panic, though, I patted her shoulder and talked to her, soft stuff, little motherly nothings. 'There, there, it's okay,' I said, 'everything is okay.'

"She sniffled a bit, she'd been crying. 'It's not okay, it'll never be okay. It hurts. It still hurts.'

"'What hurts, honey?'

"The girl didn't answer me. She just pulled in closer to me. Then I noticed that the bed seemed damp. Cold and damp, as if the girl had just come in from the rain. Maybe she had, I thought, it's a nasty night out there. But I pulled the blankets back to see from where the wetness had come."

Laura paused and got up from her chair, rubbing her arms with her hands. "Cold in here, isn't it? Since last night I just can't seem to get warm."

“Well.” John stared out the window for a second. “It *is* cold outside. This office is always cold in the winter. Was that the end of the dream?”

Laura looked over at him. “Of course not. Does that sound like a dream which would wake up the entire floor with my screaming?” She chuckled. “Apparently I have a future in the movies with that scream. Just ask anyone on my floor.”

“Finish the dream.”

“The bed had filled up with a dark, sticky liquid. I reached over and flipped on the light. As I’m sure you can guess, it was blood. The little girl lay there, dead, in a pool of her own blood. So I sat up and screamed.”

“And then?”

“All of a sudden the girl disappeared. And everyone else was wide awake.” Laura sighed. “I couldn’t get back to sleep. I’m so tired.”

“I’m sure you are.” John checked over a few pages in her file. “How long have you been on the Valium?”

“What does that have to do with the nightmare?”

“Possibly a lot. How long?”

Laura thought for a moment. “Dad started me on these when Mom died. So that would’ve been almost 20 years ago.”

“And you’ve been taking them daily since then?”

“More or less. I’ve had time periods where I haven’t taken them at all, like during my pregnancies.”

“And did you experience any drastic withdrawal effects when you went off of them?”

Laura yawned, then covered her mouth. “Sorry. I’m beat. I don’t remember anything like that. Why?”

"One of the side effects of Valium withdrawal is hallucinations. I suspect that's what happened to you last night. Especially since you describe it as very real."

"Ugh. What can we do about it? Can you prescribe something else to take care of it?" Laura hoped that he might. *Maybe then I could get some sleep.*

"Not here, Laura. Sorry. This place is designed to get you off drugs, not to prescribe new ones."

"Damn."

"How's the new roommate?"

"She's very nice. A little new-agey for my tastes, but..."

John laughed. "New-agey?"

"You know. Cassie's into new age stuff. Palm reading, tarot cards, purification rituals." Laura made a face.

"And you don't approve?"

Laura shook her head. "My approval has nothing to do with it. Apparently she makes a decent living doing readings and astrological charts, which places her a few rungs higher on the employment ladder than I am. I don't actually believe in all that nonsense. She's already read my aura, my palms and my cards and has predicted that I'll be doing battle in the future with evil influences." She laughed at that. "Of course I will. I already am."

"What do you mean?"

Laura rolled her eyes. "Alcoholism. Addiction. All evil influences, don't you think?"

"That's one way to think of it, yes. How is your battle going?"

"Not all that well. I'm just trying to get through the next three weeks. After that, I figure it's all up for grabs. Although, it seems to me, the cards are stacked against me, anyway."

"Why would you say that?"

Suddenly Laura got very angry. It was all well and good for this man to ask these questions, but how was this helping? She felt about twenty times more useless than when she'd come to rehab. And infinitely more vulnerable. That nightmare last night had left her completely drained, fresh out of hope or resolve. And to know that these sorts of events might reoccur? Why bother?

She got up from her seat again and walked over to the window, tracing a design on the glass, then turned around and folded her arms. "Where's my incentive to do better? I know no one believes this, but my life was fine before they forced me to be here. Now that I've been "helped" I can look forward to what? Hallucinations and cravings for the rest of my life? What good is that? Drinking isn't all that bad — at least it's not heroin or anything like that. Drinking is legal, provided I'm not driving. And it's socially acceptable." She glared at John, daring him to refute her statements. How dared he sit there all smug in his comfy chair at his big fancy desk and tell her how to live?

He started to speak, then seemed to think better of it and just returned her stare for a while. His mouth shaped a sad smile. "I know you don't want to be here, Laura. Do you think that anyone does? Now what really has you this upset? Although you'll be happy to know that you're right on schedule — now's the time for anger.

"I'm starting to believe that it's always a good time for anger, *Doctor.* Can I go now?"

"It's up to you, Laura. Always has been. No one can force you to join in. No one can force you to heal. See you tomorrow."

"Maybe." Laura slammed his office door on the way out, knowing full well that she was acting like a spoiled child and not caring a bit. She didn't even know why she felt so angry.

She avoided the other groups in the common areas, although she'd been scheduled for several of the events this afternoon. She walked right past the gym, ran up the stairs to her room and slammed that door as well. Thanks to last night, this place wasn't quite the haven it had been. And thanks to the knowledge that she might be having hallucinations, now she didn't feel safe anywhere.

She sat in the chair next to the window, staring out and trying to think it all through. Watching the trees on the edges of the rehab center whipping around in the strong winds, she realized what the problem was. Laura had no control. Over anything at all in her life. She'd been taken hostage by the events around her for so long, ruled by the genes which dictated her very being, blindsided by the control she'd relinquished, starting with her parents, and then Tony. One day the bottom just fell out. She had no way to hold on to the ground, nothing on which to base her life, no beliefs to carry her.

"Matthew," she whispered his name to the empty room. She needn't hallucinate about dead children — all she had to do was dredge her memory and there one was. Tears ran down her face, and she wiped them away, angry again. "I can't think about him. Not here, not now."

Fortunately at that moment Cassie breezed in. "What's happening, Laura? You missed the lecture." The she stopped and looked at Laura's face. "I'm sorry. Are you okay?"

Laura sniffed and wiped her face with her sleeve. "Yeah. I yelled at Bryant."

Cassie smiled a gentle smile. "That's what you're supposed to do. You need to get angry. It's all part of the healing process. Didn't you get the memo?"

Laura took in a deep ragged breath and began to sob. Cassie came over and knelt by the chair taking Laura into her arms in a soft embrace, letting her cry it all out.

Laura and Cassie grew closer after that day, supporting each other through the following weeks. Their relationship achieved a happy balance — Laura's skepticism played off of Cassie's beliefs, bringing them both to common ground. They talked about everything, no subject was too sensitive to explore. Except perhaps the subject of Cassie's family. No one ever came to visit her, so Laura assumed she had none, until the day a letter arrived that upset Cassie.

"Bad news?" Laura asked gently.

"Yeah. Pretty bad. My sister says I'm being evicted from my apartment — she picked up the notice when she drove by to check on things."

"You have a sister?"

"Yeah. But don't ask. Anyway, I'm always running a little late on my rent, but I really thought the landlady would let it slide until I got out of here." Cassie sighed. "Apparently not."

"What will you do? Stay with your sister."

Cassie frowned and shook her head. "Out of the question. So I've no idea what I'll do."

"Do you have any friends in the area?"

"Most of my friends are online ones. So no."

Laura smiled. "Not true. I'm in the area. Why don't you come and stay with me?"

Cassie's face lightened. "Really? You wouldn't mind?"

Laura reached over and touched Cassie's hand. "It's not a problem. I have the whole house all to myself. There's lots of room and I could use the company. I spend way too much time alone."

"Great. I can't thank you enough." Cassie crinkled up the letter from her sister and tossed it across the room. "Time for our deep breathing seminar. You coming?"

CHAPTER TEN

Despite the friendship she and Cassie shared, Laura was thrilled when rehab was over. The feeling of freedom amazed her and frightened her at the same time. She hardly knew what she would do with herself.

On the drive home, Laura was quiet and Mike respected her silence. She made a mental list of all the things she needed to take care of: she needed a job, first of all, one close to her house so she could walk if necessary. Then she planned to ask Tony for joint custody of the girls. If he didn't agree, she'd find an attorney and sue for joint custody of the girls. If it came to that, it wasn't going to be easy, but it was well worth the effort. She'd blown it with Tony for good, but could still salvage her relationship with her daughters.

Laura smiled to herself, thinking how nice it would be to see them both on a fairly regular schedule and began making plans for where they would sleep and how she would decorate their room. She was so deep in thought she barely noticed they'd pulled into her driveway.

"We're here," Mike said.

"Great. I'm so happy to be home."

Laura got out of the car and walked up the sidewalk, pulling her keys out of her purse and opening up the front door to her house. Mike followed her and carried her suitcase.

"That's easy for you, isn't it? Opening the door?" he asked, coming in behind her.

She smiled at him. "Yeah. You put the key in the lock, turn the knob and *voila*! The door, she is opened."

"Very funny, babe." He shut the door behind him. "It's just that it would never open up without a fight when I tried to get in."

"Maybe," Laura said absently, sorting through the stack of mail, "the house doesn't like you."

Mike snorted. "Yeah, right. So are you really happy to be home?"

"Very. Thanks for looking after things while I was gone. And thanks for coming to spring me."

"My pleasure." He walked up behind her and put his arms around her waist, pulling her close to him, nuzzling her neck. "I really missed you."

Anubis chose that moment to come over to them and weave around all four of their legs. Mike stepped back and Laura stooped down, scratching the cat around his ears. He meowed, then purred, bumping up against her hand. "I missed you too, baby."

"Was that comment for me?" Mike asked. "Or the cat?"

Laura chuckled as she stood up and turned around to face him. "Both of you, of course."

After Mike left, Laura sat down at the dining room table with the Sunday paper, sipping her second cup of coffee. She felt almost dizzy from the caffeine buzz. "One month away from the stuff," she said to the cat, nudging him off of the section of the paper she'd been reading, "and I'm already a weakling. I'll have to get some decaf when I go to the store."

She got up from the table and found a pen in one of her kitchen drawers, then sat back down to look at the want ads. She wasn't sure what she was qualified to do — anything in sales was out of the question, since she couldn't drive yet. Her real estate license had been revoked for a full year. And since public transportation in the suburbs was limited, any job would need to be nearby. She frowned. “Doesn't leave that many options, does it, kitty?” She gave him a pat. “I wonder why I even bother.”

Prior to rehab, that sort of thought often led to depression and more drinking. Laura stopped, took a deep breath and used one of the methods she'd been taught. Visualizing a switch in her mind that turned off negative thoughts, she immediately changed gears and began to list the benefits. “I can always work in food services or retail; there are lots of places within walking distance. There will be openings, since the holidays are coming. And I'll get to meet people on a daily basis — maybe it's a good a chance to make new acquaintances.”

Laura sat back in her chair and gave a small laugh. “That actually worked. Cool. Probably best, though, that I walk around and see what there is. Otherwise, I'll waste a lot of time reading the ads and not get anywhere.”

She rose from her chair again, walked into the kitchen and dumped the rest of her coffee into the sink. *Makes me too jittery,* she thought, realizing that her hands were shaking. She washed them at the kitchen sink, the warm water helped to relax her. The doorbell rang while she was drying them off.

She opened the door to a petite blonde, dressed in a short leather jacket and a pair of designer jeans. “Hi, I'm Carolyn Crosby,” the woman introduced herself. “We live on Maple Grove, two houses from the corner. I saw that you were home, so I thought I'd stop by.”

“Laura Wagner,” Laura started to put her hand out, but saw that it was still shaking. Instead she opened the door a little wider. “Come in, please,” Laura said. “It's nice to meet you.”

Carolyn smiled, stepping into the house and looking around curiously, showing perfectly straight, white teeth.

Laura closed the door behind her and led her into the living room. Carolyn chose Laura's favorite chair to sit in, so Laura sat down on the edge of the couch. "What can I do for you?"

"I wanted to ask you about that light in your basement."

"Light?"

"The fluorescent one? We can see the sliding glass door down there from our family room. Anyway, the light's been flickering a lot lately. And I wanted to make sure you knew it was happening. Maybe you need to change the bulb?"

Laura shook her head. "There isn't a fluorescent bulb down there."

Carolyn laughed rather unpleasantly. "Then you either need to stop flicking it on and off or you need to call an electrician."

"I've been away for the last few weeks, actually. How long has this been happening?"

"For a few months now, at least. While this house stood empty, of course, it didn't happen."

Laura nodded. "No electricity, for one thing."

"But now there is. And obviously there's some sort of problem."

"Well, I can assure you I've not been doing it."

"No, no, I didn't mean to imply that," Carolyn corrected.

Sure you didn't. You think I'm some crazy lady turning the lights on and off on a whim. Laura gave her what she hoped was a warm, grateful smile. "Anyway, I'm glad you told me. And I'll call an electrician tomorrow."

"Thanks." Carolyn looked around, obviously not quite ready to leave.

"Would you like a cup of coffee? I just made a fresh pot," Laura offered.

"Thanks," Carolyn smiled. "I'd love one."

Laura stood and moved toward the kitchen. Surprisingly, Carolyn followed.

Laura took a clean mug down from the shelf and poured it full. "Do you take anything in it?

"No, thanks, black is fine."

Laura handed her the steaming mug and started toward the living room.

"Aren't you having any?" Carolyn asked.

"No, I'm done. The caffeine makes me jittery."

Carolyn laughed as she set the mug on a coaster on the coffee table and sat down in Laura's chair again. "Jittery is what keeps me going." Carolyn took a sip and made an appreciative sigh. "I don't get enough coffee on the weekends, since I have to share the pot with my husband. Anyway, you said you were away? I thought I saw a car coming and going here."

"You probably did. My boyfriend," Laura couldn't help the smile that word drew, "was here, feeding the cat and checking up on stuff."

"Good idea. You don't think he was flicking the lights on and off, do you?"

Laura pictured Mike frantically flipping the switch at the top of the stairs. She choked back a laugh. "Not likely."

Carolyn settled back onto the chair, gripping her coffee mug between both hands. "Is he at all handy? Maybe he can check the wiring for you?"

"He's a policeman." Laura said. "I suspect electricity is beyond his expertise."

Carolyn nodded vigorously. "Oh. I knew I'd seen him before. That's Officer Gallagher, right?"

"You know him?"

"He does assemblies at the local schools. You know, anti-drug stuff. Half of the teenage girls have a huge crush on him." Carolyn gave a snicker. "Hell, I suspect half of the women around here do as well."

Laura smiled, not quite knowing what to say. Fortunately, Carolyn had no such problem.

"He seems very nice. Is he?"

"I haven't known him for all that long, really. But he's like my knight in shining armor."

Carolyn gave what seemed to be an envious sigh.

"So," Laura said, embarrassed and changing the subject. "Have you been in the neighborhood long?"

"I moved in after," Carolyn said.

"After?"

"You know. After. The disappearances?"

"Ah. Mike mentioned something about that."

Carolyn shook her head. "I heard it was awful. People were afraid to let their kids out. Do you have kids?"

"Yeah, two girls, twelve and eight."

"No kidding. Me, too! That's amazing. But they're not living here, are they?"

"No, they're with their father. They live over in Sewickley — not all that far away." *But it might as well be clear across country.*

"He got custody? That's kind of unusual, isn't it?"

Laura could tell that Carolyn was prying, that she wanted the dirt on her relatively new neighbor, so the story could be repeated at the various coffee gatherings they must have here. Laura didn't want to be a topic at the gatherings. "Yeah. He had a great lawyer."

"I guess that happens. Too bad. Do you see them much?"

Back on safe ground again, Laura smiled. “They'll be coming to spend about six days or so with me in two weeks. Tony — that's my ex — is getting remarried and he and Susan — his new wife — wanted a romantic European honeymoon.”

“That's very nice of you, Laura. I think if my husband divorced me and remarried, I'd not help out at all.”

Laura shook her head. “I'm not doing it for him; I'm doing it for the girls.”

“Of course.” Carolyn got up. “I should be getting back home. Thanks for the coffee. And the talk. Make sure you get that light checked out.”

“Will do.”

Carolyn took one last look around the house. “Next time I'll ask you for the tour. This house is a bit different from all the others in the neighborhood. This plot is where the original farmhouse stood and the developers merely remodeled the old house to match the style of the other houses they planned to build.”

“Interesting. I knew the house was older than the rest of the development. Wondered why it didn't seem that old. I didn't know the whole story, though.” *Or maybe I did and forgot it,* she thought. *I may have been a real estate agent, but I was also a drunk.*

“Of course, before you moved in, the house stood empty for a while.”

“I bought it from the bank -- a foreclosure.”

“Makes sense. The last people to live here were an older couple, Dolores and Bert Wellman; they owned the original tract of land that sold to the developers of Woodland Heights. Rumor has it that the man gambled away all of the money and they were forced to stay here. Apparently, they were like their house — didn't quite fit in. It's a bit of a sad story. They also say that after all the money was gone, he left her for a younger woman. And she, well, she..." Carolyn shook her head. "She just wasted away.

"That is sad."

"And...well..." Carolyn stopped abruptly and pointedly looked at her watch. "I'd better go," she scrunched up her face. "I've got the in-laws coming for dinner and I need to scrub the bathrooms before they show. Besides, we need to save stuff to talk about at a later date, right?"

She walked out to the kitchen and put her cup in the sink. "Here," she said, picking up Laura's pen from the counter, "this is my phone number." She wrote it down on a scrap of paper stuck to the refrigerator. "Call me soon. And let me know for sure when your girls get here. They can come up and play with mine. Or, since they're getting too old to 'play,' they can hang out. Or whatever it is that kids do these days."

Laura stood at the open door and waved as Carolyn walked up the street. Interesting, indeed. Carolyn had more to say, Laura was sure of it.

CHAPTER ELEVEN

Mike shuffled the papers on his desk, knowing it wasn't going to get him any closer to going home. Or rather, going to Laura's house. He'd had a romantic evening planned, but now that would have to wait. The department devised new reports every six months or so and each time Mike and his co-workers would spend a few extra nights figuring it all out. He sighed and picked up the phone.

Laura answered on the third ring — she sounded half asleep. "I'm sorry," Mike said, "did I wake you?"

Laura gave a low laugh. "Almost. I've been waiting up for you."

"Well, damn. I'm going to be here for at least another hour. Maybe two. Can I have a rain check for tonight?"

"Anytime."

"How did your day go?"

"Good. I met a neighbor, went shopping, put in an application at the grocery store, interviewed and got the job..."

"Great! That was fast work."

"They were hiring. And I can walk there. The pay's not that great, but it's a start. After that, I came home, ate some dinner and Renee picked me up for the meeting tonight. Then it was back home again and a nice relaxing hot shower. Since then, I've been sitting in a chair, watching television and dozing off. And if you're not going to make it tonight, I guess I'll just get to bed."

"Are you okay?"

"Yeah. Actually I am."

Mike detected surprise in her voice. "Good. First day out can be a problem."

Laura yawned. "I had some rocky moments, but managed to get through them. And for the first time in my life, I was happy grocery stores, in this state at least, don't sell alcohol."

"Yeah. I'm going to let you go now, babe. You sound exhausted."

"I am."

"You know you can call me if you need me, right? Or Renee? Don't torture yourself with the cravings. Help is only a call away."

Laura chuckled. "Yeah, I'll reach out and touch someone. Thanks, Mike. I can't tell you how much this means to me — I'm not sure I'd have gotten through it all without you."

"Happy to be of service, ma'am. Night."

Mike hung up the phone, feeling a bit relieved that Laura was doing as well as she said. He hoped that she'd call someone if she got into trouble. Then again, he thought he'd managed to get rid of her stash, including the many bottles of Valium he'd found. He wished, though, that he could've spent this night with her. Whether they made love or not, he wanted to be there, wanted to just lie next to her, drink in the scent of her hair and watch her sleep. Somehow in the short time they'd known each other, she'd gotten under his skin. He couldn't now imagine life without her and looked forward to a long future with her.

A little too soon for that, cowboy, he thought, *don't rush the lady — you'll scare her away.*

He smiled. Laura seemed such a spooky little thing, so fragile, almost ethereal. Then he went back to shuffling his papers. "I need to finish this up tonight," he muttered, "so I'm not stuck here tomorrow as well."

Cassie arrived on Laura's doorstep late Friday afternoon. Despite the plans they'd made, Laura hadn't really expected Cassie to be moving in. But here she was. The company would be nice, at least.

Laura smiled and opened the door wide. Cassie hesitated at the portal, but Laura reached out and gave her a hug, which pulled her in completely. "It's good to see you," Laura said. "How'd the last week in go for you?"

Cassie rolled her eyes and made a sound of exasperation. "Those people really started to get to me after a while. My new roommate turned out to be a newly converted born-again. And while I appreciate the thoughts of her Lord giving her strength, I didn't need to hear about it 24/7. Not all of us are Christians, after all."

Laura laughed. "I can't say I'm sorry I missed it. Other than that, how are you doing?"

"Well. I can tell that *you're* doing okay, you've got a nice warm aura around you. Things good with Mike? And don't you look pretty? Are you going out?"

"Better than good. Thank you. And yes." Laura had dressed with special care for tonight and she spun around to give Cassie a full view of the little red cocktail dress. "But why don't you come in all the way and get settled. You're in the second bedroom — that's the one across the hall from the bathroom — and I cleared space in the closet for your belongings." Laura looked down at the suitcase Cassie had brought in. "Is this all you have?"

"There's some stuff still out in the car; but I left most of it in storage. Staying here is only temporary. I do greatly appreciate the offer, but I wish the house were more..."

"More what?"

"Welcoming? Inviting? It needs warmth, it needs lightening up." Laura frowned and Cassie hastily backtracked. "Nothing to do with you, Laura, and nothing to do with your preparations. It's not your fault at all. The bad vibes hanging in the air are much uglier than you could ever be even at your worst. If this house were a person, you'd cross the street to avoid contact." Cassie bit her bottom lip. "I'm sorry, Laura, the words aren't coming out right. I hope you know that I mean well. Anyway, it's probably nothing that can't be fixed with the proper purification. I can do that, if you'll allow me."

Laura tried not to take offense at her words, but some of the good feeling of Cassie being here had worn off. "Knock yourself out. Short of burning the place down, you're free to purify away. I just want you to make yourself at home the best you can."

"I'm sorry. I'm being tactless and blunt, as usual. Thank you for allowing me to stay with you for a time. And I'm sure we'll manage just fine." Cassie reached down and picked up her suitcase, nodding her head in the direction of the hall. "Lead on!"

Laura sat on the bed, watching Cassie unpack, feeling somewhat guilty about snapping at her earlier. She'd brought more accessories than clothes: candles, books, jars of oils, four decks of tarot cards, and a laptop computer. Cassie used the nightstand to set this up. "You have wireless here, right?"

Laura nodded. "Yeah, I used to need it for work. But now that I'm no longer in real estate, I barely even turn the computer on. Didn't cancel the service, though, so you should be set."

"Great. I can keep the business going, at least. Save up some cash and get a new place to live. I don't want to be a bother to you any longer than necessary."

"You're not a bother. I'm glad to have someone else here — we'll each have a built-in support group."

Cassie hung up her sparse collection of clothes in the closet. "So you're looking mighty spiffy," she said, "what's the occasion?"

"Mike's taking me out to a fancy restaurant. To celebrate."

"Celebrate what?"

"I don't know. Maybe for surviving rehab. Maybe for staying sober for five days. Maybe he's trying to seduce me with good food and a romantic atmosphere."

Cassie laughed. "Leading you into temptation?"

Laura got up from the bed and smoothed the skirt of her dress over her thighs. "Oh please, I hope so. God, it's been a long time. Will you be okay here by yourself?"

"I'm fine." Anubis chose that moment to jump up on Cassie's bed and rub up against her. She looked down at the animal. "And you must be Anubis the Bonehead. What a sweet boy you are."

"Are you sure? I might be late. I hope so, anyway."

"We'll be fine," she patted the cat again and he purred. "Just Anubis and me. So you have fun. Write down the WiFi password before you go. And if I don't see you until tomorrow morning, I won't be upset. I will, however, expect a full report."

"I can't promise that. But thanks. And yes, don't wait up."

Mike smiled at Laura across the table and reached for her hand. "You look so beautiful tonight," he said.

Laura laughed and blushed. "You've said that already. Several times."

"And I'll keep saying it since it's true. You haven't caught the looks from the other men here? You're one hot babe."

"It's the dress," she said with a small shrug that caused one of the straps of her dress to fall off her shoulder. She pushed it back up. "Red is one of those colors that men notice."

"What's filling the dress isn't all that bad either." He reached for the bottle sitting in the ice bucket on the table. "More bubbly, my dear?"

Laura laughed as he refilled her glass. He was so sweet; he'd asked the waiter to bring a large bottle of sparkling water for them to drink. Oddly enough, although there was no alcohol involved, the trappings made a difference. The restaurant was upscale and expensive so making a big show of drinking water added to the festive feeling. And since the restaurant used dimmed lighting, she and Mike didn't seem any different from the other diners. She could admit to herself now that she'd worried about this dinner, worried about being in a situation where ordinarily she'd have drunk something. Or several somethings. But Mike, it seemed, had thought of everything.

"If I didn't know better, Officer Gallagher, I'd think you were trying to take advantage of me."

"Me? Take advantage? I'll have you know my mother raised a gentleman."

"Damn. And here I'd been hoping all night..."

"Shall I ask for the check?"

Laura choked a bit on her water, laughing. "We haven't eaten yet."

"Yeah, I know."

"But afterwards, maybe we could go back to your place." Laura had not been to Mike's apartment, didn't really even know where it was. For any other man, that might have been a danger signal. She hadn't dated much since the divorce, but a time or two she'd been stung by men she'd met in bars who turned out later to be married or living with someone. She felt sure that Mike wasn't married or involved. Still, she'd like to see his home. "Since Cassie is at mine, I mean."

Mike made a bit of a face. "Is she staying long?"

"Don't you like her?"

"I don't know her, Laura. And neither do you. I worry about you, that's all."

Laura twisted her mouth. "I can take care of myself." *Don't go there, Mike,* she silently prayed — the blatant falseness of that statement was so obvious. She knew and he knew: someday it might be true, but right now she was hanging on the edge. *Just let it go.*

Mike took a sip of his water and set his glass back down. The waiter came then with their food. "Thank you," Laura said, smiling up at him, "everything smells wonderful."

"My pleasure, Miss."

The awkwardness of their conversation disappeared and they ate in comfortable silence. Laura couldn't remember a meal that had tasted as good as this one. She suspected it was the company rather than the skill of the chef. That plus the fact this was the first dinner out in a long while she'd eaten when sober. *Maybe this not drinking isn't all that horrible, after all.* Deep down inside, Laura didn't believe it for a second, but it was a good thought while she could hold it. The fact was, she trembled from head to toe, craving just one drop, just one little sip of what the other people around her were casually drinking. Suddenly, Laura lost her appetite.

She ducked her head and wiped her mouth with her napkin, laying it back by the side of her plate.

Mike looked over at her. "Something wrong? You're only about half way through that steak."

Laura shook her head. "It tasted wonderful, but I'm full." She tried a feeble laugh. "This is more than I normally eat in a week."

"Ah," Mike said. "I understand." He reached across the table and touched her hand. "It does get easier, you know. Eventually. If you want it to." He signaled for the waiter.

Laura sighed. She didn't want this evening to come to an end. "We don't have to leave unless you're ready, Mike. I'm fine."

She looked down at her hands; one held the stem of her water glass firmly, the other grasped at the end of the table as if she were hanging on to herself and to her life by a hair. *Not as if,* she thought and made an effort to loosen her grip, *I am hanging on. And just barely managing.*

He cleared his throat and she looked over at him. She could tell from the look on his face that he knew she wasn't fine. "It's not a problem, Laura. I'm finished too." He patted his flat stomach and smiled over at her. "Can't afford to get fat. Besides, we can get a doggy bag — restaurant food always tastes best the second day."

Laura's stomach twisted up in anticipation as she entered Mike's apartment. She wasn't sure what she'd expected, a sort of modern bachelor pad, perhaps, but this place certainly wasn't that. Furnished with overstuffed furniture and a big screen television, Mike's home teemed with a huge variety of houseplants, all of them lush and vibrant. "I guess you have a green thumb. I'm impressed."

Mike gave a laugh and took Laura's coat, hanging it up in the hallway closet. "It's a hobby, something I picked up after rehab. All of the passion, drive and obsession with which I pursued my drinking — and believe me, I was a raging drunk — I redirected into one pitiful house plant that my sponsor had given me. And that plant, to my great surprise, responded and thrived. So I bought more which all grew as well. It's therapeutic. A shame that I'm a cop — I could probably grow some awesome marijuana." He laughed. "Anyway, when I see them, I'm reminded of all of the pain and torture I went through and how it all turned out to be worthwhile in the end. It had fostered new life, not just in me, but in the world around me."

Laura looked around again, then back at Mike and smiled. The knots in her stomach eased. She even forgot her cravings, her own particular pain and torture, for a moment. She crossed the room and took his face in her hands. "You're a good man, Mike Gallagher. Too good for me, at least..."

He stopped her words with a kiss. "Never," he whispered into her ear, giving her shivers, good shivers, "never say that again. You happen to be talking about the woman I love."

Making love to Mike turned out to be every bit as good as she'd imagined. It had been so long since she'd been intimate with anyone; and she could barely remember when she'd had sex without being drunk. As if she was having sex for the very first time, every touch, every kiss seemed heightened. The intensity overwhelmed her, making her feel lost and slightly embarrassed by the sheer intimacy. She almost wanted to close her eyes and just let her emotions wash her away, but she didn't want to miss a thing. The look in Mike's eyes as he loved her, coaxing one orgasm out of her after another, was too exciting to miss. The experience seemed to last forever and to take no time at all. When he finally collapsed on her, spent and sweating, she smiled and sighed. He held her, stroking her hair, whispering endearments; she fell asleep in his arms.

Mike felt Laura get out of bed and leaned up on one elbow to watch her. She seemed unaware of him watching; instead she picked up her shawl from where it lay on the floor and draped it over her, hugging the edges close to her. She walked as far as the doorway, but hesitated there, as if unsure of where she was.

"First door on the right," he called softly to her, assuming it she wanted the bathroom.

She looked over her shoulder at where he lay; her hair feathered around her cheek and her face glowed softly in the hall light. She looked beautiful, even with the dark circles and the haunted look in her eyes. She put a finger to her lips. "Shhhh. Listen. Do you hear that?"

Mike shook his head, he didn't hear anything.

"It's a baby. Crying."

He listened again and could hear nothing. But she didn't seem to notice him and listened again, her head cocked to one side, a distant look crossed her face. "It's Matthew. I'm sure of it. I have to go to him."

Mike realized then that Laura was dreaming. He got out of bed and touched her shoulder lightly. She trembled under his hand. "Laura?"

She woke up with a start. "What's happening?"

He draped an arm around her — she felt ice cold. "You had a bad dream, sweetheart, come back to bed now."

Laura rubbed her hand over her eyes, then snuggled into Mike. "It didn't feel like a dream," she said, shivering. "Or maybe I got up to turn the heat on — it's damn cold in here."

Mike nuzzled her neck. "It's nice and warm under the covers." He led her back to the bed and pulled the covers up over her shoulders. She fell asleep almost as soon as she lay down. He stayed awake for quite a while, watching her breathe, in and out, and wishing he could do something to help her, something to make her transition to a sober life easier. Wishing he could stop the nightmares.

He wondered how long Laura had been having these walking nightmares, wondered when they would end. But most of all, he wondered who Matthew was.

CHAPTER TWELVE

Laura woke the next morning, confused about her surroundings. Then she remembered and smiled — she was at Mike's place. She stretched and slid out of bed, finding an oversized sweatshirt in the closet to wear. The smell of coffee drew her to the kitchen, where Mike stood over the stove, making eggs and bacon.

"Wow," Laura said, accepting a mug of coffee from him and sitting down at one of the bar stools at his kitchen counter, "that smells really good."

Mike set his fork down and came over to give her a quick kiss. "So do you. How are you feeling this morning?"

"Great," Laura said, taking a sip from her cup, "I slept like a baby."

Mike raised an eyebrow. "I take it you don't remember your nightmare?"

Laura shook her head. "No, I remember falling asleep. Then waking up just a few minutes ago. Nothing at all in between. Did I have a bad night?"

"Not particularly bad, really. Restless, maybe. You were up and walking around, but weren't really here, if you know what I mean. You heard a baby crying. And you thought it was Matthew."

"Matthew?" Laura's voice quavered slightly. "You're right, that is a bad nightmare." She set her cup down and rubbed her hands over her eyes, making a slight moaning noise.

"Who's Matthew?"

"My son. He died at only two months old — crib death."

Mike nodded. "You'd said you lost a baby, but I assumed it was a miscarriage." He walked over behind her and wrapped his arms around her neck, pulling her back against him.

She leaned into him, putting a hand up and lightly stroking his cheek. "It was," she paused, sighed, and continued, "horrible." No one word could describe the event — but cataclysmic came close. For Laura and her family, it was singly the most tragic event they'd ever experienced. And for her marriage it was a death knell. Laura preferred not to think about any of it — alcohol had always dulled the edge of the pain, made it easier to bear. "I guess I'm not surprised it should come to the surface now. I've spent most of the time since he died living at the bottom of a bottle. And now there is no bottle to live in."

"I'm sorry," Mike said, "there's nothing else I can say to make this feel better, is there?"

"It's okay." Every fiber of Laura's body screamed at this lie. "It's old news and I'd rather not talk about right now. Or ever. Regardless of what the counselors say, talking doesn't help. All that does is bring it back up to the surface."

He moved away from her and back to the stove. "Breakfast?"

She smiled. "Absolutely."

They were halfway through their meal when Mike's phone rang. He looked at the clock — it was still early. "Must be the precinct calling. Or a wrong number." He stood up and answered it. "Gallagher here," he said and listened for a little bit. "Hi, Cassie, yes, she's here." He held his hand over the receiver. "Obviously it's for you," Mike said. "She sounds upset about something."

Laura barely had a chance to say hello, when Cassie started in. "I'm sorry to call you so early in the morning, but I thought you'd want to know that Tony called in the middle of the night last night. Your daughter apparently had a particularly nasty nightmare, involving, as best as I can make out, you and a dead baby?"

"That's really weird," Laura said, but didn't elaborate. Cassie didn't need to know that she and Lizzy seemed to be sharing the same night terrors.

"Yeah," Cassie said. "Anyway, I gave Tony the number over there — found it on your speed dial — but he said he wasn't going to bother you. Apparently your cell phone wasn't picking up either."

Laura nodded. "I had it turned off."

There was a pause on Cassie's end of the phone. "Well, he sounded really angry. No offense, Laura, but he can be a real asshole, can't he? He just couldn't believe that you might not be at home when he needed you. Or rather, when Lizzy needed you. I tried to explain you had a life, too, and that it was pretty late to call, but he hung up on me."

Laura gave a soft chuckle. "That's about par for the course, Cassie. He's been particularly touchy lately. I'll give him a call when we're done. Other than that, how'd your night go?"

Laura heard Cassie take in a breath. "We did okay, I guess. For a fairly new house, this place sure has its share of creaks and noises. Finally I quit chasing the sounds down, lit some calming incense and fell asleep watching television. Only to have Tony call and wake me up."

"Sorry," Laura said. "About all of it." She didn't see the need to explain to Cassie that the house really wasn't a new construction. "I'll be home in a bit — need anything from the store?"

"Nope," Cassie said. "I checked out the food situation and we seem to be in good shape for dinner. I'll cook if you don't mind."

"That'd be heavenly, Cassie. Thanks."

Laura sighed when she hung up the phone.

"Trouble?" Mike filled up her coffee cup again and patted the bar stool for her to sit down again. "Finish your food before it gets too cold."

Making a face, Laura shook her head. "I should really call Tony soon." She explained the call to Mike and she noticed his eyes grow angry.

"You don't need to call him right away. Seems like he expects you to be sitting around waiting for his every move. I'm sure Lizzy is fine, or he'd have called here as well. As far as his being upset about you being here," Mike shrugged, "tough shit. And you shouldn't apologize for it either — we're both single, consenting adults. So what if he doesn't like it? He's not exactly living the life of a monk, is he? Shacked up with your old college roommate?"

"Whew," Laura said with a small laugh, setting the phone down and sitting next to him again. "Tell me what you really think, Mike, why don't you? Although at least I know you've actually been listening when I've been talking." She took another bite of her eggs. "I'm sure Tony's just concerned about Lizzy. Her nightmares can be very intense. He's also probably stressing about the wedding. And about leaving the girls with me while he and Susan go to Europe. So for no other reason than to reassure him about my fitness as a mother, I should call. Otherwise, he might decide to cancel their visit. I really want to see them."

"I understand. I do. I can't help getting angry, though, when people walk all over you."

Laura smiled. “I do get angry, Mike, all by myself. But I pick my moments.”

“Fair enough. I only want you to be happy. So call the bastard if it makes you feel better, but finish your breakfast first. You must be hungry.”

Laura took another bite. “Starved, actually. And the eggs are fantastic. What a pleasant surprise to find you’re as good at cooking as you are at...other things.”

“And what things would those be?”

Laura blushed but didn’t answer. Instead she finished her plate, picked it and Mike’s up and put them both in the sink. Then she dialed Tony’s number.

He answered on the first ring. “Hi, Tony,” Laura said, “it’s me. I understand you were trying to reach me. What’s up?”

“Where are you? And who is this Cassie person who answered your phone?”

“Cassie is staying with me for a bit,” Laura said, “and I’m at Mike’s house. What’s up?”

“Lizzy wanted to talk to you. Insisted she couldn’t go back to sleep unless she did.”

“Cassie gave you the number over here. Why didn’t you call then?”

“God only knows what you were doing, Laura. I can’t keep up with you.”

Laura could hear Susan talking in the background. “I think you can guess what I was doing, Tony. Most likely the same thing you and Susan were. I can hear that she’s there. So drop the injured ex-spouse tone, okay? I’m not going to let you make me feel guilty for trying to put my life back together.”

“That’s not what I was doing, Laura, and you know it.”

Laura gave a low, rather unpleasant chuckle. “I know no such thing, Tony.” There was a pause on both ends of the line. Changing the subject, Laura spoke again first. “How’re the wedding plans coming along?”

“Not too bad,” Tony sounded relieved at the new topic. “You haven’t RSVP’d yet. Will you be coming?”

“I doubt it. I’m supposed to be working that day. But you’re still bringing the girls on Sunday, right?” Laura held her breath for the answer.

Tony sighed into the phone. “I don’t know, Laura. They’ve been a bit of a handful lately. Are you sure you’re up to it?”

Laura remembered that code quite well. “I’m sober, Tony. Completely clean and sober. I haven’t had a drink for over thirty days. Haven’t had a Valium in that time either. I worked hard at this, you know. I attend AA meetings, I have a sponsor, I’m 100% committed to staying sober. You might show just a little bit of interest, offer just a small bit of support. It wouldn’t kill you to be a human being for once. And if you can’t do that, then at least recognize that I *am* the mother of those girls and I have a right and a need to see them. They’re not tiny babies, after all.”

“Yeah, you’re right.” Tony’s voice hesitated — admitting he might be wrong about something was difficult.

Laura nodded and smiled. “So, I can expect them sometime next Sunday morning?”

“Sure.” He paused again then cleared his throat. “I’m glad you’re doing this well, Laura. I really am. We wanted to get up and visit you in rehab at least once, but with school and the wedding stuff, things are crazy around here.”

“I’ll bet.” *Let him off the hook, Laura,* she told herself. *You can’t expect him to apologize much more than he already has.* “Visitors’ Day was always pretty hectic, anyway. I need to go now, I think. Call me and let me know what time you'll be coming by, okay? And tell Susan I said 'hi.'"

Laura hung up the phone. Mike looked over at her while he washed those few breakfast dishes. "Good conversation?"

Laura smiled and gave a satisfied nod. "Yeah, it was. Satisfying."

Mike snickered. "Sounded to me like you kicked his ass. Good girl. I'm proud of you."

CHAPTER THIRTEEN

Things settled into a routine at Laura's house. Cassie kept to herself mostly, closed away in her room. The smell of burning sage continually filled the hallway; Laura grew used to the odor and to having a stranger of sorts living in her home. When they were together, they got along fine, as long as Laura didn't take anything that Cassie said too seriously. She allowed the self-proclaimed psychic to read her cards and her palms. The outcomes of these exercises were inevitably filled with doom and gloom, people falling out of burning towers or pierced with swords. *They're all only pictures on cards,* Laura would think. She had no room in her life for otherworldly influences; everyday temptations proved to be a difficult enough task to master.

Getting to sleep at night seemed nearly impossible. Although she kept herself busy during the days — with work, preparation for her daughters' visit, as many meetings as she could attend, and all of the other household chores — and would be exhausted when she lay down, sleep just wouldn't come. Laura would toss and turn, each nerve and muscle in her body itching, crying out for help, help in the form of a pill or a long glass of something. Anything. She missed the slow burn of a shot of bourbon or scotch, missed the way it would hit her stomach and spread its numbing warmth all the way down to her toes.

Mike had been working nights this week, and she had day shift so she didn't even have the comfort of his presence, the warmth of his body next to hers. She missed him as well.

The weather turned bitterly cold on Wednesday, a frigid snap unusual for October, but not completely unheard of in this area. To make matters worse, the circuit breaker to her furnace kept switching itself off, usually in the middle of the night, which would necessitate a trip down the cellar stairs into the dim, cobwebby, and now frigid gloom. While it was true that she wasn't sleeping during those times, she'd have gladly forgone the whole thing. The fifth time this happened, she remembered her visit with Carolyn and the problem the neighbor had noticed with her lights.

Between her job, Cassie's presence, and Mike, Laura never had a chance to get to know Carolyn better. They'd shared a few rushed phone calls, but that was all. Laura still was torn between wanting to know her neighbor better and wanting to avoid what seemed to be good old-fashioned snooping. Still, Carolyn had been a good resource for information and seemed happy to recommend a local handyman.

The handyman spent several hours in the cellar, coming up with no good explanation for the problem, at least not to Laura's understanding. But with the bill for over five hundred dollars he also issued her his personal guarantee that it probably wouldn't be happening much from now on. "When it got so cold all of a sudden," he explained, "your older circuit breakers just couldn't handle the overload. But I patched it up the best I could without rewiring the whole damn place, which, trust me, you didn't want me to do. I couldn't find nothing wrong with the lights, though, so maybe your neighbor was seeing things. You should be okay, so long's you're not trying to run too many things at once. Have you had this problem before?"

Laura shook her head. "Not really — I've not been here that long."

"The people before you, maybe?"

"I've no idea. The house sat empty for five years before I bought it."

"Five years?" The handyman laughed. "What happened? A murder spree in the cellar?"

"Excuse me?"

"You know, like that movie about the haunted house in New York, I think. And that house only stood empty for one year before new folks moved in with the ghosts." He paused for a second then nodded. "Anyways, that's likely your problem."

"Excuse me?" Laura repeated. "You must be as crazy as my roommate. Are you trying to tell me that there are ghosts down here in my basement playing with the circuit breakers?"

The man laughed again, louder this time, the noise echoing off the cellar walls. This man seriously creeped Laura out; so much so that she had goose bumps up and down her arms.

"Nope, lady, that's not it at all. Although that'd be fun, don't you think? Me, I don't believe in none of that stuff — I just watch the movies. What I really meant was that if the house stood empty for five years without having the furnace run or serviced, that's likely to be your biggest problem. Anyway, with the maintenance I gave it today, you should be just fine." He chuckled again to himself. "Ghosts playing with the circuit breakers. That's a good one. I should write that up on the service ticket, just to give dispatch a good laugh."

Laura looked at the bill in her hand — all it said was routine maintenance. "You'll take a check, right?"

"No problem."

She escorted him up the stairs and then later out the door with check in hand. Cassie came out of her room and gave Laura a little smile. "Maybe he's right."

“That there are ghosts? Give me a break.”

Cassie shook her head. “This house is poisoned. You know as well as I do that strange things have happened to you here.”

“True,” Laura said, thinking back over nights of bad dreams and odd noises, of feeling cold chills shooting down her spine, of sitting on the couch and catching movement out of the side of her eye. To say nothing of the banging of the cellar door all day and night. Although with the addition of a new, tighter fitting deadbolt, the noise had ceased.

So, yes, odd things had happened. But she also had experienced similar events elsewhere. In rehab and at Mike’s house, she’d had some fairly nasty dreams, and a lot of touch-and-go moments which led her to chalk it all up to withdrawal of some sort. Cassie, of course, had the same problem. “But I hardly think you and I are good judges right now of what is real and what is not. We’d be jumpy anywhere. So, if it’s all the same to you, I vote for not burning down my house anytime soon. We’ll need more proof than a couple of ex-addicts could come up with.”

Cassie just stared at her. “That’s a bit of a low blow, Laura. If you only stopped to think, you’d know I was right. This house is poisoned,” she repeated, “I’ve done the best I could to shield us, but it may be more than I can handle.”

“Maybe,” Laura said the first thought that came into her mind, “you should just move out if it’s so horrible.”

Cassie blinked, tears forming in her eyes. “That’s not fair. I have no place else to go.”

Laura instantly regretted the words. “Oh, God, I’m so sorry, that was a rude thing to say. I don’t really want you to leave, Cassie. Just give it a chance, okay? Give it another week or so, when we’ve detoxed a bit more and we’ll look at it again.”

Cassie nodded. "You might be right, I've been a little off my game lately. So what are we doing for dinner? What should I cook?"

Laura could tell that she hadn't convinced Cassie, but she seemed willing to drop the subject and that was good enough for now.

Tony and Susan stopped by the house early Sunday morning to drop the girls off. Tony carried their bags in and set them down in the front hallway. "We can't stay, I'm afraid, we got a bit of a late start this morning and our flight leaves in about two hours. What with us flying out of the country, I figure security will be tricky. House looks nice, though. Maybe I can have the tour when we get back?"

Laura had hugged both of her girls, spending perhaps a little extra time with Lizzy, who looked tired and pale. "Wedding go okay?"

Tony nodded, "Yeah. We had fun — you really should have come."

"I had to work," Laura said, "I've not been there long enough to ask for a day off." *To say nothing of how little interest I had in attending.*

"Girls?" Lizzy and Amanda went to him. He hugged each of them, gave them a quick kiss. "Be good for your mother, okay? And remember what we talked about."

"Bye, Dad. Have fun." The girls stood at the door and waved as he got into the car with Susan and drove away. Then they turned away from the door and looked at Laura.

"Feeling okay, Mom?" Amanda asked.

"I'm fine, sweetheart. Better than fine, actually." Laura picked up one of their suitcases and Amanda picked up the other. "Let's get you two settled in. You'll be sharing a room — I hope that's okay."

Amanda rolled her eyes. "I thought you had three bedrooms."

"I do, but I have a friend staying with me now. I figured your father would tell you."

Lizzy laughed. "He told us to be good and to not make you crazy. Is your friend the cop?"

"Well," Laura said, "I do know a policeman and you'll be meeting him at some point. But this is another friend. A girl friend I met at rehab."

"Friends are good," Lizzy said solemnly. "They keep you from being alone."

Amanda laid claim to half of the room, taking the bed closest to the window, unpacking her clothes in the top two dresser drawers. "This is my part of the room, Lizzy. You stay away and we'll do fine."

Lizzy looked around. "I'm cool," she said. "Where's your cat, Mommy?"

Laura lifted Lizzy's suitcase to the top of the bed and opened it. "Anubis? He's around here somewhere. Do you want me to unpack your clothes?"

"Sure. Anubis is a funny name for a cat. What's it mean?"

Amanda chimed in. "We read about Egypt in school last month, Anubis is one of those gods they had. He's got a dog's head and he lives in Hell."

"It's not exactly Hell," Laura explained. "He presides over the afterlife. And he has a jackal's head," Laura said, putting the rest of Lizzy's clothes in the last available drawer.

"But he *is* a cat, right. Maybe he's the god of ghosts?"

Laura smiled, "Not really, sweetheart. I tell you what — I have a book here somewhere with all of that kind of information in it. We'll find it when we finish here." The last thing to come out of Lizzy's suitcase was a bedraggled faded blue velour bear. "You still have B Bear?" Laura smiled — Lizzy had received the stuffed bear on her third birthday and it had been her favorite toy since.

"She won't let us throw it away, Mom," Amanda said. "It's gross."

"It's mine," Lizzy took the bear from Laura and placed it in the position of honor right on top of her pillow. "And he's not gross; he's well-loved."

"Whatever."

Laura heard the cat door click. "Here's Anubis now, I think." Seconds later, he jumped up on Lizzy's bed. "He doesn't look like a jackal," she said, and reached out a tentative hand to pat him.

Amanda moved away abruptly. "Susan says cats carry all sorts of germs and that they're nasty, sneaking animals. She said not to get too cozy with him."

Laura could hear the cat purr, completely oblivious to Susan's opinion of him. *A good lesson*, Laura thought. Lizzy was entranced, as Anubis probably intended. When he had thoroughly charmed her, he moved on to Amanda. Within five minutes, Susan's opinion of cats no longer mattered.

"Can he sleep in here with us, Mom?" Amanda scratched him under the chin.

"Leave your door open and he'll come and go. He likes to patrol the house."

Lizzy laughed, and sat down next to the cat on Amanda's bed. "He's a watch cat!"

"What's for dinner?" Amanda asked.

"Mike's coming by a little bit later on and is taking us all out. You can pick the place, as long as it's not very expensive."

"Pizza?"

"Sure, we can do pizza, if that's what you both want."

The girls nodded. "In the meantime," Laura said, "I've got some soda and stuff out in the kitchen. I want you two to think of this as your home. So do whatever you'd do at home."

Laura paused. "Just stay out of the cellar, okay?"

"Why?"

"No real reason — it's messy and cold and spidery down there. And there's nothing of interest — just the litter box, the washer and dryer, and boxes of junk left over from the move. Plus the stairs are kind of treacherous and the lights are funny. There's plenty of stuff to keep you occupied up here and you girls are old enough to stay out of places you don't need to be, right?"

Lizzy nodded and Amanda made her standard "whatever" reply. "Can we watch television?"

"Whatever," Laura said with a small laugh and the girls headed out to the living room, leaving Anubis behind. He looked up at her and blinked.

"I wonder," she said quietly to him, "whether I should have said anything about the cellar at all. Now it's a forbidden thing which might make it more interesting."

The cat had no answer, so Laura gave him a final pat and headed out the living room to join the girls.

CHAPTER FOURTEEN

Tony had made arrangements to have the girls picked up each morning and driven to school, saying their school, a private academy, didn't allow them many days off without good cause. Fortunately, the school was closed the last two days of the week for teacher in-service and Laura was able to adjust her work schedule accordingly.

Pizza night had gone well, with Mike making almost as big an impression with the girls as the cat had. Cassie had been unable to accompany them; she'd had to leave the house entirely to go stay with her sister's family for about a week, while her sister recovered from emergency surgery. Cassie might not get along with her sister or want to live with her, but in a crisis family was family.

Tuesday had been a rotten day for Laura. Predictions of a snow storm to occur later on that evening had everyone in the area hitting the grocery store for food and supplies. Although she didn't smoke, she took her break outside, just to clear her head. "Why is it," she said to one of the young men who bagged the groceries at her register, "that people buy eggs, milk, bread and toilet paper when a storm is coming?"

The boy nodded and laughed. "Yeah, no kidding. Like they're all just dying to make breakfast or something. French toast, maybe."

Snow warnings also seemed to make people grumpier than usual, especially when they happened as early in the season as this. By the time Laura had finished her shift, she'd been yelled at, accused of ringing up an order wrong, blamed for the high prices and called stupid. She felt ready to throw something. Instead, she picked up some emergency provisions herself, although hers consisted of a few two-liter bottles of soda, some orange juice, a box of cereal, milk, and a family-sized macaroni and cheese dinner.

As she had every day after work, Laura walked past the liquor store. Ordinarily, she would quicken her pace, and leave it behind her — out of sight, out of mind — but today it was so cold and the bags were so heavy, that she stopped under the awning above the door. She set the bags down on the ground and flexed her fingers, looking into the window. The craving washing over her was so strong she wondered it didn't knock her down. She had the cash; she should just go in and buy a little bottle, a little drop of something to put into coffee on a cold winter day, a reward for working hard and walking home. Laura took a deep breath and put a hand to the door, then jumped back as if she'd been burned. She stepped back, put her hand in her pocket and pulled out her cell phone, hitting the speed dial number for Renee.

"Hello?"

The relief Laura felt at the sound of her voice felt almost as strong as the craving. "Renee? It's me. Laura."

"Hey, sweetie. How are you today? Are you enjoying having your daughters visit?"

Laura sighed. "I'm standing outside the liquor store. I've had the most horrible day and a drink would go down so good right now. Is it so terrible of me to want to go in and get something?"

"It's normal, Laura. But it would be bad for you. And you know that. Want me to come and pick you up?"

Laura thought about that. “I’m not too far from home, I can make it. Hold on a second, okay?” She dug around in her purse and found the cell phone headset and plugged it in. After getting the gear into place, she picked up her bags again. “Are you still there?”

“Always. What’s happening?”

“I’m walking away. Talk to me while I walk home.”

Renee asked questions about the girls’ visit and they set up a coffee date for later in the week. By the time Laura was a block away from her house, the craving, while not completely gone, had subdued. Softened. Laura held control, just the way it should be.

She thanked Renee, clicked off the phone and stopped for a second to adjust her hold on the plastic handles of the bags. Then she trudged the rest of the way home, scuffling her feet through piles of frozen leaves sitting on the sidewalks. A few small flakes of snow started falling when she put her key in the door. The girls had made plans to stay for a while after school each day while they were here, so they didn’t need to come home to an empty house. Plus, Laura remembered that Mike had trouble with the lock and didn’t want either Lizzy or Amanda stuck outside waiting for her to arrive.

The house was freezing inside, as usual. A look at the thermostat confirmed her suspicion that the heater had not run all day. “Damn circuit breakers,” she said as she unlocked the cellar door and flipped on the light. She sighed. “I do not want to go down those stairs right now.” Anubis came over to her and butted up against her leg. “Yeah, you heard me right, Bonehead. I don’t want to go down there. But I have to. Come with me?”

Laura started down the stairs, trailed by the black cat. “What a good boy,” she said, “and what a smart kitty. You understand every word I say, don’t you?” She flipped the circuit breaker for the furnace and it clicked on, hissing and sighing and finally rumbling into action.

"Stay on this time, dammit." Remembering the talk she'd had with the electrician the other day, she gave a little chuckle. "And you ghosts quit playing with it!"

She regretted the words almost before she'd finished saying them. Somehow even joking about that situation freaked her out. The hair on her arms and on the back of her neck tingled and stood on end. "Okay," she whispered, "I'm leaving," and ran up the stairs as quickly as possible, slamming the door when she reached the upstairs and throwing both deadbolts.

Anubis came through the cat door and gave her a dirty look. "Sorry I left you down there, baby, but..." He reached up, pawed her leg, and she picked him up, snuggling him, burying her face in his rich warm fur. "How about some dinner?"

After Laura and the girls had eaten, they settled in the living room with cups of cocoa and played a few board games until the cat, attracted by the sound of the dice, started moving the playing pieces. Finally he scooped a paw around Lizzy's piece and pulled it over to the finishing line.

"I win!"

Amanda twisted her mouth. "Not really, nitwit."

"Don't call your sister names," Laura said absently. "And it's late anyway — time for bed."

"But," Lizzy protested, "we probably don't have school tomorrow." Both girls had been watching the weather reports on and off for most of the night, anticipating a snow day.

"We'll see about that tomorrow."

By the time Amanda and Lizzy got settled in, Laura's nerves were jangling. The constant bickering bothered her, although she knew that it was normal for children of their ages. Developmentally,

Amanda was so much further along than Lizzy; their interests were so totally different, it was no wonder they didn't get along. *But enough is enough,* Laura thought. *I don't need this after battling with the job and the cravings all day.* She ached with tiredness; she'd give her right arm for just one little Valium. *Or a nice shot of scotch.*

She took a deep breath, then several more. That relaxed her. Still she didn't know how much longer she could deal with everything. "One day at a time," she murmured to herself on her way back to wish the girls a good night. "One day at a time." She gave a little snort. *Too bad they don't have a saying to cover the nights. The nights are far worse than the days ever are.*

Tonight Laura had no problem falling asleep, as if the exertions of her day had balanced out the frustrations. She remembered starting one of her deep breathing exercises and then she was gone, deep into a sound sleep. Part of the problem with sleeping so well, though, was that it allowed the mind to dream. As Laura's did.

Everything starts out well enough — the day in the dream is sunny and warm. Worries about the furnace and the circuit breaker problems are a whole year away. She and the girls and Mike are having a picnic, at the same place he took her that day before rehab. She fixes herself a plate full of the best smelling food, but Mike takes it away from her. "No time to eat, babe," he says in the dream. "The storm is coming."

Laura looks up to the sky, surprised he would say such a thing. Not a cloud in sight. She shakes her head. And the rain starts, pouring down out of a cloudless sky. Before she realizes what is happening, the lovely park they'd been in turns into a gully filled with rushing water. First one girl, then the other is carried away by the growing torrent. Mike holds on to her. "Save the girls," she screams, barely audible over the roaring water. "Too late," he says, and lets go, allowing the rushing water to carry him away. Her head goes under the water and when she comes back up to the surface, she's no longer outside. She is, instead, in the cellar of her house. The water is draining away, leaving the bodies of Mike and the girls behind. "No! "You can't have them. Give them back!"

She has no idea to whom she speaks. But there is an answer. A whisper. Then many whispers. A door opens up in the concrete block cellar wall. Greenish fog comes pouring out, covering the floor, twining its way up Laura's legs, slowly, almost sensually. She sighs, all the anger and grief pulled out of her, as if the fog, and the shapes she now sees in that fog, sap her of strength. It feels so good to relax, so easy to just let it all go. The whispers grow louder. "Yes, let it go, Laura. Come with us. We can all be together. We can take you too. There's room for more..."

Laura shot straight up in bed, gasping for air. Her nightgown soaked with sweat, she blinked in the darkness. "Damn," she said, rubbing her hand over her eyes. "I guess I can thank the Valium withdrawal for that one." She swung her legs over the side of the bed, thinking she'd watch a little television and sleep on the couch, but something didn't feel right. She stopped short, listening. There, on the very edge of her hearing, was the whispering. The source of her dream. "Girls," she called out, "quiet down in there. You woke me up."

The whispering stopped, leaving an odd sharpness in the air. That also didn't feel right to Laura. Normally, the girls wouldn't listen right away and there would be giggling. Instead, silence. She got out of bed, quietly opening her door and choking back a scream. There, at the cellar door stood the figure of a little girl. It's Lizzy, she realized, and let out a breath, glad she restrained her initial reaction. As she approached the girl, she saw she stood up on her tiptoes attempting to reach the uppermost deadbolt. Lizzy turned, her eyes glazed and staring. It had been a while since Laura had witnessed one of Lizzy's night terrors, but obviously that was what this was. Lizzy's lips were moving. Laura got closer, so she could hear, even though her speech during these episodes was normally gibberish.

Not this time. "There's room for more," Lizzy whispered. "They say there's room for more, Mommy, but I don't want to go."

Laura started back for a second. Were she and Lizzy sharing the same dream? How could that be possible? She repressed her own rush of fear out of concern for her daughter. Lightly Laura touched her on the cheek, then wrapped her arm around the girl's shoulders. She could feel Lizzy quivering through the heavy flannel of her pajamas. "It's okay, sweetheart, you don't have to go. You can stay here with me."

"Mommy?" Lizzy gave a little shiver and blinked her eyes. "You're here? Are you okay?"

Laura gave a shaky laugh. "I'm fine, baby. You were having one of your bad dreams. Are *you* okay? And where else would I be?"

Lizzy's eyes rolled to the cellar door. "Down there, with them."

"Who, Lizzy?"

"I don't know, Mommy. It's just a dream."

Laura led her out to the kitchen. "I'll heat you up a little bit of cocoa and then we'll get a blanket and snuggle up on the couch. How would that be?"

The girl nodded.

"Who knows," Laura joked softly, "maybe there's actually something good on to watch."

There wasn't, but it didn't matter. Curled up next to her mother on the sofa, wrapped tightly in a warm blanket, Lizzy slept. Peacefully this time. Laura sat awake, jumping at each and every creak and sound in the house. Outside the snow fell, hissing softly as it coated the trees and the grass and the street.

"No school tomorrow then," she whispered, pulling the curtain shut after she gauged the amount of snowfall. "But I'll still have to work. I don't want to leave them home alone. Something here seems very wrong."

If Cassie were here, she might be able to help. Laura hadn't wanted to believe her before, thinking all of her fears and misgivings about the house were silly and ridiculous. But now, as the house became more and more chilling, she wondered. *What do I do if she's right?*

CHAPTER FIFTEEN

With the light of day, Laura felt differently. There had to be a logical reason why she and Lizzy were having the same dream. The obvious conclusion was not ghosts in her house. “Maybe,” she said quietly to the cat sitting on the arm of the couch, “maybe she was talking in her sleep and I heard the words, working them into my dream.” *Stranger things have happened*, she thought, *everyone has those dreams where they hear a bell or a buzzing and wake up to find that their alarm clock noise had filtered in.*

She gently eased Lizzy’s head off of her lap, where the girl had finally settled in to sleep and got up from the couch, tucking a pillow under her daughter’s head and pulling the blanket up around her neck. Laura went over to the thermostat and tapped on it, sighing. “Freezing again,” she said, “I’m going to call a real electrician today.

She turned on the television and put it on mute, flipping to the news. School closings were being listed and sure enough the girls’ school made the top of the list. Laura shook her head. “Bad timing,” she muttered to herself as she first turned on the coffee machine then threw the deadbolts on the cellar door, trudging down the stairs restart the furnace. “Just stop it,” she said, throwing the circuit breaker back to on, unsure if she was talking to the machinery and wiring or the ghosts. “Yeah, right,” she said as the furnace kicked back on. “Ghosts. That’s just ridiculous.” But somewhere in the back of her mind she heard one of the lecturers at rehab. *Denial is the first stage...*

She shook her head again as she closed the door and locked it. Laura still didn't want to leave the girls home alone today, but wasn't sure what to say if she called off. She didn't want to lie and say she was sick; nor did she want to say something like, "I can't come in, I had a nightmare." Or: "My daughter had a nightmare." And she certainly wasn't going to say "I have ghosts in my house and I can't leave the girls alone." That last one made her chuckle. She picked up her phone and dialed Mike's cell number. At the very least, he could stop by and check on Lizzy and Amanda around lunch time.

He answered on the second ring, his voice professional, his manner terse. "Gallagher."

"Hey, it's me."

"Hey, you." Laura smiled. She liked the way he said that, somehow he managed to make those two simple words sound very special.

"I wondered if you could stop by the house sometime today and make sure the girls are okay. They don't have school, but I still have to work."

"Tell you what," Mike said, "I can go one better than that. I'm working a split shift today, so I'm off at twelve and don't go back until four. I can just stay at the house and wait until you get home."

Laura felt a huge rush of relief. "That would be wonderful, Mike. Thank you. We had a bad night."

Mike's voice grew sharp. "What happened?"

"I had a nightmare and Lizzy had a nightmare and the two of us spent most of the night sacked out on the couch. The furnace circuit breaker is still not working."

"I have a buddy who is a real electrician, not some dumb schmuck handyman like that other guy you had. Where'd you find him, anyway?"

"Carolyn, one of my neighbors, recommended him."

"Well, he charged you way too much and didn't do a damn thing to fix things. I'll get my friend to stop over this afternoon and we'll see what we can do. I'm not all that handy around the house, but I can follow instructions."

Laura sighed. "That really would be great, Mike, and I'd be so grateful."

"How grateful?" The edge in his voice was replaced with a honeyed tone.

Laura giggled. "*That* grateful. Anyway, I need to get off to work here soon, although if the roads are as bad as they are saying, I doubt we'll have anyone there."

"The roads are as bad. If you were driving, you wouldn't make it."

"Yeah, luckily I'm within walking distance."

"Not all that lucky, babe, it's cold and windy out there, with lots of drifts and blowing snow. Stay pretty far on the side of the road if you can."

"Will do. And thanks."

"My pleasure."

Laura hung up the phone and heard a big yawn come from the couch. "Morning, sweetie."

"Morning, Mommy. Why am I out here?"

"You had a nightmare. Don't you remember?"

"Nope." Lizzy actually looked well rested and certainly didn't seem concerned in the least about last night's activity. Then again, she'd become accustomed to night terrors when she was younger. Maybe this episode was just an extension of those.

"What do you want for breakfast?"

"Oatmeal?" Then she stopped and ran to the window. "Snow! Do we have school?"

Laura smiled. "No school today."

"Hurrah! Let's go tell Amanda."

Laura grabbed her hand as she ran past. "Let's just let Amanda sleep, okay? She's not going to be as excited as you are."

"Oh." Lizzy's face fell. "Yeah, okay. Do you think we could go out and play in it later on?"

"Well, I have to go to work. But Mike's coming by around lunchtime and he'll be here when I get home."

Lizzy grew cautious. "Like a babysitter, you mean? We're too old..."

"Just as a friend. Maybe he wants to play in the snow too."

"That's okay then. I like him." Lizzy paused for a bit. "Are you going to marry him, like Dad and Susan?"

Laura laughed. "He hasn't asked me yet. But if he does, I'll think about it."

"You should," Lizzy nodded, "he's nice. And it won't be *if* he does, it'll be *when*. He likes you too, I can tell."

"Thanks for that vote of confidence, honey."

Amanda came out with a hopeful look on her face. "No school?"

"No school," Laura confirmed, "so if you want to crawl back into bed, that'd be fine. By the way, how did you sleep last night?"

"Great, as far as I remember."

"You didn't hear Lizzy then?"

Amanda rolled her eyes. "Did you have another nightmare, squirt? She's been having nightmares now for months, Mom. Susan says she thinks it's stress, between school and the marital situations. Not," she added quickly, "that anyone thinks it's your fault. Susan says that

Lizzy's just a bit more sensitive than I am. And she picks up on things. Like Dad and Susan and you and rehab and stuff like that."

Laura gave an internal sigh, but kept her opinions to herself. Susan *was* their step mother now, after all. *She always felt bad about not using her degrees,* Laura thought. *At least she's practicing a bit. I just wish it wasn't on Lizzy.* "Well, Lizzy has always been like that so Susan's probably right. But I've got to get to work now. You guys stay out of trouble until Mike gets here and I'll be home as soon as possible."

Rather than struggle with the key to Laura's door, Mike rang the doorbell. When he received no answer, he rang it again. Then he knocked, loudly, on the door. Still, no answer, so he pulled his key out of his pocket and fitted it into the lock. Twisting and turning the knob, he jostled the door with his hip. "Damn thing," he muttered under his breath, "I keep forgetting to change these locks."

Finally, the door yielded and he walked into the house. It was quiet, very quiet and he called for the girls. "Amanda? Lizzy?"

No answer. The house felt empty. Where could they be? Before he allowed himself his initial reaction, he walked back to the bedroom the girls shared. Amanda sat there, reading a book and listening to her music. "Hello?" Mike said and she looked up.

"Hi," she mouthed, not removing the headphones.

"Where's Lizzy?"

"What?"

"Where's Lizzy?"

Amanda looked surprised and slid the phones down around her neck. "She was just here."

Mike shook his head. "She's not in the other rooms, as far as I can tell."

"Bathroom?"

"Nope, no one in there."

"Maybe," Amanda nodded her head down the hall, "she went down to the cellar."

"The locks were still on when I walked past. Anyway, isn't the basement off limits?"

"Well, yeah, but..." Amanda thought for a minute, "she really wanted to go out and play in the snow. Maybe she got tired of waiting."

"Her coat and boots are out in the landing."

"Weird," Amanda said, "but she has to be around somewhere. People don't just disappear."

Mike felt a sharp stab of fear in his gut. *But people do disappear around here*, he thought, *or at least they did, five years ago, boys and girls around Lizzy's age. But that's over. Right? Unsolved but over.* "Exactly," Mike said, "so let's find her before your mother comes home."

They called her name and checked all the corners of the house. Outside they saw that the only footprints in the snow that led to the house were Mike's, so she couldn't have been outside. Finally, Mike threw open the locks on the cellar door and looked down the steps. There sat Lizzy, huddled in the corner at the end of the stairs, clutching a blue stuffed animal, the black cat curled up next to her. She appeared to be asleep, her eyes were closed, the rise and fall of her chest was slow and steady. "Lizzy?"

She moaned a bit in her sleep and Mike ran down the stairs and picked her up. "How on earth did you get down here with the doors locked?"

Lizzy opened her eyes, looked up at him and gave him a little smile. "Hi," she said, "I thought no one would ever find me." She shivered. "I was down here forever. And I'm so very cold."

"How about some cocoa?" Mike carried her up the stairs and settled her in on the couch, wrapping a blanket around her. "We'd have found you sooner, but the door was locked. How'd you manage it, Houdini?"

Lizzy giggled. "I went through the cat door."

"Ah," Mike said, giving the door an appraising look. "I guess you would fit, at that. That never would have occurred to me. Maybe now you should tell me why on earth you went down there in the first place."

"B Bear was down there. I'd been watching television and I wanted him with me, but when I went back to my bed, he I couldn't find him."

"B Bear?"

"It's this," Amanda reached over and poked at the toy.

"Anyway," Lizzy continued, "I wasn't sure where he was so I asked Amanda. She said the cat had been playing with him and the next time she looked up they both were gone. So I called Anubis, but he's not like a dog; he only comes if he wants to. I went to hunt them down and as I walked past the cellar door, the cat door clicked. I peeked down it and B Bear was lying at the bottom of the stairs. I knew that if Mommy saw him down there, she'd think I put him there and she'd be upset."

"We're not supposed to upset Mom," Amanda supplied, "or Dad said she might start drinking again."

Mike nodded. "It doesn't really work that way, you know. People who have a drinking problem don't really need reasons; it's more like a disease."

"Yeah, that's what Susan said. She and Dad had a very loud discussion about it one night."

"But we're getting sidetracked," Mike said, "what happened next, Lizzy?"

"I couldn't reach the upper lock, but thought I could probably fit through the flap on the cat door, so I did that. It was easy — it's a very big door for a cat. I got down the stairs just fine and picked up B Bear, but couldn't get the flap to open when I tried to crawl back into the house. I knocked on the door for a while and called for Amanda, but if she's listening to music, she can't hear."

"I found that out," Mike said. "How did you end up at the bottom of the stairs again?"

"I got really sleepy after a while, and I didn't want to fall asleep and roll down the stairs, so I went down and curled up in the corner. It's not quite so cold there. I figured someone would find me sooner or later. Anubis came over and kept me company and that made it better. But it's dark down there. There are spiders. And the furnace makes funny whispering noises."

"Yeah," Mike said, "we're getting that fixed today, I think. I have a friend who said he'd do it."

"Good," Lizzy said. "Mommy hates going down there." She paused. "Do you have to tell her where you found me?"

"Yeah, sorry, kiddo, I do."

"I knew you would, you're a policeman. But maybe she won't be mad. It wasn't really my fault Anubis stole my bear. Can you tell her that?"

"I'm pretty sure she won't be mad, Lizzy. Now," Mike stood up from where he'd been crouching next to the girl on the couch, "who wants lunch? And who wants to help me fix dinner?"

"I still can't believe she crawled through the cat door." Laura and Mike sat snuggled up on her couch; he'd returned after his second shift, and had a bowl of the stew he and the girls had made earlier. Lizzy and Amanda played outside, riding down the hill in the back yard with the large plastic discs he'd brought with him.

"Well, she did. That door is awfully big for a cat door. And you can answer me this time, right?"

Laura ducked her head in embarrassment. "It's not really a cat door; I bought the wrong size and didn't realize it until it was already installed." She paused. "I'd been drinking that day, of course."

"Of course. It's not a big deal, anyway. The door serves its purpose. I'm more upset with myself for not noticing it earlier; I'm usually more observant than that. I almost called 911 to report her missing, you know."

"I'm not surprised." Laura kissed his cheek gently. "Thanks for taking such good care of them. They really enjoyed fixing dinner with you. Even Amanda seemed enthused."

"They're good kids."

"And thanks for the snow saucers. They're really enjoying them." Laura could hear the girls' laughter along with that of the other neighborhood children who'd joined them for their impromptu sledding party. "They needed a little fun, I think. Especially Lizzy."

"Yeah. I figured they'd need something to do for the next couple of days. Although your neighbor — Carolyn? — called and wanted to talk to you about a sleep-over on Saturday night." Mike gave a chuckle. "She's quite the talker, isn't she? I didn't think I'd ever get her off the phone."

"Yeah, she's something." Laura paused, wondering how to tell Mike about what happened here last night. About how she was convinced something was wrong with this house. But she had no idea how to bring up the subject, without appearing totally nuts. And she didn't want to scare him away. *Not now,* she thought, *I couldn't bear losing him now.*

Mike noticed her silence. "What's wrong, babe?"

Laura sighed. "I'm tired, I think. It was a long day at work — boring as anything, since there were no customers to speak of and they had us reorganizing the register racks and cleaning the bread racks." She gave a little laugh. "Cleaning the bread racks? I'm too old for that nonsense. I'm going to try for a better job in the spring, once I adjust to this new sober life."

"And how is the sober life treating you?"

"I'm getting used to it, I guess. I only stop for five minutes to stare in the liquor store window instead of ten. And Renee is a joy — she's always there for me when I call. But I have bad nights. You know?"

"Yeah," Mike pulled her a little closer to him. "I do know."

"Trying to get to sleep is impossible. That stupid furnace..."

"I'm sorry about that," Mike said. "Stan did show up, but took one look at the wiring set-up and said he'd have to come back over the weekend when he had a little more time."

"You needn't be sorry, Mike. It's wonderful that you tried."

"He'll get it fixed, I'm sure of it."

"It's not just the heat, although that's a real problem. I just toss and turn and every little sound is amplified. Finally, when I do fall asleep, I seem to wake back up within an hour or two. Especially with Lizzy here — she talks and walks in her sleep. Granted, that's better than the night terrors she used to get, but it doesn't make for a restful night for me. No wonder Tony and Susan were so anxious to get away."

"That, plus the fact it is their honeymoon. Speaking of which..."

Mike pulled her to him and kissed her hard on the lips. She relaxed into his arms and gave a happy sigh. He always made everything better.

The neighborhood girls formed a semi-circle around Lizzy. Thinking it was only the cold that made her shiver, she took a deep breath. *This is a stupid game,* she thought, *I never should've said I'd play.* But she knew she couldn't back out now. Amanda, who'd been enjoying the other girls' company, would never let her forget it.

"Go ahead, Lizzy." Brittany gave her a little push forward so that Lizzy's nose almost touched the sliding glass door.

Lizzy shut her eyes and began to count silently.

One, two, three, four...

The girls around her began to chant softly. "Aunt Dolly, Aunt Dolly, Aunt Dolly..."

...twelve, thirteen, fourteen...

The girls' voices grew louder and Lizzy felt her heart beat faster and faster. She wanted to stop this stupid game. She wanted to stop it now. But she kept her eyes closed tight.

"Aunt Dolly, Aunt Dolly, Aunt Dolly..."

...eighteen, nineteen, twenty!

Lizzy finished the count. She opened her eyes. And screamed.

CHAPTER SIXTEEN

Laura jumped up out of her seat and ran out the front door in less than a second, not stopping to put on her coat or her boots. That hadn't been a scream of delight or a protest about having a handful of snow put down one's neck. It was pure terror. The distance from the front door to the backyard was short, but it seemed like miles. On the way, she envisioned all sorts of terrible scenarios: Lizzy, her finger partially severed by a sled rung; Amanda, bleeding from a head wound; broken legs, broken arms, any of a dozen accidents that could have happened.

When she got to the back yard, she was relieved there were no dark pools of blood on the white snow. What she saw seemed trivial in comparison. Lizzy stood, standing in front of the cellar door, staring in the window. The other neighborhood children stood huddled around, a few yards away from her, whispering and tittering. But Amanda stood next to her, holding her hand. "Lizzy," she said, "what is it? What did you see?"

Laura heard one of the girls whisper, "She saw the ghost. She must have."

"Shhhh," the other girl said, "be quiet, Brittany. You shouldn't have made us play that game."

But Laura had no time for their games. She picked up Lizzy, and smoothed her hair back from her face. "What is it, sweetie?"

Her teeth chattered a little. "I thought I saw a face."

"What sort of face, Lizzy?"

"I don't know. I'm cold."

"Of course you are, you're shivering. Let's go inside."

Laura gave Amanda a signal to come in as well. "Say goodnight to your friends, Mandy, and let's go get something warm to drink."

Once the girls changed out of their snow and ice encrusted clothes and both had bathed, she sat them down in the living room with a steaming cup of cocoa. "So which of you wants to tell me what you were all doing outside? That one girl said something about playing a game. What sort of game?"

"It's a stupid game," Amanda said. "They were just trying to punk Lizzy."

"Punk Lizzy?"

"You know, play a prank on her. Trick her."

Mike shook his head. "This wasn't the Aunt Dolly story, was it? We get calls from hysterical teenagers every few months on that one."

"The Aunt Dolly story?"

Mike nodded and continued, "It's like an urban legend. The hook on the door of the car or the sweater left on the tombstone by the girl ghost."

Please, no ghosts. Not tonight.

"That's exactly what it was," Lizzy said, warmer now, her fright forgotten, or at least consigned to nothing but a curiosity. "The Aunt Dolly game. You look into a pane of glass from the outside on a night of the new moon. Then you close your eyes and count to twenty. When you open them again, you see the ghost."

"And did you?" Laura's voice trembled just a bit, remembering playing similar games with her friends when she was Lizzy's age. Those games then, as now, always freaked her out.

Lizzy gave a little laugh. “I thought I saw something. But that’s probably because I expected to see something. Amanda stood right behind me and didn’t see anything at all. Did you?”

“Nah. Just Lizzy’s and my reflections in the glass, that’s all. Like I said, it’s a stupid game.”

“Are you sure?”

“Laura?” Mike looked confused. “Of course it’s just a game. What else could it be?”

“I don’t know,” she said. “I’m tired. And grouchy. And I don’t like people playing tricks on my daughters.” Her voice sounded cross, but she gave Mike a smile to soften the tone. “Anyway, I think it’s time for bed now, you two. We’ve all had too much excitement for one day. At least I know I have. I’ll come back in a few minutes to say goodnight.”

Recognizing, no doubt, the certainty in her tone, neither girl protested. She sighed, and watched them walk down the hallway, not looking forward to the night.

“Laura? Are you okay?” Mike came up behind her and massaged the back of her neck gently. “You’re really tense.”

“I can’t explain it. I have this awful feeling.”

“You sound like Cassie.”

Laura gave a soft laugh. “Yeah, I know it. But still, I wonder if I should see if Tony and Susan can come back early. I don’t want anything else to happen to spook either one of the girls. I’m hoping to apply for joint custody in a month or so; I don’t want Tony thinking I’m unfit to have them.”

“That’s not going to happen, babe.”

“Would you...” Laura felt like a fool asking the question, but she had to. “Would you stay the night? It’s easier with you here somehow. And I sure could use the company.”

Mike smiled and kissed the back of her head, hugging her to him. "If you don't think the girls would object, I'd love to. I have early shift tomorrow, though, so I'll need to sneak out at the crack of dawn."

"No need to sneak, I'll make the coffee."

"Mike?"

Laura's voice, soft though it was, woke him immediately. He sat up. "What time is it?"

"About 3:30. I'm sorry to wake you."

"I have to get up in about an hour anyway, so it's okay. What's wrong? Can't you sleep?"

"I've been wondering about that Aunt Dolly game the girls were playing. Has that been going on long?"

Mike thought for a minute. "At least as long as I've been here."

"Could it have something to do with the Dolores Wellman who once lived here? Dolly might be a shortening of Dolores."

"What do you know about Dolores Wellman?" Mike's voice came out sharper than he intended and he forced himself to tone it down, reaching over and stroking her arm, searching for the best words. "Dolores Wellman really doesn't matter, Laura — it has nothing to do with the game. It's just a silly thing that kids do. Here or anywhere else. It doesn't need to be based on any actual facts. All you need are a few kids with overactive imaginations." He didn't like her getting hung up on this or on what happened tonight. None of it was relevant. And, he knew from experience, her worry about it was part of her detox progress. There always seemed to be something a recovering addict would obsess on. This was Laura's.

"Sweetheart," he lay back down in bed and pulled her into his arms, warming her chilled body next to his warm one. "You know what this is, don't you?"

Laura ducked her head onto his chest. "The drugs talking? Or rather, the lack of drugs talking?"

"Exactly."

She gave a soft laugh, her breath tickling the hair on his chest. He smiled. That was a feeling he'd like to get used to. "I told Cassie the same thing when she acted crazy. So I know you're right. It's just, everything else feels so wrong."

"And it will for a while. Then one day, you'll wake up and you'll feel right again. Simple as that."

"But what if..."

He kissed her hard on the lips. Each moment alone with Laura seemed precious to Mike, he didn't want to spend any of it talking about local legends or the previous inhabitant of her house. *I'd like to throttle the neighborhood gossip for dropping that bit of news on Laura. Poor love has enough to deal with.* "That's enough talking," he murmured. "And now that we're both awake..."

Thursday turned out to be a good day for Laura. Lizzy'd had no nightmares and Laura had fallen back to sleep when Mike left. She finally woke around eleven, to find both girls up. They'd made themselves cereal and made coffee for her. "What a nice surprise," she said as she sipped from her cup. "And that's really good coffee. Who made it?"

"Me," said Amanda, "I make it at Dad's house all the time. It's one of my daily chores." She made a face at the word.

"Chores are good." Laura grinned at her daughter. "Especially if it means there's fresh coffee in the morning."

"Not all that fresh, Mom. It's been sitting there for two hours — we thought you'd never wake up."

"Tell her, Amanda." Lizzy sounded excited.

"Brittany's mom called and invited us to the birthday sleep-over on Saturday night. Can we go?"

Laura raised an eyebrow. "This would be the same Brittany that played that trick on you last night?"

"Please, Mommy," Lizzy begged, "it was just a trick and I'm fine. It was sort of funny anyway."

Yeah, Laura thought, *if hearing one of your children screaming bloody murder out of nowhere can be considered funny, then the whole thing was a real hoot.* "Funny isn't a word I'd use to describe the experience, but if you two want to go, I don't see any reason why you shouldn't."

"Thanks," Amanda said, sounding totally confident that yes would be her answer. "You should call up there and let them know we can come."

Laura thought for a second while she sipped her coffee. "It's a birthday party, though, we'll need to get gifts, won't we?"

"Brittany's registered at the big toy store."

"Registered?" Laura had never heard of a twelve year old girl being part of a gift registry service. *I guess I'm way behind the times.* "You mean like for a wedding or a baby shower?"

Amanda rolled her eyes, something Laura had started to consider a very bad habit. "Yeah, lots of the parents do that these days. Makes for fewer bad gifts."

"Hmmm, imagine any gift being considered bad."

"That's what I think too, Mommy." Lizzy nodded. "Gifts are always good."

Amanda gave her a nudge. "You're such a baby."

"I don't care — Brittany's a little snot."

"And you're a silly baby. If Brittany's so bad, then why do you want to go?"

"Dunno. But I do want to."

"Well, it is your last night here with me. But now that I'm better, maybe your father will let you visit more. So I guess you can go," Laura said, "both of you. Provided the bickering stops. And the eye drama." She mimicked Amanda's mannerism.

Lizzy collapsed in giggles. "That looks just like you, Mandy."

"Does not."

Laura took a deep breath. "Enough, okay? Enough."

Her voice sounded sharper than she intended and she noticed both girls exchanged a worried glance.

"I'm sorry," Amanda said.

Lizzy came over and hugged Laura. "Me too, Mommy. I'm glad you're feeling better. I want you to stay that way. So I'll be good. We'll both be good. We promise. We don't want to make you sick again."

That statement set Laura back a bit. Where did they get the idea that their behavior caused her drinking? She sighed. "Lizzy?" She reached down and stroked her hair. "Amanda? I hope you understand that my problem never had anything to do with you two. I didn't drink too much because you were bad. It wasn't your fault, it wasn't anyone's fault but my own. And the fact that for some people drinking is a very bad thing. People like your dad or Susan or lots of other people can drink and it doesn't bother them. But I can't. And I know that now. So I've stopped. I worked really hard to get this far and I'll have to work harder in the future. But I'm doing it for you, for me, for our family, because even though it might seem like we've broken into two pieces now, we're still all family. Do you understand?"

The girls seemed relieved. "Yeah," Amanda said. "You said that in your letter to us from rehab. But it's good to hear you say it in person."

"Now that we're talking serious stuff, I need to ask you both a question. Do you feel safe in this house? Or did the little scares of the last few days frighten you so much that you want to leave? I don't want you to feel trapped here — so if you want me to call your father and have him come early to get you, I will. Or I'll make arrangements to have you stay at Bridget's house until he gets home. Your choice."

Amanda looked confused. "I'm not really sure what you mean, Mom, but I'm fine. Why would I feel trapped or scared? Lizzy is just a victim of her own overactive imagination."

Laura gave a small laugh. "That sounds like something Susan would say."

"Because she does," Lizzy said, "almost every day. She makes it sound like a disease." She thought for a moment. "Imagination never hurt anyone. I like thinking how I think."

"Good."

Carolyn called that afternoon. "Laura," she started, "I'm really sorry about last night. I understand Lizzy had quite a scare."

"I did too."

"I'm sure. There's nothing worse than hearing your kid screaming and not knowing what's wrong. How is she today?"

"Fine. You know how kids are."

"Yeah. They're pretty resilient."

Laura paused. "So tell me about this Aunt Dolly game. When did the children around here start playing it? And who exactly is Aunt Dolly?"

Carolyn hesitated. "Well, I hardly know where to start. Aunt Dolly is the woman who used to live in your house. It's what all the people around here called her."

Laura nodded. "Short for Dolores. I figured that part out."

Carolyn sighed. "She died in that house. Did you know that?"

"Not really. But it makes sense." Laura bit her lower lip to take her mind off her shaking hands. "How did she die?"

"It's not a very pretty story, Laura. Maybe you don't want to know."

"Oh, I want to know." *Not really, but I think I need to know.*

"When Bert Wellman ran off, Dolores killed herself."

Laura took in a breath. "How?" The question was more like a whisper, but Carolyn heard and responded.

"She slit her wrists in the bathtub. They didn't find her for days."

Laura felt like throwing up. But she controlled her voice. "Lovely," Laura said.

"You asked." Carolyn gave a nervous giggle. "But that was over five years ago. It shouldn't make a difference."

"Right."

It makes all the difference in the world.

Almost immediately after Laura hung up, the phone rang again. This time it was Cassie.

"Hey, roomie," Laura said. "How's it going?"

"Not bad. Eleanor is recuperating quickly and she thinks she'll be up and around in a day or two." The pitch of Cassie's voice dropped. "I think she's sick of having me around already and I'm sick of being here. So I'll be back fairly soon. Sunday, probably. Anything exciting happening there?"

Laura gave a little laugh. "You could say so." She caught Cassie up on everything. "Maybe you don't want to come back after hearing all that." Laura heard the plea in her voice, but hoped Cassie wouldn't pick up on it.

"Of course I want to come back. I can't stay here for much longer or I'll go crazy." Cassie paused, then laughed. "Or crazier. Anyway, it's interesting to hear all of that about the previous owners. Maybe now that I have a name, I can help."

Laura heard a voice calling Cassie in the background.

"Well, I need to go. The timer on the stove went off and dinner's ready. See you soon."

CHAPTER SEVENTEEN

After the girls left for the birthday party, Mike and Laura attended a meeting, then returned to Laura's house with take-out food from a local Italian place. Laura preferred to eat at home rather than at a restaurant — fewer temptations, fewer reminders of what she craved. *Not, of course*, she thought, *that I need reminding.* Still, she preferred eating in and was relieved Mike understood.

She pushed her chair back from the dining room table after eating her entire order of lasagna. Picking up her empty plate and Mike's she gave a small chuckle as she walked to the kitchen. "I'm going to need to start going to Overeaters Anonymous soon, if I keep eating like this. But it tasted so good."

Mike nodded. "You're getting your appetite back; that's a good sign. But how do you feel?"

Laura hesitated, realizing she'd been so busy just trying to get through the days and the significantly more difficult nights, she hadn't actually stopped to think about her physical state. But now that Mike mentioned it, she gave herself a quick evaluation and was surprised to discover that she felt pretty good. Gone were the shakes and the nausea, her head felt clear and her body felt strong.

She put the dirty dishes in the sink, then turned around, leaned back against the counter and smiled at Mike. "I feel great. Physically at least. It's almost as if a dead weight has been lifted from me. The alcohol settles into your bones, if you know what I mean. And you end up getting used to that heaviness; you live with it on a daily basis and it becomes the norm. Now I feel lighter. Although," she patted her stomach briefly, "the scale might say something different."

"Don't worry about gaining weight. To be honest, I've never met a woman who didn't look better with a little flesh on her bones."

"Well, then you're the only man in the world who feels that way."

"Not true," Mike said, "it's usually women who get all hung up on their weight. No matter, really. And how do you feel emotionally?"

Laura sighed. "I don't know. I think I'm better in that way too, but it's hard to tell. I do feel stronger in some ways — more in control of what's going on around me. I even have times when the craving for a drink is barely there."

Liar! The thought struck Laura, almost as if from somewhere else than inside her. And with that thought, the craving she'd just denied seemed to crawl over her, engulfing her with its familiar warmth and despair. *All you really want is a drink, nothing else matters. And you don't just want a drink, do you? You need a drink. You deserve a drink. No one else really cares about what you need, or what you want, do they? So you should just take care of yourself. Send him home — he doesn't belong here. He doesn't like you anyway — you're just a way to fill his time. And fulfill his sexual needs. Dirty men, all of them. Getting what they can when they can regardless of the consequences. You don't need a man. You need a drink.*

Laura shook her head and wondered where these thoughts came from. No matter how hard she tried to think positively, that old self-doubt and self-loathing would trickle in. "That's not quite true." She tried a small smile, but her lips shook slightly. "But maybe if I keep saying it, one day it will be true."

"It will, babe. Really. Trust me."

"I hope so." Laura turned back around to the sink and rinsed the dishes. "And," she said, changing the subject, "I hope the girls are having a good time. It sure cost enough money to get an appropriate present, and I even picked one of the cheapest items on the list. Obviously Carolyn and her family aspire to a higher station than mere middle class."

Mike chuckled. "This is that sort of neighborhood. I've often wondered how you ended up here."

"The price on the house was right. More than right, actually. The bank listed it so low, I couldn't pass it up. Although, I guess, a lot of other people did. Carolyn thinks the floor plan must've thrown them off — it's not like the rest of the houses in the area; for one thing, it's an older construction, much older, with the outside shell renovated to make it match the other homes. Moving here, one would expect to get a newer home, not an older one, redone. That's a silly reason not to buy the place, but I heard sillier excuses when I worked as an agent." She paused and took in a short breath. "Or maybe people didn't buy it because of Dolores Wellman dying in here."

"That's ridiculous."

Was it? "I guess so. Anyway, when I bought the house I didn't know any of that. All I wanted was an affordable place to live — this one was so affordable, I used my divorce settlement to buy it." Laura neglected to mention she'd been drunk when she initially saw the house, drunk when she'd decided to buy it, and drunk again when they'd closed the deal. *Not,* she added to herself, *that there's anything wrong with the house. The house is fine, I'm fine, everyone is fine. Ain't life grand?*

"Laura, you don't need to justify buying this house to me. I was just thinking out loud — you don't really fit in with this particular group of suburban moms. And that has nothing to do with drinking or not drinking — you're not a superficial person. And you're not a snob. Sometimes, not fitting in is a good thing."

"I guess." Laura remained unconvinced — she'd felt like an outsider all her life. It would be nice to find a place where she felt at home. "Anyway, let's watch that movie you rented. Want some popcorn?"

"We just finished eating."

Laura laughed. "But there's always room for popcorn."

Mike looked down at Laura; she hadn't lasted long before she fell asleep there on the couch. He couldn't decide if he was disappointed or relieved. The relief came from the fact she felt relaxed and calm enough to fall asleep — it meant she was recovering from the poisons in her system. The disappointment would have been that he'd had plans for the evening. He smiled to himself and put his hand in his pocket, feeling for the small jeweler's box he'd picked up this afternoon after work. Part of him felt that perhaps it was too early for this commitment, he and Laura had only known each other for a short time. But he'd made up his mind that day he'd driven her home from the police station. *I can only hope she feels the same way,* he thought. *But it can wait. For a while, at least.* He considered that the timing might be a little bit better tomorrow anyway; the girls would be going back home with their father and their new step-mother and he'd have Laura all to himself.

Mike sighed and tapped her gently on the shoulder. "Babe, you should go back and get into bed."

She sat up and kissed him on the cheek. "Good idea," she said, "coming to join me?"

Mike shook his head. "I've got some paperwork to catch up on. I'll be there in a little bit."

"Don't stay up too late," Laura started down the hallway, then turned around in front of the cellar door. "I'll be dead to the world before too much longer." Suddenly she gave a gasp and fell to her knees. Mike jumped up off the couch in a second to help her back up.

"What happened, babe?"

Laura shook her head slightly. "That was weird. I guess I tripped, but it felt as if someone tugged on my ankle."

"Are you okay?"

She reached up her hand and stroked his cheek. Mike couldn't help but smile; her touch felt so good. "I'm fine. I won't win any awards for my gracefulness, I'm such a klutz," she chuckled, "but I'm fine. Don't be too late."

Mike checked in on her a few minutes later, she was tucked away in bed, sound asleep. Anubis, curled up at the foot of the bed, watched him with slitted eyes and purred. He nodded to the animal. "You keep her company, buddy. I need to go out to my car and pick up some files."

The files in question were those of the Woodland Heights kidnappings; Mike's obsession was becoming a joke at the station, but he couldn't shake his gut feeling that the investigation had just missed something. Maybe it was Laura's sharing of the gossip about the previous owners; or maybe the game of Aunt Dolly the girls had been playing the other night. And maybe it was just spending time in this house, one of the few in the neighborhood that had been here five years ago. He felt the answers there, just below the surface of the thousands of details and interviews that had been collected at the time. Someone just needed to look at it with new eyes. He didn't imagine the children were still alive, but he'd like to find out what happened to them, if nothing else, he'd like to find the remains. That, at least, would provide closure for the families.

And then we could all move on. An unsolved case like this always seemed to linger, settling over the area, like a dense fog, clouding vision and judgment. The uncertainty disturbed him. *Like a fog,* he thought, or *like a ghost.* Mike shook his head and gave a soft snort as he opened the car door and pulled out the folders. *I might believe in all sorts of intangibles — gut feeling, hunches, intuitions. But ghosts?* "That's just too much," he laughed to himself and let himself back into Laura's house.

Hours later he set the files back down onto Laura's coffee table. He wasn't getting anywhere, but he knew he was missing something, something important, something that tied all these children together. A common ground that might explain why them and not some others. In Mike's experience there was always a reason why. One that might not make sense to him or to others but seemed perfectly reasonable to the one responsible.

The six missing children had come from fairly different backgrounds and circumstances. One had just completed extensive chemotherapy and radiation treatment for leukemia; one had been in and out of juvenile hall for drugs and petty burglary. Two were twins, a brother and a sister, from a family with an abusive father, a man who'd been considered the prime suspect for a while, but whose alibi held tight. One was the son of a junkie, and the last, a girl whose parents were in the process of a nasty divorce.

"Such a shame," Mike said, looking at the pictures of the unlucky six children. "Like your lives weren't hard enough already." He marveled again how the last child taken, with her long, straight dark hair and slender build, so closely resembled Laura's girls, especially Lizzy. *If they'd been here five years ago, who knows?*

Bingo. It was almost as if Mike's mind made an audible click. *There* was the connection; each of these children taken had had decidedly miserable lives, either from sickness, circumstance or parental interference. And they all suffered from, not just your general childhood woes, but what could be considered life-shattering or threatening situations. What if the person taking them had been trying to help, what if in some bizarre and twisted way they'd thought they were giving the kids a better life?

Better off dead.

Then he shook his head and dropped the pictures back onto the coffee table. *What possible difference could it make? The children were still missing, most likely dead. The crime was five years old; the kidnappings, just another folder tucked away into the unsolved cases files.* He was putting too much effort into something futile; although the mystery nagged at him, deep down inside he knew that it was way too late to make any sort of difference. *It's all over and done with, I really should just give up and move on.*

Mike checked the front door lock and the thermostat, which now seemed to kick itself off only half of the time since his friend Stan had fixed it. The trick, he'd discovered was keeping it a degree or two cooler than wanted. He turned out the lights and went back into Laura's bedroom. She still slept, so he quietly took off his clothes, left them neatly folded on the chair in the corner, and crawled in next to her.

She rolled over to him and snuggled up against his chest, still asleep. Mike lay awake for a while, listening to the sounds of the house. Its shell might make it appear to be a younger house, but the inner structure knew the truth. It creaked and groaned and the damn cat door drove him crazy, clicking open or shut, startling him awake. He couldn't blame it on the cat — Anubis lay curled up at the bottom of the bed. *Must be a draft,* he thought as he finally fell asleep.

The clock read 3:30 a.m. when Laura sat up with a quick gasp. One second later the phone rang. Laura answered it and Mike could hear an agitated woman's voice in the background.

"Yeah," Laura said. She listened for a long time to the caller, whose voice seemed to grow angrier with every word. Laura's cheeks flushed red and she cleared her throat, to interrupt the tirade. "Look, Carolyn, I'm sorry this happened. I'll be right up to get them."

She shook her head and rolled her eyes when she hung up the phone.

"What's wrong, babe?" Mike asked.

"Lizzy had one of her nightmares, followed by a screaming fit." She put on her pink robe then sat down on the bed to pull on a pair of sweat pants. "Carolyn wants them to come home — they're apparently a bad influence on the other girls and I'm a terrible mother. So I'm going to go up and bring them back here."

"Bad influence?" Mike pulled on his clothes. He was angry now. In his opinion, if anyone in that group of girls was a bad influence it sure wasn't either Amanda or Lizzy. He followed Laura out to the living room and watched as she put on her snow boots and coat. "Maybe she should take a good hard look at her precious little Brittany, instead. I'll go up for them and give her a piece of my mind while I'm at it."

Laura touched his shoulder gently. "Thanks, Mike, but I'll manage."

"Then I'll go up with you."

"Not necessary. Really. You can make some cocoa, though, for when we come back."

Mike put the kettle on the burner then stood at the door to watch Laura make her way up the street. He was still angry. Trouble with the neighbors was the last thing Laura needed, especially on this last night with the girls here. He knew she worried about whether Tony would allow them to come back; having them tossed out of a slumber party might be the last straw. Although Mike knew that none of this was Laura's fault, nor was it the fault of the girls, all that he'd heard about Tony led him to believe that the fault would eventually be made to lie on Laura's shoulders. She didn't need any more guilt, undeserved though it may be.

He heard Laura's voice raised in argument with Carolyn, then heard a door slam. Two seconds later, Laura and the two girls came into view, walking sideways down the street, so as not to slip on the icy road surface. Even with this ungainly stride, Mike could tell Laura was fuming. She held Lizzy close to her while Amanda followed closely behind, carrying both of their backpacks. When they got near enough so that Mike could make out their expressions, he could see Amanda was furious as well.

He opened the door and let them in, offering an arm so that Laura could remove her boots. "What happened?"

Lizzy turned her tear-stained face up to his. "I had a bad dream and screamed and woke everyone up."

"It wasn't her fault," Amanda said indignantly. "Brittany and the others were telling ghost stories."

"What did you dream about, Lizzy?"

"Aunt Dolly." Lizzy trembled and Mike lifted her up, carrying her to the couch.

Laura scowled at him. "Do we really need to get into it?"

"It always helps to talk about things," Lizzy said. "That's what Susan says, anyway. If you tell the dream, it loses power."

Laura sighed. "Talk about it if you want, honey."

The kettle whistled and Laura got up to make them all a hot drink.

"I was in this house," Lizzy said, her voice quavering. "A nice old lady invited me in, to talk. It wasn't really me, but some other girl," she amended, "You know how dreams are."

Mike nodded and tightened his hold on her hand.

"Anyway, she gave me a cup of cocoa. It smelled funny and I didn't really want to drink it. But she insisted and I didn't want to be rude. When I drank half of it, I started to feel sick and really sleepy. She picked me up and carried me down the stairs to a little room. It smelled funny, kind of like worms after rain?"

"Yeah, I know what you mean," Mike said.

"She put me on a cot and tucked a blanket up under my chin. 'You'll be better off, sweetheart. You'll see.' Then I noticed that there were other cots in the room with other kids sleeping in them. When she closed the door, I tried to get up off the cot, but couldn't move. I called out and none of the other kids answered. Or even moved. So I called louder and louder. But no one came. My eyes felt funny, sort of fuzzy and everything got blurry."

"And then?" Mike asked.

"Then I woke up. And when I woke up, I realized that none of the other kids in the dream were sleeping. They were dead." Lizzy sniffled a bit. "It doesn't sound so scary now, I guess."

"Scary enough," Laura said as she came into the living room with a tray of mugs. She pushed aside the folder laying on the coffee table and the papers fell out.

Before Mike could pick them up, Lizzy saw one of the pictures. He felt her stiffen next to him, then reach down and pick them up. "This," she said, holding out a picture of a little girl, just a bit younger than her, "is the girl.

"What girl, honey?"

"The girl I was in the dream."

Mike tried to take the pictures away from her, but she held onto them tightly as she looked through them. She came to another one and gasped, dropping them all. She started to cry again. "And that one," she said choking back a sob and pointing to the uppermost picture, "that one is Aunt Dolly."

"Really?" Mike's interest was piqued by this identification. "Do you remember anything else?" He didn't know how, but it seemed like Lizzy had had some sort of first-person vision of one of the missing children. "Do you remember a man in the dream?"

Lizzy started to sob in earnest now. "I don't remember anything else."

"Are you sure? It's important, Lizzy. Try to remember."

The girl dissolved into a torrent of tears.

Laura came over, picked Lizzy up and held her close to her. Mike now noticed the anger on her face.

"She doesn't remember," Laura said. "And it's just a dream, anyway. Let it go, Mike."

Mike shook his head. "But this sounds like it's related to—"

Laura cut him off. "Don't say another word

Mike never remembered seeing Laura this angry before. And had never expected her to turn it on him.

"But, if Lizzy can..."

"That's it. I think it's best if you leave now. And take your papers with you. That's probably where she got all this stuff anyway. How dare you bring this into my house?"

Mike stood up, gathered his folder and gently touched Laura on the shoulder. "Laura? Calm down. It's okay."

Her eyes seemed cold and unfeeling, viewing him as if he were a stranger. Mike felt confused.

"It will be okay when you quit hounding my daughter. This has nothing to do with you. Please leave."

He thought about the ring in his pocket. He thought about how this night had not turned out at all as planned. He went to kiss Laura on the cheek, but she pulled away from him. *I have no idea what's gotten into her. But maybe she's right and I should leave.*

He got his coat and walked to the door. "I'll call tomorrow and make sure everyone's okay." Not waiting for a response, he got out as quickly as he could. He quietly closed the door behind him, got in his car and drove home.

CHAPTER EIGHTEEN

The house felt very lonely and cold without the girls. *And without Mike,* Laura thought. She missed all three of them. Several times she picked up the phone to call Mike, then thought better of it and hung up without dialing. She knew she'd overreacted, but he'd been so cold, so ruthless that last night he was there, she felt betrayed. His work, apparently, came first with him. Even a dead case, five years old.

You're better off without him. We don't need him here.

Laura went to work on Monday and attended a meeting with Renee afterwards. When the two of them arrived back at Laura's house, Cassie's car was in the driveway. Cassie seemed more relaxed than previously and she and Renee hit it off instantly, making for a pleasant evening of coffee and conversation. Laura felt pleased with the distraction, since she didn't want to talk about Mike. But soon enough, Cassie excused herself and went to bed.

Renee carried their cups to the kitchen and began to wash them out.

"You don't need to do that, Renee," Laura said.

Renee turned and smiled at her. "I know. I want to. I'm feeling a bit jumpy tonight and keeping busy helps."

"Yeah," Laura agreed. "I often feel the same."

Renee dried her hands on a kitchen towel, then turned around, looking Laura straight in the eyes. "So what happened?"

"What happened?"

"With you and Mike? He's been really grouchy and you seem subdued."

"We had a fight, I guess."

"Yeah. I figured as much. He said something about having pushed you a bit too hard. And that he wanted to give you time to cool off. Have you?"

Laura thought about that for a moment. "I think so. He wasn't pushing me — I wouldn't mind that so much," she gave a self-depreciating chuckle, "most of the time I need it — but he was pushing Lizzy. Apparently, I'm like a mother bear. I probably overreacted. And said a few things I didn't really mean. But..."

"I know. Just don't let it go too long. I may decide to take that boy for myself."

Renee gave Laura a quick kiss on the cheek. "You tell Cassie I said goodnight. And pass that kiss along to Mike. Sooner rather than later."

Laura sighed, she really did miss having him around. "I will."

After Renee left, Laura locked the front door, checked on the thermostat — it had stayed on all night, for which she was extremely grateful. Then she switched out the lights and knocked lightly on Cassie's door. When she didn't answer, Laura went to bed. She tossed and turned and finally got back up at around midnight, going out to the kitchen to make herself a cup of herbal tea. She stared at the phone, then picked it up and dialed Mike's number. *What the hell,* she thought, *I'm getting good at this apology thing.*

Mike answered the phone after one ring.

"Hi," Laura said hesitantly. "Did I wake you up?"

"No. I just got in a few minutes ago."

"Good."

There was a silence for a while, then they both said simultaneously, "I'm sorry."

Both of them laughed and the very atmosphere seemed to relax.

"I overreacted," Laura said, "I know you weren't trying to hurt or scare Lizzy."

"No," Mike said, "You didn't do anything wrong. I shouldn't have asked so many questions. I can't help it sometimes." He chuckled, the sound of his laughter over the phone warmed Laura. "They call me the bulldog at the station." He paused. "I'm glad you called, though, I wasn't sure how long I should wait. You're not getting away from me that easily."

"I don't want to get away."

"Want me to come over?"

Laura considered. "No, it's late and Cassie's already asleep."

"She back?"

"Yeah, she was here this afternoon when I got home from work. She and Renee and I had a nice visit after the meeting."

"No dire predictions of doom and gloom?"

Laura laughed. "No, not at all. She seemed quite relaxed, actually. You were right all along. We were both having trouble adjusting."

"Are you sure you don't want me to come over?"

Laura gave an almost involuntary sigh. Every inch of her wanted Mike here with her tonight and the feeling frightened her quite a bit — it felt like a craving as strong as the one she felt for alcohol, or for her precious little blue pills. "You're dangerous." She whispered the words, but he heard.

"Why?" he asked.

"You're an addiction, as bad as the ones I'm fighting."

He gave a low laugh. "Oh, but it's a good addiction, right?"

"Depends."

"On what?"

"On how hard the twelve step program is afterwards."

Mike paused. "Maybe there needn't be a program. Maybe I'll be around forever."

He's lying. Laura startled at the thought, so loud and clear and completely at odds with her emotional response to Mike's statement. *They never stay around and they're all liars.*

"Laura, are you still there?"

"Yes, I'm here. Listening."

"I wondered; the phone line sounded kind of funny, full of static and sort of screechy."

"Must be a problem with your phone — everything is fine on this end." Despite her words, she felt the skin crawl along her arms and neck; she'd heard that static on the phone line before — to her it always sounded like whispering. "Creepy."

"Yeah. Are you sure you don't want me to come over?"

Laura smiled to herself. "I'm fine, Mike, really. Just a little tired. And we both have to work tomorrow. How about a rain check? Tomorrow night maybe?"

"Sure, that would be good. Sleep well."

"You too."

This time the pause held no static. Laura heard Mike's breath over the phone and smiled again.

"Laura?"

"Yes?"

"I love you."

"And I love you." The words seemed to warm her completely — it felt good to finally say them to Mike. "Night."

Laura woke the next morning in an extraordinarily good mood. Even the addition of four new inches of snow overnight didn't faze her. *Everything is going so well,* she thought. Most nights she slept well, felt more energetic during the day and, even though her cravings still lurked right on the edge of her consciousness, she felt better able to deal with them. The house seemed quiet and the furnace stayed on. And Mike? "He loves me," she gave a little shrug of her shoulders and hugged her arms to herself. "He loves me."

Anubis came in and rubbed against her ankles, purring loudly. Laura picked him up and held him, spinning around with him. "Everything's going to be all right," she whispered into the top of his head. "We're going to be fine."

The cat door clicked open and Laura shivered, feeling a cold draft on her legs. "Or we will be, once it gets a little bit warmer around here and stops snowing. And I can get that damned draft taken care of."

She set the cat down on the counter, opened a can of cat food and scooped some out into Anubis' bowl. Then she started the coffee and absently watched the water drip into the pot. Once the machine had finished, she poured herself a cup and went to the living room, turning on the television to the weather reports. They were predicting a warming trend later on in the week.

Cassie came out of her room and poured herself a cup of coffee, sitting down on the edge of the couch. "More snow?"

"Yeah, can you believe it?"

"No. I'm just glad I don't have to go out driving in it. Thank the gods for working from home. How about you? Are you scheduled to go in today?"

Laura nodded and took a sip of her coffee. "Fortunately, I can walk to work. Of course, that was the whole purpose of working there."

"You need a new job, Laura."

"Yeah, but this will do for now. I'm just trying to keep myself busy enough so that I forget what I really want to do."

Cassie ducked her head and stared into her coffee cup. "I know how that goes. I hope it works for you."

Something in her tone of voice triggered a warning in Laura's mind. "Cassie? Are you using again?"

"No," Cassie's answer came quickly — too quickly Laura thought — her voice sounded angry, defensive and her words, rushed. "Of course not. Where would I get it?"

Anywhere. Temptation is everywhere and for a price anything can be gotten. But Laura didn't feel the need to get into this with Cassie. She wasn't responsible for Cassie's actions — she wasn't her mother, her sister, or her counselor.

"Okay," Laura said. "I was just asking. Speaking of which, Mike and I will be going to a meeting early this evening. You're welcome to join us.

"I'm sort of busy today, so probably not."

"Okay. But I can bring dinner home if you want."

"Sure, that'd be great. Do you mind if I do some laundry today?"

"Help yourself," Laura said. "But I thought you didn't like to go down into the cellar."

Cassie laughed nervously. "I was being silly. You said that yourself and you were right. I was too much into withdrawal to know what was what. I'm better now. There's nothing wrong with the cellar. Or with this house."

Laura finished her day at work and stopped by the store's deli counter to get sandwiches for her and Cassie. She'd tried to call the house all afternoon to find out what Cassie would want to eat, and when she'd gotten no answer, Laura assumed she was working either online or on her cell phone. She decided to get two meatball hoagies and two salads.

On the walk home, she noticed there were signs of warming weather, the ice that had piled up in sheets at the sides of the roads now formed a gently flowing stream of thawed water. Even though it was only mid-November, Laura couldn't help feel the sort of anticipation she got with the approach of spring. And with that thought came thoughts of Mike. She smiled as she approached her house. Maybe the girls were right. Maybe he would be proposing marriage soon. If he did, would she say yes?

"You bet your boots I will," she said to herself, opening her front door. "Cassie," she then called, "I'm home. With dinner."

Laura walked into the kitchen and set the food bags down on the counter, opening them up and pulling out the contents. "I got you a meatball sub," she called, a little louder this time. "It's still nice and hot." Her voice seemed to echo.

That's odd, Laura thought, *the house feels so empty.* But Cassie's car was in the driveway — she had to be here. Taking two plates out of the cabinet, Laura shivered, feeling someone move up behind her, catching a glimpse of movement out of the corner of her eye.

As if from a great distance she heard Cassie's voice, thin and reedy, but still recognizable as her voice.

"I was right the first time."

Laura relaxed. "There you are, Cassie. Right about what?"

But when she turned around, no one was there.

"Cassie?" She called out louder now, hearing a small note of panic begin to creep into her voice. "Cassie, are you here?"

She put the plates back down on the counter and walked down the hallway. Cassie's door was open; her laptop computer lay on the bed. Laura glanced down at it, an astrology program was running in the background and an instant message window was open. The last message on the screen said, "I've got to get the laundry — brb."

Laura nodded. She remembered now that Cassie was going to wash clothes today. Obviously, she must be in the basement.

Relieved, Laura went to the cellar door — she didn't hear the washer or dryer running, but thought maybe Cassie was down there folding her clothes. "If so," Laura said quietly, "she's a braver woman than I." Then she chuckled to herself and opened the door. The laugh died in her throat.

Cassie lay at the bottom of the stairs, her head resting in a puddle of dark liquid. Clothes were scattered everywhere on the stairs and on the floor around her. She wasn't moving.

"Oh, God," Laura ran down the stairs and bent over the woman, trying not to stand in the pool of blood. She reached down and gently touched the pulse spot on Cassie's neck. Nothing. She took her wrist and checked again. "Oh, God, Cassie, I'm so sorry."

As Laura ran back up the stairs to call 911, she thought she heard a faint, mocking laughter follow her up.

CHAPTER NINETEEN

Laura sat on the steps, holding Cassie's cold hand — it didn't seem right to just leave her lying there alone. When the paramedics showed up, Laura turned Cassie over to them and slowly climbed back up the stairs, holding back her tears. She sat down in the living room feeling distant and numb. One of the paramedics came up and spoke to her, something about the police...

Mike arrived a few minutes later, still in uniform, with two other policemen; she took one look at Mike's face and burst into tears.

"I'm actually off duty now, babe, but when I heard the call I came over without changing." Mike held her for a while, stroking her hair and rocking her gently back and forth. She never wanted him to stop, but unfortunately there were questions to be answered. Mike led her over to the couch and sat down next to her, his arm around her shoulders.

She didn't know how much time had passed before one of the other policemen reappeared. Mike nodded at the other man, gave Laura a firm squeeze, then rose to speak with him quietly on the far side of the room. He returned a few minutes later, sat down, and put his arms around her once more

"Laura, they need to ask you a few things."

She took a deep breath, nodded, and looked up to the policeman who stood nearby.

"This is Johnny Brewster; he's one of the officers on the case. Johnny, this is Laura Wagner."

Johnny nodded and extended his hand. "Pleasure to meet you, Ms. Wagner. I mean, I'm sorry it is under such sad circumstances, but... Could you tell me how you found the body?"

"I came home from work with some sandwiches and called out for her. Her car was here, she wasn't in her room, so I thought she was downstairs doing her laundry. I went down there and..." Laura began crying again.

"Are you related to the deceased?"

Laura cringed inwardly — such a terrible term — *the deceased.* "No, we're just friends. She was staying here until she could find a place of her own."

"Do you have next of kin information? And identification?"

"It's probably in her wallet. That's her purse over there." She pointed to the huge red leather satchel Cassie always carried. The man rooted through the bag, and when he pulled out her wallet, a bottle of pills fell out. He picked them up, read the label and handed them to Mike.

He, in turn showed them to Laura. She nodded. "You know, I thought she might be using again, although she denied it. That's her sister's name on the bottle; I guess she took them."

Johnny nodded. "Those alone might be reason enough to fall down the stairs. Add that to the huge basket of laundry she carried, and it's an easy accident."

"Easy?"

"Well, I didn't really mean easy. Understandable is probably a better word. She got high and fell. Happens all the time."

Laura noticed his tone changed when he found the drugs. *Addicts don't get sympathy, apparently. This jerk probably thinks she deserved to die.*

Better off dead.

She shook her head slightly. No need to start in thinking those sorts of thoughts.

"Well, ma'am, this is obviously an accidental death. I mean, the coroner will have to rule on that eventually, but for now... We are getting some pictures before...well, the paramedics will be removing the body soon and then we'll be on our way."

Mike cleared his throat. "Do you need anything else, buddy?"

"No, uh..." Johnny shook his head. "We'll give the sister a call from the station." The young policeman abruptly murmured a "thank you" and excused himself.

Mike stood up. "I'm going to go down to help while they finish up." He reached down and touched her cheek. "Are you going to be okay?"

"Yes, I think so. What's that guy's problem anyway?"

"You have to forgive Johnny. He's brand new and this is his first death of any sort. I suspect he's terrified of it all."

"So am I."

"It's going to be okay, Laura. It was just a horrible accident."

"I know," whispered Laura. *At least, I hope I know.* Despite her fear, she managed a small smile.

Mike kissed her forehead. "Be right back."

"Oh, no," Laura said, jumping up from the couch, "that reminds me. Cassie was in the middle of an instant message chat when she left to go downstairs. When I went to look for her, I saw it on her laptop screen. I should probably let that person know that she won't be back. Ever." She started to cry again as she rushed down the hallway, careful not to look through the open door and down the stairs.

Laura felt uncomfortable using Cassie's computer, it was almost like reading someone else's mail. But she didn't want whatever friend Cassie'd been chatting with not to know. She sat down on the bed and pulled the computer over to her. The other person seemed to have signed off or left the keyboard, but the window was still open. Laura typed in "Cassie's had an accident. Call me." She added her name and number and hoped that would be good enough, then closed the machine with a sigh.

The warming trend continued and on the day of Cassie's funeral, it began to rain. The world seemed a dreary, soggy mess to Laura; the past week had gone by in a teary blur. She longed for something to take the edge off her misery — a drink, a pill, anything. Mike had been working nights, and Laura days, so she hadn't even had him for company. With only Anubis around, she felt engulfed in an overwhelming atmosphere of sadness.

When she dropped off to sleep at night, she thought she heard rustling and whispering and stifled sobbing along with a faint mocking laughter — all of them right at the edge of her hearing threshold, like the sound of a television set with the volume turned down to near silence. None of it was really concrete enough to make her believe she heard it and didn't dream it. Mike, those few times he'd been to see her, heard nothing. So she chalked it up to nerves. And the lack of drugs, most especially the Valium, still playing havoc with her system. She didn't allow herself to think "What if?"

Cassie's funeral was sparsely attended. Laura offered her condolences to the sister and her husband; they gave no response other than a nod. She assumed they were still in shock. *Or* she thought, observing their serious but emotionless expressions, *maybe they're angry. Angry at me or at Cassie or at the world in general.* Laura could tell from this brief meeting why Cassie had not spent much time with her sister — the two of them were like night and day.

As she walked back to the cab she'd hired, a soft male voice called her name. She turned and saw a youngish man, thin and lanky, with scraggly brown hair. "Laura?" he said again and she nodded.

"I'm Dennis. We talked the other day, remember?"

Laura nodded. *Cassie's friend from the internet.* She extended her hand. "Yes, of course I remember. Hi, Dennis. I'm pleased to meet you — it's just too bad it had to be in this situation."

"Yeah." Dennis shifted slightly. "I wanted to ask you a favor and I hope you won't be offended."

"Ask away," Laura smiled, "I'm not that easily offended."

"Cassie always talked about your house. About the presence or presences she felt there. Do you think I could come over at some point and see for myself? She was more into astrological charts and tarot cards than supernatural occurrences. I, on the other hand, well, I'm a sort of paranormal investigator."

Laura thought for a moment. *Do I want a total stranger traipsing through my house? Do I want to hear what he has to say? Why would I want to give credence to the belief that my house is haunted by an evil presence?* "I don't know," she said finally. "I'm not sure I believe in any of this stuff. The house is odd, yes, but most or all of it has a rational explanation, I think. So you'll probably be wasting your time."

"Understood. But I don't mind."

Laura shook her head. "I think I'm going to decline the offer, Dennis. Things are better left as they are."

Dennis gave her a sad smile. "Cassie said you were a stubborn little thing. Always clinging to the belief that the world is a rational place."

Laura laughed at that. "I'm not so sure about that. But maybe that's what I seemed like to Cassie. I miss her."

"Yeah, me too." His voice broke a bit and he blinked back tears.

His sadness, so lacking in the others there, touched Laura. *What harm could he do?* "Tell you what," she said, "I'll think about your offer and let you know. If you don't hear from me in a week or so, please call me."

"Thanks so much. Is that your taxi? I could drive you home if you'd like."

Laura shook her head. "The driver would kill me. He's been waiting all this time." She extended her hand again and they shook. "I'll call you. Take care."

With the warmer weather and the steady rain, the snow melted quickly, so much so that green started to show in Laura's front yard. That sight of green might have cheered her, but the continuing downpours were depressing. She called Mike as soon as she got home.

"Gallagher here." He answered the phone as he always did, but it never ceased to bring a smile to her face.

"Hey," she said, "I'm home. Want to come over for dinner when your shift is done?"

"Sure. Are you cooking?"

Laura gave a snort of amusement. "Doubtful. I was thinking along the lines of some sort of take-out."

"That can be arranged. How'd the funeral go?"

"Sad." Laura sighed. "Cassie's sister seemed completely unconcerned. But I met a paranormal investigator who wants to check out my house."

"You told him no, right?"

“Of course.” She wondered to herself if she should have taken Dennis up on his offer. What harm could it have done?

“Good. The last thing in the world you need after all of this is to have some stranger getting you all upset over nothing.”

“Yeah.” Laura paused and noticed that Anubis sat directly in front of the cat door. His ears were flat up against his head and he meowed at her. “Hold on a second, Mike. Bonehead wants something.”

“Silly cat,” she heard Mike say affectionately as she put the phone down on the counter.

“So what is it, cat? Box needs changed?” Laura reached over to the door, clicked open the locks and peered down the steps. The light shone strangely on the floor, making the concrete seem glossy. Then she noticed a few pieces of clothing floating. “Oh, shit. I can’t believe it.”

“What is it, Laura?” Even with the phone on the counter some distance away, she could hear the concern in Mike’s voice. She shook her head and closed and relocked the door. “I’ll put a box for you in the bathroom up here, kitty. I’m sorry, I know you don’t like to get your feet wet.”

Laura picked the phone back up. “Mike? I’m fine. But the cellar is completely flooded. It must be almost eight inches deep already. Maybe there was too much water, with the melting snow and rain, for the sump pump to take care of it. Or,” she dreaded the thought of having to spend more money for house repairs, “maybe I need a new sump pump. Or something.”

“How about a new house?”

Laura gave a humorless laugh. “That’s sounding more and more like a good idea with each passing day. But for now, I guess I’d better call someone and see if they’ll come over. This should qualify as an emergency.”

"I'd think so. Just stay out of the cellar until I get there, okay?"

If Laura had hated going down into the basement before Cassie's death, now she dreaded it. Since then, she had avoided it as much as possible, even though every effort had been made to remove any reminder of the tragic accident. As soon as the police investigation was over, Mike had arranged for a professional cleaning crew to scour away all traces. His buddy, the electrician, had hung new fluorescent fixtures that brightly illuminated the laundry and cat box area. It helped, but not much.

Now going down there meant wading through eight inches of murky water. *No way is that going to happen.* "Somehow I don't think we need to worry about that. See you soon."

Mike arrived an hour later with take out from the nearby Chinese restaurant. And an hour after that, the plumber Laura called showed up. He put on a pair of rubber boots, waded over to the far corner of the cellar, and spent about five seconds assessing the situation while Laura stood on the middle stair and watched. He reached down, removed the cover on the pump and pushed a button. Laura could hear the pump turn back on and hear the movement of the water. "That'll do you for now, Ms. Wagner," the plumber said. "But if I were you, I'd get that pump replaced. You're lucky it's still working at all — looks to me to be about twenty years old or so."

"Yeah, it's my lucky day," she said, heading back up the stairs, followed by the man. "How much will a new pump set me back?"

He quoted the price. She did the mental math. It would almost completely deplete her savings, but having a cellar that stayed dry was important. "Fine," she said, "can you do it fairly soon?"

"I can start tomorrow if you like. It's probably no more than a one day job to replace the pump. If you wanted French drains it would be more, of course. Both in money and time."

Laura shook her head. "I have to work tomorrow. So I don't know..."

"I've got the day off tomorrow, so I can be here," Mike said. "What time?"

Once all the arrangements had been made, the plumber left and Mike checked on the water level before relocking the door. "Yeah, it seems to be draining pretty well. I think we can stay dry enough tonight."

"Finally," Laura said, sighing, "some good news. I really could use a drink."

"Can't help you there, but how about a hug?" Mike held out his arms and she went to him and snuggled up to his chest. He stroked her hair away from her face. "You've been having a rough time, babe. I'm sorry. But things have got to improve, right?"

"Shhhh," Laura said, putting a finger up to his lips, "don't say that. I said that to myself right before I found Cassie."

Laura began to cry again, a soft sobbing that nevertheless seemed to echo off walls. Mike put an arm around, took her back to bed and tucked the covers up around her, then sat down on the edge of the bed.

"Stay tonight?"

"Yes," he reached over and stroked her hair again, "of course I will. And things will get better, just wait and see."

CHAPTER TWENTY

Laura did feel better in the morning. Waking up to the smell of hot coffee brewing helped, as did finding Mike up and in the kitchen, fixing them both some breakfast.

He sat her down gently down at the table as if she might break. Laura reached up and pulled his face down to hers for a long, hard kiss. "You're too good to be true, sweetheart."

He turned away and picked up the plates from the counter, setting one in front of both of them. "We're not all bastards, Laura."

She took a bite of her eggs. "Who's we? Men? Cops?"

He smiled. "Both. Neither. Don't talk with your mouth full."

Laura giggled. "Too bad I have to get to work in less than an hour."

"I'll be here when you get home. And if the plumber is done by then..."

"That reminds me. You might as well have him start the French drains while he's at it. I can scrape up the money from somewhere. No sense doing half of the job."

She thought how domestic this whole conversation sounded and how comfortable she was with that thought. Laura sopped up the rest of egg yolk with her last piece of toast, then got up and carried the plate to the sink. "Thank you for a wonderful breakfast. I could get used to this, you know."

"That's the plan, babe."

Laura carried that conversation and the warmth it brought her throughout the day. It wasn't much of a conversation, really, but maybe in the whole scheme of things, what it represented — kindness and love and someone who cared about what happened to her — could be thought of as a trivial thing. But it made all the difference in the world. She thought back to when this all started and how despairing she'd been. How willing she'd been to throw her life away. And now each and every moment spent with the man, who she'd thought at that time had ruined her life, were precious. Amazing.

Laura gave a broad smile to her customer, startling her out of her own problems and eliciting a smile in return. Laura felt good.

So good, in fact, that she only paused for a few minutes in front of the liquor store on her way home. All of her good feelings evaporated, and she thought about Cassie, of how her craving had caused her to steal her sister's pills and how the use of those pills had caused her to fall down the stairs to her death. The worst part of these thoughts, though, was Laura's internal admission that she understood why Cassie had done it. *If Mike wasn't around, if I didn't have the joint custody of the girls in my sights, that could have just as easily been me.* Laura shivered and tried to push the negative thoughts out of her mind, tried to recapture her earlier happiness. But the mood was gone. And its absence led Laura into the old familiar thoughts of despair and the futility of life.

She turned her key in the door, so lost in her thoughts she scarcely remembered the rest of her walk home.

Better off dead.

Mike greeted her at the door with a big kiss and a hug. She could hear the sound of hammer against concrete bouncing off the cellar walls. "I guess the plumber's still here," Laura said, wincing at the next clang to echo.

Mike laughed. “What was your first clue?”

“How long has that noise been going on? How can you stand it?”

“He just started that a few minutes before you came in.”

“Lucky me.” Laura took off her coat, hung it up in the closet, and sat down on the bench near the door to take her boots off.

“Bad day?”

“Actually it was a pretty good day.” She gave him a sad little smile. “Entirely your doing. But on the way home I have to pass the liquor store and I started to think about Cassie and life and death and everything. I wonder why any of us try.”

“Laura, babe, we try because that’s what you have to do to live. Keep moving forward, keep looking forward and only take it one day at a time.”

She sighed. “I know, I know. But, Mike, I’m so very tired.”

He took her by the shoulders. “It’s okay to be tired. But you can’t give up. I couldn’t bear it.”

Laura smiled a genuine smile. “Okay. But just for you.”

“And for your girls.”

“Yeah, for them too.”

“Soon, Laura, all of this will be behind you and we can be a family. You and me and Amanda and Lizzy.” He reached into his pocket and pulled out a small black box, “I’ve been carrying this around for weeks now and it never seemed to be the right time, but I can’t wait forever for the perfect moment...”

Laura felt a great swell of happiness. Finally he was proposing. He snapped the box open. “Laura,” he said earnestly, taking out the ring and sliding it onto her finger, “will you marry me?”

“I thought you’d never ask. Yes, of course.” She went into his arms and raised her head to kiss him.

At that moment, though, the cellar door opened.

"Ms. Wagner?"

She pulled away from Mike. "What's up?"

"Did you know you had a door in the cellar? Cemented over with concrete?"

"Um, no. I had no idea. Why would anyone do that? And to where does it lead, do you think?"

"Root cellar most likely. This house is the original farmhouse, you know. That's why it's different from all the others."

"So I've heard. Okay, let's go down and see what you've found. It's like a secret treasure hunt."

Laura put her foot on the first step and shivered, feeling a wave a nausea come over her. She swallowed hard and climbed down the rest of the stairs. *Why am I so scared?* she wondered. *It's only a root cellar like the guy said. Nothing to be frightened about.*

But the room had an odd odor. An odd feel. She stared at the pile of broken concrete strewn beneath the old wooden door. She took in a deep breath, afraid to let it out. Laura put her hand to the door, and felt a jolt of pain, almost electric in its feel.

"I lost my balance," the plumber said, his voice sounding indistinct and far away, "and accidentally hit the door with the sledgehammer. The surface just crumbled away to nothing. Weird."

Run away, she told herself. *Turn around and go back up the stairs. Run away. Hide. Don't open that door.*

Her hand reached over and touched an old rusted latch. The door swung inward, but caught halfway on an old bundle of dirty, tattered rags tossed on the floor. Laura blinked, coughed and covered her mouth and nose with her hand. A putrid odor washed over her.

The room itself was dank and dark, but sunlight shone through the sliding glass doors and fell on the room's contents. For a few seconds, her eyes took in the sight without having to comprehend what she saw. At first she saw only what she was capable of seeing: the bundle of old rags, the low shelves covered with blankets. She saw six little shelves with six more bundles of rags, tossed aside carelessly. Six white china cups with tiny red rose buds were carefully lined up on the floor — all of them showing a black crusty stain at their bottoms.

Laura drew in another ragged breath and only when she exhaled did she notice a tiny hand, grey and skeletal, peeking out beneath one of the blankets.

"Oh, dear God."

She ran up the stairs and dashed into the bathroom. She cried almost as violently as she vomited. Laura didn't think it would ever subside.

"Oh, dear God. They're children."

Better off dead.

"No!"

Mike had noticed the silence in the cellar. Then he heard Laura's painful cry. Seconds later she flew out of the cellar door and into the bathroom. He heard her crying and vomiting. He went to the bathroom door, pushed it open a bit. "Laura?"

She shook her head. "Downstairs," she whispered, "they need you downstairs."

He passed the plumber on the stairs. The man's face looked ashen and tears trailed through the dust on his cheeks. Mike nodded to him. "Stay here," he said, "while I check this out. Don't leave — depending on what's going on, we might need a statement from you before you go."

"I'm not going anywhere," the plumber said, holding his hand out so that Mike could set how badly it shook. "Doubt I could drive anyways."

Mike smelled the decay before he even got to the door. He took one look inside and pulled his cell phone out of his pocket, hitting the speed dial number for the police station. *No wonder Laura reacted the way she did,* he thought, taking a scarf from the clothesline and wrapping it around his mouth and nose. He felt like vomiting himself, but in times of crisis, his police training took over. He knew from experience that he'd react to the situation later on and would end up paying the price for the repression of emotions. For now he had to do his job.

Still, when he clicked his phone shut, all he could do for a few more minutes was stare in disbelief. *This,* he thought, before finally closing off his mind to the horror, *this is the kind of shit that made me drink in the first place.*

A soft meowing woke him out of his dark thoughts. "Hey, Bonehead," Mike said picking him up, "this place is off limits for you for a while." He carried the cat back up the stairs and put him into the bedroom Laura's girls had occupied during their visit, then closed the door.

"Laura," he said to her small trembling form crouched over on the couch, "are you okay, babe?"

She turned her face up to him; her skin, blotchy and red. "No," she said, "how does one recover from something like this? But don't worry about me. You go and do your thing — take care of those poor children." She attempted a smile, but burst back into tears instead. "Poor little kids."

"I can't leave until the rest of the guys from the station and the FBI get here. But when they do, I'll get you out of here, okay?"

"Please."

"For now, though, are you all right?"

"Well," Laura sniffed and dabbed at her eyes with a soggy tissue. "Considering what's down in my cellar, I'm doing okay." She paused and sniffed again. "I can barely grasp any of it right now. Maybe once I do..."

Mike nodded and looked over at the plumber seated at the other end of Laura's couch. "Can I get you anything?"

The man blinked. "A good stiff drink would be nice."

"Sorry, we're clean out. How about a fresh cup of coffee?"

Laura stood up, gathered all the used tissues from the couch and floor area. "I'll make it. Have to do something, don't I? And the place will be crawling with people in a bit. The least I can do is give them some coffee."

Walking across the room seemed like such an effort. Rather than taking a direct route to the kitchen and walking past the cellar door, Laura went through the dining room. She felt glad to have something to occupy herself, even if it was only making coffee. She wondered how many law enforcement types they could fit into that room. *Better them than me,* she thought. *I'll never go down into that cellar again.*

Suddenly, she had a sharp stab of bitter amusement. *I should have let Cassie burn down the house. Then she'd be alive and I'd never have known I had the bodies of six children buried in the basement.* She shivered again, but kept back her tears. Instead, she set out mugs and spoons on her counter, along with napkins, sweeteners and milk, for the officers and agents.

Mike came back upstairs with a roll of duct tape in his hand. He sealed the outside of the cat door.

"Uh oh," Laura said, "the cat's not down there, is he?"

"Nope, I carried him up and locked him in the girls' room. But I don't want him down there, so I figured I'd tape up his entrance."

"Good idea. His cat box is up here anyway since the flood. Happily, I put it in the girls' room as well." She smiled at Mike, then frowned. "Will I be able to take him with me? I really don't want to leave him behind."

"I'm not supposed to have any sort of pet, but I think this qualifies as an emergency."

Laura relaxed slightly. "Good. He's family, after all. So what happens now?"

"The guys from my station should be here soon and then I can get you out of here. They might want to ask you some questions, but it's only routine. Obviously you had nothing to do with what happened down there."

Laura shivered. Ever since they'd made the discovery she'd been so cold. "Should I pack a few things?"

Mike nodded. "It may take them a day or two to get everything here under control. Then once everything's been inventoried and removed, you should be able to come back."

"I'm not sure I want to. But a few days away is a great idea, either way."

Someone knocked heavily on the front door; Laura gave an audible gasp and jumped. Mike stroked her arm then went to answer the door.

After all the questions had been asked and answered, Mike helped Laura gather her stuff and put Anubis in his cat carrier, getting scratched up in the process.

"I'm sorry," Laura said, "he's usually well-mannered as you know. But he hates riding in the car. And he knows that's where he's going when I get the crate out."

"No harm done, babe. If someone tried to stuff me into a little plastic cage, I'd probably scratch too."

I wish I had a safe little cage to retreat to, Laura thought, and gave a little laugh. Mike's apartment was tiny, so her wish would soon be granted.

They smuggled the cat in to Mike's place and brought the cat supplies and Laura's clothes in a suitcase. He fussed over her, until she kissed him and sent him on his way. He seemed eager to get back; she knew that he'd been horrified over what had been found. But she also suspected he was excited by the prospect of such a big case being dropped right in his lap. She didn't understand it. *You'd better start trying,* she told herself, *pretty soon you're going to be a cop's wife.*

Smiling at that thought, she hung up the few clothes she'd brought in Mike's small but neat closet. Then she set up the cat box in his bathroom, put food and water out in the kitchen, and opened up the cage to let Anubis out.

He looked around, sniffed at the house plants a bit, then leapt up to the back of Mike's leather recliner, curled up with his tail over his eyes and promptly fell asleep.

Not for the first time in the last few weeks, Laura envied him. She wasn't sure she'd ever be able to sleep again.

The investigation continued for three days, at the end of which the evidence pointed to Dolores Wellman murdering the children and her husband, then walling up the root cellar and eventually committing suicide in the bathtub. It would be months before solid IDs for the victims could be established and the official rulings made, but the facts were unofficially obvious.

What details Laura couldn't get from the news, Mike supplied, watered down for her consumption. "Somehow she got them to come with her to the house — the trees were fairly thick then, since construction around the old house hadn't yet begun — and gave them a cup of cocoa with poison. Then she carried them downstairs, laid them on the cots and covered them over with a blanket. The coroner thinks they died quickly, without suffering."

"That's something, I guess." Laura and Mike were eating dinner, together for a change, in his small apartment. Frozen dinners weren't really much of a meal, but to finally have him working reasonable hours made it feel like a feast. "And it will be a comfort of sorts. It always helped me when Matthew died — knowing he just fell asleep and never woke up. Not, of course, that one ever really recovers from the death of a child."

"Yeah." Mike reached across the table and gave Laura's hand a brief squeeze. "Anyway, those are the facts we know for sure. Why Bert Wellman joined the children is still unknown. We're speculating that he wasn't involved in the actual kidnappings or murders. He might have just found the bodies and confronted his wife. We do know that his skull was crushed with a blunt, heavy object — probably a shovel."

"Why did she do it? Not just Bert, but all of it?"

"Unfortunately, we'll never know for sure. And she's not talking."

I'm not so sure about that. Laura kept her thoughts about the possible presence of a ghost or ghosts in her house to herself. She loved Mike dearly, but realized that he was one-hundred percent skeptical on the subject of the supernatural — just as she had once been...

"I meant to ask you, babe. Did you want me to get someone to come in and cement that wall over again? With the investigation closed, the room doesn't need to remain open. The house would definitely be easier to sell as a result."

"Sell? Do you really think, after all the news and media coverage, anyone in their right mind would want to buy it?"

"Well, you're the expert, so probably not. But it might be worth a try."

"In a year or two, maybe. But right now? Trust me — they won't be buying. Regardless of that, let's definitely do the wall. I'll have to go back there sooner or later, and it'll make it easier for me. I still carry the picture of those poor children in my mind and I don't need anything else to remind me."

"You're going back? Leaving me so soon?"

Laura smiled. "I'd hoped you come with me. We can't all stay in this teeny apartment for much longer."

Mike nodded. "I'm off tomorrow, I'll make arrangements for the wall. We can probably move back in after the weekend. Are you sure you want to do this?"

Tears gathered in Laura's eyes. "Pretty sure." Her voice trembled, so she cleared her throat. "There's no reason to expect that anything else bad will happen. Yes, the whole event is tragic and I wish it never had happened — especially not in my house. But five years is a long time and life goes on, right?"

"True."

"Do I sound heartless?"

"Laura, I've heard you crying at night over this. I lie next to you in bed while you thrash about in nightmares. This has affected you deeply and you are anything but heartless. So you don't have to worry about that. I think everything will be fine."

CHAPTER TWENTY ONE

Walking back into the house on Monday seemed odd to Laura. She'd been to work; a late afternoon fog had rolled in on her walk home leaving her feeling disoriented and detached. Her first step over the threshold was tentative; in spite of her previous career in real estate, empty houses always unnerved her, and this particular one made her more nervous than most. She took a deep breath, said a small quiet prayer and plunged in.

So far so good. No negative feelings flooded over her. The house seemed quiet — and unlike previous times it wasn't an uneasy, watchful quiet, but rather a peaceful calm. Laura exhaled.

She could see Mike had been busy on his day off. Although she didn't go down the stairs to see the wall — plenty of time for that after he arrived home — she saw the washer and dryer had been moved upstairs and installed in the small room off the kitchen. He'd also set up an area for the cat with food and water bowls and, back in the corner, a litter box. Tears welled up in her eyes she was so pleased. *Perfect,* she thought, *I never need to go down those stairs again.*

She listened to the messages on her machine, all of which she'd covered earlier when Mike told her who'd called. Her dad had called to say he wasn't going to be home over Thanksgiving. Tony had called to make sure she was okay after having seen her house on the news and invited her to spend Thanksgiving with them. As much as she'd like to see the girls, she had to turn him down, due to her and Mike's work schedules. Then Carolyn, after seeing all the official vehicles parked outside, expressed concern. A second call came from her after she'd watched the news — she offered her condolences, and then her apologies for the argument they'd had the night of the sleep over. She too was going to be away over the next weekend; in fact most of the families in the neighborhood were headed out of town, to celebrate the holiday at parents' or grandparents' homes. "It'll be a ghost town around here," Carolyn said.

"Thanks a lot," Laura said to the answering machine. "I didn't really need to hear that."

The final message was one Mike hadn't told her about, since it had come in earlier in the day. "Laura? This is Dennis Maxwell. We met at Cassie's funeral, remember? I saw this story on the news about the house where they found those missing children. That's your house, right? I might be able to help. Call me."

She picked up the phone, cycled through the last calls and redialed his number. "Dennis," she said when he answered. "This is Laura Wagner."

"Laura, I hoped you'd call. That *is* your house, right?"

She sighed. "Yeah."

"You know, that whole situation explains so much of what Cassie talked about. I'd really like to come over and check it out."

Laura thought for a moment. *Would his visit make things worse? Everything is quiet now, maybe I should just let sleeping dogs lie.* "Well," she hesitated, "I really don't know."

"You have nothing to lose. I suspect that after the bodies were discovered, the souls were released. And that your house is perfectly fine now. How does it feel?"

"Calm," Laura admitted with surprise, "and peaceful. Could it be that simple?"

"Hope so," Dennis said. "And how do *you* feel?"

"Also fairly calm and peaceful. I don't have an entire soundtrack of negative thoughts running through my brain. Of course, a lot of that has to do with being sober."

"Yep. But I can still come over. And maybe give you a clean bill of health." Dennis chuckled a bit. "Or whatever it is. A clean supernatural slate, perhaps."

"I'm still not sure I believe in any of this."

"You don't need to believe for it to be real. But if you're at all uneasy, I think I can help."

Laura sighed again. "Okay. When did you want to come over?"

Dennis laughed. "I can come now, if you'd like. My overburdened social schedule seems to have hit a clear patch."

"Do you know where it is?"

He hesitated. "I'm sort of afraid to admit, in case you think I'm some sort of paranormal stalker, but I've driven past your house several times since the news hit. I know exactly where you are."

Laura looked at the clock. Provided Mike didn't have to work overtime, he'd be home in about an hour. And while she didn't want him to think she'd gone off the deep end about the house, she also wanted him present. Just in case. "Come by in about an hour and a half. Maybe we'll order some pizza."

Laura tried to call Mike, but his cell phone didn't seem to be working. And since both he and Dennis arrived at the house at the same time, she hadn't a chance to warn him. Mike surprised her, though, by not finding her invitation to Dennis completely off base. "Better safe than sorry," he said. "Plus, if it helps you sleep better at night, babe, then I'm all for it."

Dennis chuckled a bit. “But you don’t believe in any of it, do you?”

Mike shook his head. “I don’t. I see enough real life horror in my line of work that I don’t need to attribute any of it to supernatural sources. Shit happens and when it does, you can usually find a logical explanation or a person to blame.”

Dennis’ mouth twisted into a dry smile. “I can tell you’re a skeptic. No problem.” He shifted his briefcase from one hand to another, zipped it open and pulled out a few hand-held, high-tech-looking items. Mike showed an interest now that gadgetry was involved. Unlike the materials Cassie worked with — cards, astrological charts, incense and candles — these tools supposedly measured “scientifically” with no room for interpretation.

Laura smiled to herself. “Shall I order some pizza while you two are setting up?”

As much as they’d been on opposite sides of the supernatural fence before, they apparently both agreed that electronic devices were the answer. “Sure,” Mike said. “I’ll help Dennis get started.”

“Cassie said most of the incidents revolved around the cellar?” Dennis adjusted his glasses, pushing them back to the bridge of his nose. “And that’s where the remains were found, right?”

Mike nodded. Laura looked up from the phone — the pizza place had put her on hold. “That’s right.”

Dennis studied the door, the many locks on it, and the duct-taped cat door. “Where’s your cat?”

“Oh, no.” Mike headed for the front door. “I forgot about him, he’s in his crate out in the car. I’ll be right back.”

“Poor thing,” Laura said, not really all that concerned.

Dennis looked over at her. “He’ll be okay. Your boyfriend is a cop, right? Seems a decent sort, if somewhat skeptical.”

“Yeah. He’s a great guy.”

"Cassie never said one way or the other. Just that he was around."

Mike walked back into the house, carrying Anubis in his plastic crate and started to open it up.

"Might be better to keep him inside there for a while," Dennis said, "that way I can be sure he doesn't set anything off."

Laura hung up the phone. "Pizza'll be about twenty minutes. We can't leave him in there, he hates the cage." She took the cat from Mike and cradled him in her arms. "I'll put him in the bedroom. We're not doing anything back there, are we?"

Dennis looked up at her. "Anything unusual happen there?"

Laura suppressed a giggle; she'd seen that movie. "Not really. You guys set up — I'm going to spend a little time with this poor mistreated kitty." When she said that, Anubis gave a pitiful little mew and Laura laughed. "Yeah, complain all you want, Bonehead. We all know you're spoiled rotten."

"I'm glad I'm here," she heard Mike say before she went into the girls' bedroom. "Laura hates going down to that cellar."

No kidding.

All in all, it had been an enjoyable evening. They spent some time talking about Cassie, but that felt natural and right. She'd touched all of their lives in some way and now she was gone. But they shared as much laughter as tears. Dennis finally went on his way, with their promise to call him, should any of the alarms go off. "I don't actually expect that to happen," he'd said as they saw him out. "If there was ever any sort of supernatural presence in this house, it's gone now. As far as I can tell."

"Just the same," Laura said to Mike when she locked the door. "If I hear one suspicious sound from the cellar, I'm out of here."

The following morning, Laura woke up completely enveloped with warmth. Mike had fallen asleep, cradled into her back, his one arm still draped around her waist. Anubis lay in front of her, snuggled up against the blankets at her stomach level. She gave a contented sigh. She'd had a good night's sleep.

That she could be this happy, that she could apparently lead a relatively normal life, despite her addictions, despite the sadness and death that had visited this house, amazed Laura. Never in a million years would she have imagined on that bleak day back in June her life would change so much. Nor would she have imagined that for the most part, the changes were good.

She slid out from underneath Mike's arm and gave the cat a nudge, then padded out to the kitchen to start the coffee. Looking at the calendar while the water dripped, she realized Thanksgiving was in two days. "I should take that turkey out of the freezer now." She and Mike had decided to just stay at home for the day. They'd had numerous invitations; in addition to Tony's invite, Renee had asked them, along with several of Mike's coworkers, but, with all the recent excitement, they'd opted instead for a low-key stay-at-home holiday. Most of the houses to which they'd been asked would be serving varying amounts of alcohol and Laura wasn't sure she was up to that challenge just yet.

"Better to stay here, where I won't be as tempted. To say nothing of not wanting to answer everyone's questions about the discovery of the children." Even the best-intentioned of people seemed to have an almost ghoulish fascination with the story and Laura did not want to talk about it. Not yet. The fear and sadness were still too new.

"Besides," she bent down to scratch Anubis, who'd followed her out to the kitchen, "the weather looks like it might be nasty. Just what we need, huh? More snow."

Laura heard a ring sound and she jumped, unable to identify the ring at first and worried for a few seconds that it might be an alarm from the cellar. Another ring and she identified the source — Mike's cell phone. "I'm not used to that yet." She picked up the phone and carried it back to the bedroom. Mike sat up in bed. "For you," she said, handing him the phone and giving him a kiss on the cheek. "I've got the coffee brewing, so come on out when you're done."

When Mike came out, she knew something was wrong by his expression. "What's wrong, honey?"

"My Aunt Betty died. We'll need to go to the funeral in Ohio."

"Oh, Mike, I'm so sorry." *More death.* "When?"

"She died last night. They didn't want to wake me in the middle of the night. The funeral is on Friday, so I'll need to leave here either today or tomorrow. I've got some leave left, so work won't be a problem."

Laura did a little pouting face. "I don't get leave. And with all the days I've been missing lately, I'm lucky I still have a job."

"So you can't come with me?"

Laura shook her head. "Probably not. Do you mind?"

"Yes, I do mind. I don't want to leave you here all alone. I can manage fine but is there someone you can stay with? Or maybe you can just go over to my apartment."

"Mike, my love, contrary to popular opinion, I can take care of myself." Her irritation showed in her voice. She'd been on her own for a fairly long time and it was difficult to have to relinquish some of that independence.

Fortunately he seemed to understand her feelings. "I know, Laura. But you're so important to me that I worry when I'm not with you."

"You shouldn't worry. I'll be fine. I'll miss you, of course. But it'll only be for a few days, right? It's a shame you're leaving on our first holiday together, but we'll celebrate when you get back. The turkey's not going anywhere. And neither am I."

"Good."

"Maybe you can call one night and read me a bedtime story." Laura smiled. "You know, I think I fell in love with you that night."

Mike chuckled. "Yeah, that book gets them every time."

Mike knew that Laura was attempting to be braver than she felt. He also knew that she valued her independence; otherwise he might have been a bit more forceful in asking her to come with him. On the other hand, he didn't really think she needed to go to another funeral, so soon after Cassie's, so soon after they found the room in the cellar. She seemed to be holding up remarkably well; he didn't see one good reason to insist she come along with him. At least not one good unselfish reason.

"Promise me," he said to her as he got ready to leave, "that if you need help, of any sort, you'll get it. I don't care how small the problem is, call someone. Renee or the neighbors or some other friend of yours. Call Tony if you have to. Or Dennis, and he can pick up his equipment while he's at it."

"I promise."

He reached out and pulled her into his arms, rocking her slightly. "I'm going to miss you, babe."

Laura smiled up at him. He loved the look in her eyes when she was happy. "I'm going to miss you too. Hurry back."

Laura stood in the doorway and waved to him as he drove away. He honked the horn and waved back, thinking how beautiful she looked, standing there. *I hope she'll be okay,* he thought, *and that if she gets into trouble, she'll keep her promise and call someone.* He knew the extent of her stubbornness, though; it was a quality both of them shared. “She’ll do fine,” he said the words out loud, almost as if to convince himself of their truth.

CHAPTER TWENTY TWO

Tuesday dragged for Laura. Due to the upcoming holiday, the biggest food day of the year, the day's work had been exhausting. By the time she arrived home, she felt drained. "I never want to see another turkey for as long as I live," she said to Anubis while she scooped out his cat food.

She'd initially intended to attend a meeting with Renee, but a message on her answering machine told her that her sponsor had gone out of town for the weekend. "You and everyone else," Laura said. "I'm starting to feel like I'm the only one around."

Which is not bad, really, she thought. *At least I don't have that paranoid feeling like someone is watching me.* She assumed that had been related to the detox from her Valium.

Laura sighed. It would be wonderful if she could just take a few pills and zone out for the rest of the evening.

Why don't you? You deserve a break — you've had a rough time of it lately.

She shook her head. No sense thinking of that, even if she wanted to go down that path again, she had no pills. Instead, she made herself a cup of peppermint tea, spread a piece of bread with some peanut butter and settled in front of the television.

The phone woke her some time later. She rushed to pick it up, not sure how long it had been ringing.

"Laura?" Mike's voice on the other end of the line sounded like heaven to her.

"Hi, sweetie. How was your trip?"

"Lots and lots of traffic, but other than that, I did okay. What are you doing? Did you go to your meeting with Renee?"

"She's out of town." Laura felt a whine creep into her voice. "Everyone is out of town."

Mike gave a low laugh. "You could have come with me, you know."

"Yeah. I should have. But there were turkeys and pies to sell — if I weren't here, who would do it? Half the people at work are gone, as well."

"Sorry, babe. At least you have Thursday off."

Laura sighed. "I miss you. You'll be home on Saturday, right?"

"Should be — a lot depends on the weather, though. They're still threatening us with another huge snow."

There was a long pause on the phone. "Mike?"

His voice cut back in mid-sentence. "...right after the service."

"What?"

"Reception here is bad. I said, I miss you so much already, I might just leave right after the service. And I'd better go, the signal is getting weaker. I love you."

"I love you, too," Laura said.

She sighed when she hung up. *Stupid cell phone.* Of course, the funeral was being held out in the boondocks of Ohio, in a tiny little town she'd never heard of before, which didn't seem to be near much of anything and obviously didn't have a huge wireless network. She should have gone along with him. "I can't believe I stayed home all by myself just so I could go to work."

Laura didn't quite know why keeping that job should be so important to her. Possibly because it was one of the first things in her adult life that she'd done while sober. That made it feel much more monumental a task. The decision had been made, regardless of how she'd reached it. She yawned, too tired to analyze it, too tired to do much of anything but splash a little water on her face, brush her teeth and go to bed.

Anubis snuggled up next to her, his purring lulled her right to sleep.

Early the next morning, Laura woke up to hear a steady, slow beeping. Not her clock, nor the smoke detector, she didn't recognize the sound. She threw the covers back, slipped on her pink terry cloth robe and went down the hallway to the kitchen to see what it was.

"Great." As she feared, the beeping came from the cellar. She remembered now they were supposed to change the tape in one of Dennis' machines — he'd had given Mike specific instructions on how to do it, but she hadn't paid attention. "I do not want to go down there and mess with this."

She pulled Dennis' card from where it hung on the refrigerator and dialed his number. He answered on the first ring.

"Morning."

"Dennis? Hi, it's Laura Wagner. Your machines are beeping."

"Really?" He sounded excited. "Is it a frantic beeping or rhythmic?"

"Rhythmic. I think the tape needs to be changed, but Mike is out of town. Can you take care of it?"

"Sure, no problem. I can come right over if you'd like."

"Yes, please," Laura said, "I'm going to need to leave for work in a few hours."

"Be right there."

True to his word, Dennis arrived about fifteen minutes later, barely giving Laura time to get the coffee started and get dressed. She reluctantly followed him halfway downstairs at his request, so that he could show her what needed to be done, just in case he wasn't around next time. He fiddled with a few dials, switched out the reel to reel tape spool for a fresh one, pushed a couple of buttons, slid a disk out of one of the machines and put a new one in.

Laura stood uncertainly on the bottom step. "Do I have to do all that?"

Dennis shook his head. "Not really. If it beeps again, you can just push this button," he pointed it out for her, "and it'll stop. I can come over afterwards and set it all back up again. If it's even necessary. Based on my preliminary readings, none of this is really needed. There doesn't seem to be any activity worth recording."

Although she'd never expected him to find anything, Laura felt relieved. "That's good news."

Dennis chuckled. "For you maybe. I hoped for a little more excitement."

"I can live just fine without excitement, thank you very much."

"I'm sure. Anyway, thanks for letting me set all this up. I appreciate the effort."

"I could say I'm sorry you're disappointed, but that would be a lie. I'm thrilled to death with your results." She stopped and smiled. "No pun intended."

Laura's work day didn't prove quite as exhausting as the previous day. The store was still crowded with people, but most of the orders were small ones — one or two items, little things they'd forgotten the last shopping trip. But the constant stream of customers made the day go by quickly and Laura's shift seemed over before she knew it. One of her coworkers gave her a ride, so she made it inside and managed to get some lights turned on before dusk.

The cold and crisp air seemed to validate the weather prediction of heavy snows on the way. "But that's not a problem for us, is it, Bonehead?" She absently stroked the cat's head — Anubis had curled up on her lap almost as soon as she'd sat down on the couch. "We've got nowhere to go and nothing to do. That's nice." After a while, she got up from the couch, put a frozen dinner into the microwave and picked up the phone.

First, she dialed Mike's cell, but the call went into his voice mail. "Hi," she said at the tone. "It's just me. I guess your phone isn't on. Or you're out of range. Anyway..." Laura paused. "I miss you. Call me when you can." Then she called Tony's house — Lizzy answered the phone.

"Mommy!"

"Hi, Pixie. How are you doing?"

"Great," Lizzy's happiness came through loud and clear. "I was just asking Daddy if we could call you tonight. I'm helping Susan with the pies. Are you cooking?"

"Not tonight, or even tomorrow. My friend Mike's gone out of town, so we'll have Thanksgiving when he gets back."

"We liked him a lot, Mom. Are you going to marry him?"

Laura smiled. "Maybe. How's school?"

"It's good." Lizzy giggled. "We don't have to go until Monday."

In the background Laura could hear the other people in the house talking: Tony laughing, Amanda chattering, Susan's soft voice giving some sort of instructions, probably a cooking lesson to the girls. Suddenly her plans of doing absolutely nothing all by herself didn't seem like independence. Rather, they seemed desperate and sad. Her loneliness hit her deep in the stomach, a sharp pang, like hunger, like craving. Laura squeezed her eyes closed tightly to hold back tears.

"Mom? Are you still there?"

"Yeah, sweetie, I am. I just miss you so much. I miss everyone."

"You could've had dinner here. Daddy and Susan wanted you to come."

Again, Laura heard Tony's voice in the background. "Is that your mom? I want to talk to her."

"Mom? Dad wants to talk to you. And I have to go, it's time to put the pumpkin gunk into the pie."

"Yum. Pumpkin gunk sounds great. I love you, baby. Put your dad on now."

"I love you too, Mom." Laura smiled, hearing Amanda scream what she always did in this exchange.

"I love you more, Mom!"

Laura was laughing when Tony got on the phone. "Having fun?" she asked.

"Loads of it. I wanted to ask you over again. Both you and Mike."

"Mike's out of town for the weekend — his aunt died."

"I'm sorry to hear that. I really hate to think of you being all alone on a holiday. Why don't you let me come over and get you so you can at least eat with us? There's no reason we all can't be together as a family."

Laura thought for a moment. Maybe it wouldn't be all that bad, there wasn't really any reason in the world they couldn't all be civilized and get along. She bore neither Susan nor Tony any grudge, except where the custody of the girls was concerned. And even that seemed an understandable safeguard back when she still drank.

She sighed. "I don't know. I'm not sure I'm quite ready for holiday celebrations."

"You don't need to drink, you know. Because some of us do is no reason for you to imbibe." He made it sound so reasonable, like she could take it or leave it. Unfortunately, it just wasn't that easy.

"But I'll want to, Tony. And I'm not quite sure I'm strong enough to resist it completely, so for now, I'm staying away from situations where I'll be tempted to fall back into old habits."

"How's Mike?"

Laura wondered if she heard a bit of jealousy in his voice. "Other than the funeral, he's fine. We're engaged."

"What? When did this happen? Congratulations."

"Thanks. I should have told you last time we spoke, but I was a bit overwhelmed with what was going on."

"Is that all over now?"

"Yes. But I don't want to talk about it."

"Fair enough."

"Come on, Dad." Laura heard Amanda calling. "We've got the game board all set up. Bye, Mom, talk to you later."

Laura shook her head. "Tell her I said bye. I just love these long distance conversations."

"Yeah, well, I need to go." Gales of laughter drifted over the phone lines to Laura. "We're playing team backgammon."

"Have fun."

Laura hung up the phone, feeling much worse than she had before she called. It's not that she wanted them all to be unhappy, and she certainly didn't begrudge them their family time. "I don't know what my problem is, except, damn," she said, leaning back against the counter. "I sure could use a drink."

Normally, she pushed thoughts like that out of her mind, but the tricks she used didn't seem to be working tonight. She spent a long time staring into her kitchen cupboards, one after another, searching for what she knew wasn't there. After taking about four deep breaths, she calmed down, closed the cabinet doors, and put the tea kettle on to boil. "Chamomile tonight, I think." *Not as good as hot cider and rum or coffee and a flavored liquor. Not even as good as a shot of whiskey. Or a beer. Or a glass of wine.*

"Stop it," she said.

Face it, Laura, you're a failure. You're useless. No one loves you, no one cares if you live or die. You're better off...

"Stop it!" Laura closed her eyes. "That's not true." She opened her eyes and looked at the ring on her finger, trying to recapture the happiness she felt with Mike.

But even he couldn't stay around, could he? He gets what he wants and he's out the door.

"That's not fair." She took in another deep breath, slowly pulling in the air, visualizing it filtering into her lungs, cleansing and soothing. She blew it back out, imagining all the negative thoughts being expelled with it. Then she closed her eyes and started the prayer. "God grant me the serenity..."

When she'd finished, she opened her eyes again and felt much better. The teakettle whistled and she poured the hot water into her mug, inhaling the calming scent of chamomile and herbs. She would get through this.

The beeper in the cellar went off again. "Oh, shit," she said, "that's the last thing in the world I need right now."

Anubis came to her in the kitchen, ears laying flat against his head, his pupils dilated. "Yeah," she said, looking down at him, "I know. It's an annoying sound. I'll fix it."

She opened the door, flipped on the light, fully expecting it to flare out. When it didn't, she took it as a good omen and walked down the stairs, slowly and carefully, and walked over to the machine with the button that Dennis had shown her that morning. Laura pushed the button and the noise stopped. "And that's that," she said, with a smug little smile and nod. "All fixed." She turned around to go back up the stairs, but couldn't resist a final comment. "Take that."

At that moment, she felt a rush of cold air at her back and all of the machines around her began to beep at once. Not a rhythmic tone this time. No, this time the machines blinked red and green, and all of their alarms sounded off, frantically.

"Oh, shit," she said again. "Dennis was wrong."

Laura heard that low laugh she'd often thought she'd imagined. So very close to her. Breathing in her ear. Standing right behind her. She spun around and felt as if someone or something struck her right in the back of her knee. She fell to the floor, crumpled onto her right ankle and felt it crack. Pain shot up her leg and screamed into her brain. The air around her grew colder still and she smelled something unpleasant, like rotting leaves. Or rotting flesh. Seven bodies neatly sealed up in a room.

She might have passed out for a while, she wasn't entirely sure. When she did finally attempt to open her eyes and raise her head she noticed the machines had stopped. Everything seemed deathly quiet.

Just lie down for a while, Laura. Go to sleep and let it go. The pain, the anger, the cravings, the disappointments, the failures. You don't need it. Let it go.

Better off dead.

"No." She pushed herself up into a sitting position and looked at her right leg, marveling at how her foot now seemed attached at a different angle. She tried to stand, but that one leg wouldn't support her weight, so she crawled, dragging herself over to the stairs. Holding onto the railing, she pulled herself up, one step after another. Each time her ankle banged against the stairs, she choked back a cry of agony and felt as if she were being pulled down, almost as if someone with an icy grip were holding her back. *I want the pain to stop,* she thought, *at least until I get up the stairs.* So many steps to take. So much pain.

Halfway up, she looked up and saw the door was closed. She lay her head down and cried.

That's it. Give it up.

Laura shook her head. Dragged herself up another step and then another. When she arrived at the top stair, she dripped with sweat and her whole body trembled. She reached up to turn the doorknob, but it wouldn't turn. "Dammit," she said, pounding the door with her fist, "I'm not going to die down here."

She looked at the cat door and realized she'd probably fit through it. *Probably the one time a mistake made while drunk actually paid off.* She pushed the door. It didn't move. She remembered then that Mike had duct taped it shut. She pushed harder and was rewarded with a ripping sound. She held the door open with one hand, while pulling herself up with the other and pushing off with her left leg. Half way through the door, she felt that icy grasp on her broken ankle again.

Suddenly Laura wasn't frightened anymore. She was angry. She kicked back with her good foot and felt as if she'd made a connection. She didn't care what or who it was that she kicked — she just knew it felt good to fight back. That strength carried her the rest of the way through the door and into the kitchen. Pulling herself up, she leaned against the counter, balancing on her left leg and picked up the phone.

After the call, she dragged herself over to the front door, unlocked it, and leaned up against the wall, finally allowing herself to close her eyes.

CHAPTER TWENTY THREE

On the ambulance ride to the hospital, Laura tried to stay awake. The paramedic riding in the back with her kept urging her to rest, telling her that everything was okay now. But she didn't want to fall asleep, not just yet. "How bad is it?" she asked.

"Pretty bad," he said, "Based on the way the ankle is twisted completely out of alignment, I'd guess you broke two or more bones. And your leg is all bruised. I've never seen anything quite like it. Must be from climbing up the stairs, but I swear it looks like someone grabbed you hard enough to leave a bruise the shape of their hand. You were alone there, right?"

Laura gave a pained laugh. "Just me and my shadow."

The emergency room doctor set her ankle, put a splint on it and instructed her to come back in three days so that they could put the cast on. They also provided crutches. After some discussion of her addictions, he gave her a prescription for pain pills. "Non-narcotic," he assured her, "so there shouldn't be too much of a problem to quit them when you need to. And more importantly they'll dull the pain. At least for a while." He handed her a few sample packets of medication. "These should hold you over until the pharmacies open. How on earth did you manage to crawl up the cellar steps? I can't even imagine how much pain you must've been in."

Either that, Laura thought, *or lie on that cold concrete floor and die.* "I managed," she said. "I had to."

Once she'd been discharged, they put her in a wheelchair and pushed her up to the nurses' station. "Have you got someone to pick you up, hon?" the nurse asked. "The roads are getting really bad out there."

"My fiancé is out of town," Laura said, "but I might be able to get my ex-husband to pick me up."

"Where will he be coming from?"

"Sewickley. Across the river."

The nurse shook her head. "Not tonight, he won't. They closed the bridges an hour ago. Black ice. It's a bad night out there. Do you have anyone closer you can ask?"

Laura thought and sighed. "Not really. I guess I could call a cab."

"I'll do that for you, hon. You just sit comfy for a while."

While she waited for the taxi to arrive, Laura made her plans. She'd get the cab to take her home, ask him to wait while she went inside and picked up some clothes and Anubis, then have him take her to the closest hotel. She didn't have keys to Mike's apartment — she hadn't stayed there long enough to worry about getting a set made. So she could go to a hotel. Or back to the house. *Not the house,* she thought, *anyplace but there.*

An hour went by before the cab showed up. "You're my last fare for the night," the driver said, as he gently loaded her into the back seat. "It's nasty out here. Most folks stayed at home."

Laura gave a humorless laugh. "I'd still be there, if I hadn't broken my ankle."

"Good point. I can't imagine you could help that. Are you comfortable?"

"Reasonably so, yes."

"Good. Sit back and enjoy the ride, if you can. We might do a little sliding, but this is an older cab so it's heavier and holds the road better. Plus, I've been driving winters in this town most of my adult life. You're in good hands."

Laura smiled. "Great. Thanks."

By the time they arrived at Laura's house over an hour had passed, and the sun was just beginning to come up. The driver turned off the meter about halfway through the trip. "No sense making you pay for the weather," he said. "You can make it up to me in the tip." He winked at her in the rear view mirror.

When he pulled into her driveway, she paid him and asked him to wait. "Can you wait for me? Please? I need to get inside and pick up a few things, then I need to go to a hotel. Anywhere that's close."

He helped her up the front walk, got her inside the front door. "I'll just be a minute or two," she promised.

The driver scowled, but nodded and went back out to the cab.

Moving around with the crutches was awkward, but she threw some clothes into a suitcase. She opened the door on Anubis' crate and called for him. Most times he came to her when she first entered the door, hoping that she'd feed him. But this time she couldn't find him anywhere. Laura even went so far as open the cellar door in case he was down there, then she opened open a new can of cat food on the electric can opener. "Damn," she said, hobbling down the hall again to check the bedrooms. She slammed the cellar door shut again on her way. "If you're down there, cat, you're on your own." She called him again, then limped back over to the front door, sliding her suitcase in front of her.

When she opened the door, she saw that the cab was gone. "Shit. Now what do I do?"

She tried Mike's cell phone, only to get sent to his message system again. She clicked down the receiver, then banged it on the counter out of frustration. "He's probably out of range still," she said to herself. "Cell phones are useless things." Then she called for another cab.

"Sorry," the dispatcher said, not sounding sorry at all. "We're not running service right now. It's..."

"Yeah, yeah, I know," Laura said, "it's nasty out there." She hung up the phone. "But it's even nastier in here. Now what do I do?"

She felt tears welling up in her eyes — the frantic activity had started her ankle throbbing and sharp stabs of pain threatened to overwhelm her. *Stop,* she said to herself, *breath.*

Thanking the person at rehab who conducted the breathing seminar, she felt herself relaxing, focusing. *Now think.*

"First things first," she said, the reasonable sound of her voice calming her, "deal with the pain." She limped over to where she'd left her purse and carried it back to the kitchen. Dumping the entire contents on the counter, she picked up the packets of medicine the doctor had given her. In the process, though, another bottle of pills fell out, from the bottom of the bag where the lining had ripped. Valium. Apparently the nurse at rehab check-in wasn't as thorough as she thought. Valium! She caught in her breath and reached for them. Her hands trembled as she undid the child-proof lid; she poured the contents into her hands and counted: twenty perfect little blue pills. Just the sight of them made her want to cry in relief. They were exactly what she needed. And they would make everything all right again.

Laura filled up a glass of water, counted out two of the pills, scooping the rest of the precious contents back into the bottle. She had her hand to her mouth, when she heard that low laugh she'd heard before.

Go ahead. Take them, Laura. All of them.

She jumped hearing that voice again in her head and dropped the pills down the kitchen drain. She put her hands up against her eyes and pressed, gritting her teeth and drawing in a painful breath. “No,” she said, her voice weak, almost a whisper.

All of them. It will be all right. You’ll be better off.

“No! Dammit. Stop it!” With a huge effort, she poured the rest of the bottle down the drain, ran the water and the disposal. “All gone,” she said, weak from battling herself, the ghostly influence and the overwhelming craving. “I don’t need them anymore.” She opened the packet of non-narcotic painkillers and downed two of them.

Laura leaned back up against the counter, panting, surprised to discover she sweated and shivered at the same time. The cat door clicked and she sprang up on her feet, forgetting about the splint for a moment, paying for her forgetfulness in a sharp stab of pain. Anubis emerged, as if from the gates of hell and came up to her to sniff at the splint on her foot. She smiled, happy to see him. Happy? Hell, she was thrilled to see one other living creature in this house of the dead. “Now you show up, Bonehead. Where were you before?”

He jumped up to the counter and she scratched his head. “Probably wouldn’t have been any hotel rooms available anyway, but it seemed like a good plan at the time. Now what do we do?”

The painkillers seemed to be working; the pain in her ankle and leg had settled down to a dull ache, persistent but not consuming. Laura picked up the phone and dialed Mike’s cell number again, getting a rush of excitement when it rang. But the feeling was short-lived when the call dropped back into his voice mail. She didn’t leave a message, but knew that he’d know she called.

“So,” she said, cranking her head to one side to look at the cat, “who should we call now?” She dialed Renee, her answering machine picked up. She dialed Carolyn and got another machine. Her father?

Although she knew he's gone away, she called him anyway, just to hear another friendly voice.

The machines in the cellar began to beep again and Laura wanted to scream in frustration. "I guess I could call Dennis," she said. "Maybe he could get here. Or at least talk to me and tell me what to do."

Dennis wasn't all that helpful. "Get out of that house."

"How?"

"Walk if you have to."

"Dennis, I broke my ankle. I can barely get around on the carpet." She looked out the window. The wind had picked up and the snow continued to fall; she couldn't see any of the houses around her. She couldn't see a single light, or a car, or another living soul. She felt as if she'd been cast adrift in a white, endless sea.

"Oh." Dennis' voice sounded flat. "Yeah, that's right. Still, maybe one of your neighbors could help, if you can get that far. And if you really can't get out, at least stay out of the cellar. Most of the malevolence seems to be centered there; it's the scene that the spirit returns to time and time again." His enthusiasm revived with his mention of the ghost. "Laura, oh my God, you won't believe what I saw on the tapes."

"Um, Dennis? I probably would believe it now. But this isn't helping me." Laura wanted to reach through the phone and smack him. This whole thing may have been a fascinating study to him — but she was stuck right in the middle of it all. Fascinating wasn't a word she'd choose to describe the emotions involved. Terror, yes, that played a big part of it, but that terror mixed with pain and despair. And underlying all of that, there flowed a strong current of anger. Laura didn't know if what she felt was her anger. Or the spirit's.

And at this point, she didn't think it made much of a difference. "Who do you think this is? Or was?"

"I only caught a single aura on the tapes, a single voice. The children's spirits should now be at rest. And since the aura has a definite female feel about it, I doubt that it's Bert Wellman. So that leaves Dolores."

"Aunt Dolly."

"What?"

"Nothing, it's just a game the kids around here play. That I know now isn't a game." Laura shuddered to think that she'd exposed her children to that woman, dead or not. "So you think I should leave?"

"Absolutely. But if you can't, then stay upstairs. Stay warm and try not to listen, try not to open yourself to stray thoughts or visions." His voice grew sad. "I suspect that's how she got to Cassie — she'd gone back to using and that made her mind susceptible. But you're clean, right?"

"Yes." Laura gave a silent thanks that she'd dumped the Valium. "I guess I'll put my coat and boots, or rather boot, on and see if I can get somewhere else."

"How about your car?"

"It's in the garage. To get there, I'll need to go down through the cellar."

"You can't get to it from outside?"

"Oh, yeah. I can. If I can make it down the driveway without killing myself. But saying I made it there, I couldn't drive anywhere."

"No, but you could sit in the car and wait for the roads to clear so that someone could get to you."

"True. Good thought. Thanks, Dennis."

"Laura?"

"Yeah?"

"Good luck. Call me if you can't get out. At the very least, I can provide a human voice to listen to."

"Thanks."

Laura hung up the phone and looked over at Anubis, where he sat grooming himself. "So what do you think, cat? Should we try to make it outside or take our chances in here?"

She opened up the refrigerator and got out a can of cat food, filling his bowl, then gave him fresh water. "You'll have to stay here, I think. You should be fine. Go sleep somewhere." She gave a little laugh. "You know more about this than any of us, don't you? Too bad you're not talking."

Laura put on her coat and slid on her one snow boot. For the foot in the splint, she wrapped it up with a scarf, then wrapped the whole thing up in a plastic garbage bag. "Won't help my traction at all, but I'm not walking around outside with bare toes." She put on a hat, a scarf, put her keys into her purse, hanging that around her neck. Then she found her gloves, got her crutches together and opened the front door.

An icy blast of cold air hit her. She heard the cat dart away, tearing down the hallway. She sighed and stepped out onto the first step.

Within no more than a second, she slipped and fell, flat on her back with enough force to knock the wind out of her for a minute or two. Laura pulled herself back up again and went back down. "Okay," she muttered, "I'm obviously not getting anywhere standing upright. Maybe I could crawl."

Getting down the driveway proved easy, she just allowed gravity and the ice to carry her along. Snow had drifted up against the garage door, though, and once she dug out enough to get to the door handle, she saw that the ice completely coated the keyhole. "Well, this isn't going to work."

She crawled back up the driveway, feeling colder and more tired with each passing minute. Snow had found its way into her boot, and that foot and her hands were frozen. Working her way back up to the front door seemed to take forever, but once she got there, she managed to sit up and look around. The sky had grown so overcast the automatic street lights had turned on, they were the only signs of life she could see. “I’m going to either freeze to death out here, or crack my head open. Either way, I’d be better off inside. There at least I have a fighting chance.”

Once back inside, it took Laura forever to warm up. Eventually, though, she managed to change her clothes and when she stopped shivering, she went to the kitchen to make herself a cup of cocoa. The sweet scent of chocolate made her smile, brought back memories of when her girls were here. She tried not to think about the other memories, the other cups of cocoa that had been drunk in this house, but the vision of the broken china cups in the hidden room downstairs flashed unbidden into her mind. Laura shivered again.

As if to punctuate her thoughts, the cellar door banged impatiently in its frame. “Shut up,” Laura said, “I’m not coming down there. Make as much noise as you like.”

She settled in on the couch, with the cat curled up next to her and watched the weather on television, sipping her cocoa. Anubis purred contentedly. “We’re right back where we started, cat. Happy?”

The cat may have been happy, but Laura was far from it. Her leg still hurt and her fingers and toes were just thawing out, with the accompanying pins and needles feeling. And her heart raced. She practiced her deep breathing and managed to calm it down a bit.

When the phone rang, she must’ve jumped about two feet. “Don’t hang up,” she said, as she struggled to reach the phone in time. Her voice sounded breathless when she picked it up.

"Hello?"

"Laura?" She felt a huge rush of relief on hearing Mike's voice.

"Oh, Mike. I'm so glad to hear from you."

"The cell reception here is practically non-existent. But I heard about the snow and wondered how you were doing."

Laura paused. What should she tell him? He'd never be able to make it to her and he might be in an accident if he did try. If he got hurt, she'd never forgive herself. And if he died...she couldn't even think about that. "I'm doing fine. I sprained my ankle and had to go to the emergency room. But they fixed me up and I managed to get a cab back here before the roads were closed. Anubis and I are just sitting on the couch, drinking cocoa and watching TV. I miss you though."

"I miss you too, babe." His voice grew faint. "I'm losing my signal again, but I just wanted to make sure you were okay. I worry."

"I'm fine, love. How are you?"

But he never answered. The line hissed, screeched, and filled up with that low hum of a whisper she'd heard before. Then the line was dead.

Laura tried to call Mike back, but couldn't even get a dial tone, getting a fast busy tone instead. She sighed and hung up the phone. Glancing at the closed cellar door, she made a face and pounded her fist on it once. It rattled and a cold blast of air washed over her feet. Laura shook her head. "Forget it. I'm not going down there."

CHAPTER TWENTY FOUR

Laura reached a strange level of detachment several hours after her trip outside in the snow. Part of it, she suspected, had to do with the painkillers she'd taken. The doctor had warned that they might make her drowsy. Then she realized she hadn't had any sleep for almost twenty-four hours. She decided she'd go back to bed right after taking her next dose of pills. Until then, she continued to watch television, continued to try to ignore the sounds coming from the cellar.

First all of Dennis' machines went off at once — a horrible cacophony of noise that grated on Laura's nerves. The door would bang, and the cat door would click open and shut. At one point, she went back to the door and duct taped the whole thing, hoping to cut back on the drafts that caused the noise. After that, she began to hear the footsteps, going up and down the stairs. For a while she counted each step, but that became too nerve-wracking; eventually she just turned the television up louder.

Every few minutes, she would check out the front window to see if a snow plow had come through, or if any of the neighboring houses showed signs of habitation. It seemed totally absurd to her that everyone would be away on the same weekend. She saw smoke rising from a couple of chimneys about three blocks away, if the snow let up, she might walk that way. For now, she had to stay stuck where she was, but at least the house provided relative warmth and shelter from the weather.

The time finally came for her next dose of pills and she washed them down with the last swallow of her cooled cocoa. Then she hobbled back to the bedroom and crawled into bed, fully clothed. The sounds from the basement continued. "Shut up," she said and giggled, more than a little woozy from the pills, "don't make me come down there." *Not surprising I should feel this way,* she thought, *I've been so long without any sort of drugs.* But she abandoned herself to the lightheaded feeling; she hoped she could sleep for a while, and prayed that when she woke up, everything would be better.

Her dreams were twisted, deep black roads winding through her sleep. Ultimately they had but one destination — like an endless loop, they kept depositing her back here, standing in front of that damned cellar door, her hand to the knob, her heart pounding in her ears. Over and over, she found herself, poised on the brink of the stairs. Everything felt cloudy, hazy and Laura couldn't tell whether she was dreaming or not.

Yes, that's it. You're dreaming. Just go with it, Laura. Let it take you where you want to go.

Where did she want to go?

Somewhere she could rest.

One step at a time, she thought, *but why does each step have to hurt so much?* She felt a spasm of pain through her leg with each count. *One, two, three...* Laura gave a soft laugh. *Another twelve step process.* But at the end of this one, she could rest. For as long as she wanted.

Forever, Laura, if you want. Just lie down and rest.

She curled up on the cold cellar floor and lay her head down, but when her cheek hit the concrete, she jolted awake. "Shit," she said, sitting up and looking around, realizing that she'd come to the one place in the world she wanted to avoid. Had she been sleep walking? Or was it an effect of the drugs they'd given her. It hardly mattered how. But why was she here?

You're looking for peace. And rest. Away from the pain of living.

It sounded so good to Laura. Life was hard and lately she'd been so tired. But she also knew now that the easy way out wasn't always the right way.

There is no right or wrong, Laura. Just life and death. And you carry more death than most. Accept it.

"What do you want from me?"

I want what's best for you, dear. That's all I ever wanted. For you. And for everyone.

Laura closed her eyes, and felt a cold hand brush her hair back from her face.

And what's best for you is what you want. What you've been looking for most of your life. Death.

Her eyes snapped open. "That's not true."

The cellar echoed with a low, bone-chilling laughter. *Be honest, Laura. You've been chasing after death since you were fifteen. Drinking it, swallowing it, letting it fill your veins and filter through your blood.*

"But that's not the way I am right now. I'm better — I've taken control of my life. I'm happy now."

Are you?

"Yes."

Don't lie to me, girl. I can tell.

Laura felt a wisp of air pass over her face, and a light tickle on her legs, as if they'd been brushed by a piece of cloth. Then two icy hands grabbed her face. She winced, recognizing the touch, and tried to pull back, but the ghost's grip was too strong.

Her eyes struggled to see the form of the person or presence near her, but all she could see was a patch of mist, through which the afternoon sun shone. “Let go of me,” she spat the words between gritted teeth.

That low laughed echoed through the room, but the grip remained strong. *I don’t know why you’re fighting me, Laura. It’s not as if your life is worth saving.*

As if to punctuate her words, the ghost drew forth some of the most depressing images from Laura’s past; they played out in front of her like ghostly images filmed with a bad camera. Her mother’s death and funeral, all tears and the sickly smell of the baskets of dying flowers. The ugly suspicion that her father had caused the accident and Laura’s steadfast denial of that situation, leading almost immediately to her drug and alcohol abuse. The lost nights and days, the waking up in unknown places, drenched in her own sweat and vomit. The number of times she’d tried to stop, followed by failure after failure, leading to despair and disillusionment. Fast forwarding through the good years, the ghost chose only to show the bad. Small things loomed large and assumed an almost cosmic importance — the arguments with Tony, disagreements with the girls, feelings of complete inadequacy, utter guilt — all adding to Laura’s general despair. Then the visions focused on the death of Matthew. The pictures slowed then, and Laura felt as if she saw it all a frame at a time, a succession of portraits of his death. That sweet little body, her sweet little boy, so little, so defenseless, so cold and lifeless. She saw her frenzied attempts to force air back into his silent lungs, *breathe, dammit, breathe!* She felt the events tearing at her stomach and her heart, the anger, the grief, the seemingly endless stream of burning tears and the dry, sandy ache of eyes that could cry no longer.

And with each vision, Laura felt herself grow colder, weaker, as if the visions were draining off her life's blood. She gasped for air.

The spirit delved deeper into Laura's soul, pulling up fears she never knew existed. She saw herself, here in the basement, the door to the root cellar no longer sealed. The picture that had been burned into her memory seemed different now. This time there were only two little cots, two little china cups with red rose buds and a toxic black stain on the bottom. She saw herself go over to the small, still forms on the cots and tenderly pull up the blankets, kissing each cold cheek. As she kissed them, she named them. Amanda. Lizzy. And on the floor, bleeding out his life from his shattered skull, Mike.

"No." Laura cried out, gripping her hands together, feeling her nails dig into the flesh of her palms. "This is what you did. I didn't. This is not real."

As real as anything. I pulled it all out of you — this is what life really is. So you see, you really would be better off dead.

Far off in the distance, Laura heard a phone ring, heard her message on the machine. "Mom? Happy Thanksgiving! We're snowed in. We can't even open the front door!" Lizzy's excited voice filtered down to her; suddenly the tightness in her chest eased and she could breathe again. "Mom? Are you there?"

"I'm here, baby." Laura felt some of her strength return.

"Okay, I guess you're not home. Call me back. I love you, Mommy."

Laura smiled. "That's what life is, Dolores." She took another few deep and calming breaths in and out. Then she reached her hands out and envisioned touching the ghost, cradling Dolly's face as the ghost had Laura's, but with a different intent. If the spirit really did feed off of hatred and despair and sadness, Laura thought she might just turn the tables.

She cleared her mind, trying to wash away the previous images of death. At first it was difficult to concentrate and project her thoughts — recent events kept interfering. The desire to curl up into a fetal position right there on the floor almost overpowered her. But Laura knew if she did that, she wouldn't survive.

Better off dead. But the potency of the ghost's thoughts seemed dimmer now.

"No," Laura said, finding small moments in her life, little bits of good to balance out the bad.

The births of her children, every one of them different, but every one of them a joy, the pain forgotten, their tiny bodies curled up against her chest and the happy tears.

But eventually they die, came the protest.

"Everything dies eventually. What's important is that they lived." Laura smiled, pulling up the warmth the memories held, envisioning it flowing into the hands cradled around coldness and death. "They lived."

She pulled up more, the contented sound of her babies nursing, their sweet scent after a bath, their first laugh, their first step. Little things, trivial things that had gone unnoticed the first time around, still held close in memories and brought out into the light. A first kiss, the touch of a kitten's fur, a patch of sunlight shining in the window on a winter's day. Laura thought of rehab and the strength she found there — in herself and in others. And although she might have wished she never went down that particular path, she had no regrets. Good did come out of it. She thought of Mike, of his kindness, of the way the sound of his voice never failed to make her smile. She remembered his love, his acceptance of her, his patience.

The spirit seemed to waver under her fingers and she dropped her guard and lost her grip for a second. Even given such a small window of escape, the ghost took advantage of Laura's loss of focus to revive some of its former strength. It swelled and raged, flooding Laura with its memories, showing her visions of the dead children. Scenes of Dolly, sweet little old Aunt Dolly, luring the children to her house on one pretext or another. Laura felt with a shock the spirit's total confidence in its own virtue. Dolly truly believed she was doing good work. She knew deep down that this was her purpose in life — to help these children get past the horrors of their daily life, to lead them to the comfort and peace of death. She thought she did them a kindness and that her actions provided the mercy the world could not. *Better off dead.*

How do I fight such convictions? Laura wondered, a spark of panic entering her thoughts. Dolly was oblivious to the truth, caught up in her own righteous justifications. Laura had to tear away at the substance of the ghost's self-delusions.

I have to show her the truth of her actions, Laura thought. *I've had a lot of practice with self-delusional thoughts. I certainly should know how to break through them.* Laura took a deep breath, taking time to feel the air enter her lungs, then exhaled slowly and repeated the action several times until her mind felt clear and fresh.

Reaching out to grasp the spirit again, Laura washed her mind of fear, but held onto the sorrow. Not her sorrow this time, but that of the parents of the dead children.

"Sorrow isn't necessarily bad," she said, pleased to hear that her voice sounded firm and strong. "Those children were loved, they were missed. Not one parent, not one person would have wished they had never been born." She pulled scenes from her mind, the parents on television, talking of their children when they were found. Then she drew on her imagination and pictured those same children, not dead, but alive and thriving. She focused on images of those children growing, learning, maturing, leading useful lives. Leading lives of love and purpose, not always perfect lives, but full and proper.

Laura felt a faltering in the spirit. *They were better off dead.*

"And was Bert better off dead? What was wrong with him that he should die and you should live?"

Bert? He's not dead. He left me. Dolly's voice wavered, trying to maintain the delusions on which she built her life, trying to hold onto the madness that caused her to murder so many.

"He didn't leave you. You killed him. They found his body in the root cellar with the others. You need to remember this, Dolly."

The room filled with huge wave of dismay and confusion. Then the haze of Dolly's thoughts seemed to clear. Laura saw Bert Wellman, alive and well, staring in horror at what his wife had been hiding in the cellar. She saw him confront Dolly and watched her deny his accusations, first in confusion and then in defiance. "You're not well, sweetheart," Laura heard him saying. "I should have seen this. But we can get you help. And we can get these children," his voice broke, "these poor children back to their families where they belong." He turned and stared at his wife. Laura could see the tears in his eyes, could see the odd mixture of love, pity and disgust with which he looked at Dolly.

Dolly saw it too, but the emotions didn't touch her. Instead, she raised her hand and struck him. "What do you know? I did this because these children were better off here than where they were."

"Oh, Dolly. You don't believe that. You couldn't. What's happened to you?"

Laura felt tears run down her face as she watched Dolores Wellman pick up the shovel leaning against the wall and smash him on the head. He crumpled under the blow, but Dolly kept hitting him, over and over, until his face disappeared, leaving behind only a bloody pulpy mass. She dropped the shovel and stared down at the dead body of her husband. Without any shred of remorse showing on her face, she tugged at his pants leg and rolled him into the root cellar. Then she shut the door and dusted off her hands, nodding in satisfaction as if she'd just done a good deed.

"But you killed him, Dolly."

I didn't. He left me. Still, the spirit attempted to hold onto the madness she'd known during life.

"No, Dolly. You killed him. Smashed his head in with a shovel. Then closed him in the root cellar and left him.

Oh, God. The words were a wail of grief and a cry of understanding. *I killed him. I killed them all.* There was a long pause, during which Laura felt like all of the air was being sucked out of the cellar. *Oh, God.* Dolores raged, *I killed them. Even Bert. I killed them all. What have I done?*

Whatever form Laura had held between her hands, seemed then to drop away. She heard another cry of dismay and then a soft weeping. Taking in a deep breath, she closed her eyes and said a silent prayer, a prayer for the living and the dead. "God grant us the serenity..."

When the prayer had finished, the cold of the cellar seemed to ease. From beneath her still-closed eyes, Laura saw a brief light, like a flash from a camera or a bolt of lightning. The weeping, which had grown softer and softer during the prayer, stopped abruptly and the surrounding air that had been cramped and restrictive, eased. She opened her eyes and looked around her. The cellar felt like a new space, clean and fresh.

Laura felt completely alone, but also completely at ease. Her leg hurt like hell; she was cold, bruised and as exhausted as if she'd run ten miles or more. Laura laughed. "And starving," she said as she dragged herself over to the wall and pulled herself up from the floor.

She limped over to the stairs, taking each one slowly, counting them as she did, leaving the darkness behind.

EPILOGUE

Laura pulled into the driveway of her house. Getting out of the car, she looked around the neighborhood. One year ago to the day, they had been in the middle of the worst winter storm in decades. Now, although the skies were grey and the trees were bare, the temperature was still mild and everything just felt better. In spite of this day's events, she stepped lightly and put her key into the front lock, opening the door without feeling the overwhelming oppression that used to be there. Inside the house felt warm and welcoming.

"Mike?" She set her bag down on the entry table and shrugged out of her jacket, hanging it on a hook by the door.

"In the kitchen."

Laura inhaled. "Wow, that smells amazing!" She walked into the hallway and leaned up against what used to be the cellar door, now sealed up and covered over with drywall and plaster. She watched Mike, dressed in jeans, tee shirt, and apron, take the massive turkey out of the oven. "And looks tremendous."

He stood back for a second and assessed the bird. "Needs a little more time, I think." He placed some foil over the top and put it back into the oven. "Tony called. They're going to be late."

"So what else is new? How'd your day go? It feels calm."

Mike shrugged. "Everything's pretty quiet, actually. A bit of rattling, but nothing else. To be honest, I sort of expected a little more activity, considering the day. But, I'm not complaining. How are you doing?"

Laura sighed and Mike walked over to her, wrapping his arms around her and holding her closely. "Rough one today?" He whispered the question into Laura's hair, knowing the answer from the tenseness of her shoulders. He gave a small laugh. "At least you weren't stuck selling turkeys this year."

"True. Even ghost hunting is better than retail." Laura laughed herself, before sobering up again thinking back on her day. "But this one is going to be a rough case."

"Aren't they all? You could just go back to real estate full time, you know."

Laura nodded. "I know, but if I can help, I have to do it."

Mike smiled, kissed her on the forehead, and went back into the kitchen. He stirred one of the pots on the stove and checked under the lid of another. "So what's going on?"

"Just a single entity this time. But it's a little girl, apparently. Dennis is excited. He thinks we might have caught her on film. But, oh, Mike, she's so lost and alone. And so very angry. She doesn't seem to know what happened to her and I'm not sure if I can help her. I'm not sure if she'll ever be able to go home."

"You can't help them all, Laura. We both know after last year that some of them just don't want to leave." As if to punctuate his words, the wall Laura leaned against rattled and banged, and the kitchen grew colder, so much colder that her breath became visible.

Ignoring the cold, Laura cocked her head to one side, concentrating, and heard the whispering start. The voices were softer these days, and less persistent, more like a sigh than a scream. But they never went completely away. She held them off, the best she could. She took a deep breath and let it out, turning to face the wall.

She ran her fingers gently over the pictures hanging there: six small frames holding school photos of children and a larger one of Bert and Dolores Wellman, in better times, standing hand in hand on the front porch of the house.

"Hush," she said quietly, holding her hand against the door for a minute or two until the rattling subsided and the whispers dropped to the faintest of sounds. "Be calm, Dolores, everything is all right." Laura struck a match and lit a votive candle on the small shelf below the pictures. "Shhhh," she said. "You're okay. Everything is okay. I know you're here. And I'll never forget."

www.ingramcontent.com/pod-product-compliance
Lightning Source LLC
LaVergne TN
LVHW020709110826
845149LV00012B/2179

* 9 7 8 0 9 8 6 0 8 6 8 1 6 *